MISSOURI MAMA

Edwards was within twenty yards. McCoy wanted to gun the man down with four shots to the heart the way Edwards had the last bank president, but McCoy was a lawman and had to call out for Edwards to surrender first.

His instructions had been to bring Edwards back alive. They wanted a show trial in Boise to prove that it was a tough town on bank robbers. He'd do his damnedest.

Then McCoy could see the dripping beard of the outlaw, the familiar face, the black eyes and too large nose and even the sneer.

McCoy took out his six-gun and laid it beside the rock. It was time.

"You're under arrest, Edwards," Spur bellowed. "Don't move or you're a dead man!"

FREE PRESS FILLY

As Spur turned the bay mare and moved toward the barn, he saw a glint of metal to the left behind a pair of pine trees. Automatically he grabbed the rifle out of the boot and dove off the bay.

Just as he dove he felt a bullet whip through the air where his head had been a fraction of a second before. The sound of the shot came almost on top of the bullet and with it came another pair of shots, and Spur figured there was a gunman amid the pine trees and another in the barn.

The gun from the trees blasted again twice, and this time screamed as if in sudden pain and then let the screams grow weaker and weaker until they faded out. He drew his six-gun, held it by his side and waited.

The *Spur Double* Series from *Leisure Books*:

SPUR

MISSOURI MAMA
FREE PRESS FILLY

DIRK FLETCHER

LEISURE BOOKS　　　**NEW YORK CITY**

A LEISURE BOOK®

June 1996

Published by

Dorchester Publishing Co., Inc.
276 Fifth Avenue
New York, NY 10001

SPUR

MISSOURI MAMA

Chapter One

United States Secret Service Agent Spur McCoy didn't feel the rain anymore. He was soaked to his long johns, his boots were a soggy bog, and his hat had fallen off so many times in the scramble through this damned brush in the wilds of Idaho that his hair was wet as well.

He lay now in a small ravine watching the slow movements of his target below. Blade Edwards had slipped through the net thrown around him for five years, but now McCoy was going to grab the slippery son of a bitch. He had been wanted for bank robbery for more than six years. At the last bank he had killed three people and laughed about it as he fled.

If at all possible, McCoy wanted this to be the end of the trail for Edwards who bragged that he would never be taken alive. McCoy wondered what tricks he had up his soggy sleeve this time.

Edwards kept moving upward. He had no idea that McCoy had surged past him in the last thunderstorm. Lightning had smashed down a dozen of the tall fir trees, and the usually even-tempered Idaho drizzle turned into a downpour that made rushing streams in even the smallest gullies.

McCoy had holstered his Peacemaker .45, slung his Spencer repeating rifle over his shoulder and charged up this lonesome Idaho hillside through the heart of the cloudburst to get in front of the fugitive and have a place of his own choosing for the final showdown.

It had worked, since Edwards evidently had taken some protection during the downpour. Spur had chosen his spot carefully. He knew that Edwards was on foot and working hard up the slopes to get over Snowfall Pass and to the tiny town of Snowfall on the other side. For years it had been a gathering point for drifters and men on the run from every crime in the book. They tolerated one another and permitted no law whatsoever in the vicinity. It served as a safe haven for from 15 to 50 outlaws, depending on the time of year and the heat of the chase.

McCoy lay in his chosen spot and watched the fugitive working his way slowly up the narrow valley. It was little more than a canyon, and a rushing stream ten feet wide still boiled down the center of it.

Edwards kept just to the side of the water where the ground was the most level and trudged upward. He had a rifle slung over his shoulder muzzle down and a six-gun holstered on his left hip. The government man would make no mistakes this time. He had let Edwards get away once two years ago due to a gun

Edwards had hidden in his crotch. Never again.

McCoy had picked a spot where two boulders sat with a crevice about a foot wide between them. It was a made-to-order firing slot. He had bent down a foot-high young fir in front of the rocks, and he had a perfect field of fire.

His spot was less than 50 feet from the edge of the stream, and Edwards was now trudging uphill on this side of the water.

McCoy felt more water dripping through his slicker, his leather jacket, his shirt and long johns. He brushed wetness off his eyebrows and checked on Blade Edwards through the continuing soft rainfall.

The killer kept coming, head down, sure of himself now. He must have figured that last shootout at the base of the mountain had put down McCoy who had cried out in pain once, but Edwards had not investigated to see if he had wounded or killed the government agent.

Now things would be different. There was absolutely no cover except the water itself in the small gully. At this point it narrowed to 100 feet across, and the water wouldn't be deep enough to cover an ankle-high boot.

McCoy shifted the Spencer slightly to track the fugitive. Edwards was 50 yards downhill working slowly upward. McCoy had sighted in this weapon three days ago. It fired a shade high and to the right at 100 yards. At 50 feet there would be little drift. He made sure the safety was off and checked the breech. One round was loaded, and seven more of the .52 caliber stingers were in the tube through the stock. He could fire eight times, as fast as he could work the lever under the trigger.

Now Edwards was within 20 yards. McCoy wanted to gun the man down with four shots to the heart the way Edwards had the last bank president, but McCoy was a lawman and had to call out for Edwards to surrender first. The killer wouldn't give up. So Spur's first shot would be in the shoulder while he was fairly stationary. Hopefully he could put Edwards down right away.

McCoy's instructions had been to bring the man back alive. They wanted a show trial in Boise to prove that it was a tough town on bank robbers. He'd do his damnedest.

Ten yards.

Then McCoy could see the dripping beard of the outlaw, the familiar face, the black eyes and too large nose and even the sneer coming through the beard.

McCoy took out his six-gun and laid it beside the rock. It was time.

"You're under arrest, Edwards," Spur bellowed. "Don't move or you're a dead man."

Even before he got out the third word, the killer made his play. He whipped up the rifle and triggered a shot at the rocks as he dove down the slope.

McCoy tracked him and fired, just as Edwards's slug chipped stone off the inside of the rock a foot over McCoy's head. The agent levered another round in as the killer rolled and fired. This time he saw the bullet hit Edwards in the left shoulder. Edwards kept rolling. McCoy lifted to fire again when another round from the fugitive chipped more shards inside the right boulder, spraying his cheek with sharp splinters of rock.

McCoy wiped blood off his cheek and dropped lower, firing a third time. This one caught Edwards just as he surged to his feet. It took him in the right shoulder and jolted the rifle from his hand.

The big .52 caliber bullet at such close range slammed Edwards to the ground where he lay panting, the fine rain still falling, diluting the blood that showed on his shoulder even through his clothes.

"Give it up, Edwards. You're outgunned this time. Take your chances with a jury."

"Got more of a chance with you, McCoy. Thought I had you that last go-round. You faked that hit, right?"

"Throw out your six-gun and your hidden weapons, Edwards, then we'll talk."

"Got nothing hidden."

"Sure, and a goose doesn't have feathers. All I have to do is deliver you alive. I can put a slug into your right kneecap. You want to walk back down the mountain hopping all the way?"

Slowly Edwards tossed his six-gun up the slope.

"Easy now. Sit up if you have to, but I want to see at least two derringers," McCoy barked.

Edwards eased upward so he sat in the slowly falling rain. Water dripped off the slouch brown hat. His eyes glared at McCoy's position, then he slid a derringer from his jacket pocket under the slicker.

"That's all I got," Edwards called.

"Like hell. You always carry two, sometimes three. Get another one out or that kneecap goes."

"Damnit, McCoy, you know me too well. In my crotch. Take me a minute."

McCoy kept the Spencer trained on the man as he fumbled with his clothes. A moment later a derringer slid out of his hand and landed six feet away. It would have done him no good to fire either of them at this range.

"Now, stand up and walk this way. When you get within twenty feet of the rocks, I want you to turn around and put both hands behind you."

"Damn you, McCoy. You don't give a man a chance."

"That's the whole idea, Edwards. The same way you shot down those three in that last bank job."

"They talked back to me."

"You're talking back to me, Edwards. Now get over here and we both can get out of this rain."

Edwards moved slowly, shuffling toward McCoy. When he was there he stopped.

"This close enough?"

"Yeah, turn around."

McCoy had the Spencer trained on the man's left shoulder. This would be the time if Edwards was going to try anything else. The robber seemed to sigh, then he flexed both arm and started to put them behind him. When moved his left arm again, a derringer slid into his hand from his sleeve, and the two weapons went off almost at the same time.

Edward's half-aimed slug from the derringer tore through McCoy's slicker, his jacket's left sleeve and shirt before it sliced a groove in his left shoulder. It burned like hell.

McCoy's own round had found its mark on the gunman's left shoulder, spinning him backward ten feet down the slope. McCoy saw the derringer fly out of Edward's hand, and the secret agent came from behind the boulders and charged forward.

Edwards lay on his back screaming. McCoy planted one soggy boot in the middle of his back, pulled handcuffs from his belt and quickly cuffed the man's hands behind him.

"Edwards, it's the end of the game for you. The only thing you have to look forward to now is a nice dry jail cell and a hangman's noose. At least you have to walk back to the horses. That's the only reason I didn't shoot you in the leg."

It took McCoy the rest of the day to get back to the small town of Riley, Idaho. The sheriff took charge of Edwards for the night, and two days later McCoy turned Edwards over to the federal court in Boise, Idaho.

He wired his office in St. Louis and got back a curt reply that he had no messages waiting from him from General Halleck, the number two man in the United Secret Service and his boss in Washington.

McCoy grinned. For the first time in six months he had a chance to get back to his office in St. Louis and sleep in his own bed again. It didn't happen often. He wondered if Lucinda would still be there.

Chapter Two

Agent Spur McCoy's office in St. Louis, Missouri, consisted of space leased by the government on a yearly basis in the venerable Claymore Hotel. It was really two rooms—one to live in and a second, smaller room where he could receive mail, have a desk and represent Capital Investigations of Washington D.C., the cover name for the United States Secret Service.

McCoy had wired ahead, and when he arrived in the office Thursday morning, he found it open, the room aired out, and the mail neatly sorted and stacked. Behind this miracle of work stood Priscilla Quincy, a small lady of 24 with short red hair, a winsome smile and a neat and trim little figure. She smiled and nodded.

"Good morning, Agent McCoy."

"You're the best helper in the world, Quincy. I see you have things in good shape. First, any work orders from the general?"

"For once, Mr. McCoy, not a single one. Isn't that great? You can have some time to repair your weapons, buy new clothes and have a small rest between assignments for a change."

Her glorious smile was worth the long train ride. "The rest of the mail?"

"I put it into three piles: throw away, read only if interested, and two scented envelopes mailed from right here in St. Louis."

"Two scented letters . . . well, yes, I'll take those. Why don't I see to the rest of my mail after my bath and some clean clothes? I just got off the Limited from Omaha and points west."

"Mr. McCoy?"

He had just opened the connecting door into his room and now turned and nodded. "Yes?"

"It's good to have you back. You do look a little thin. I've got a great roast beef dinner I can have ready for you about six . . . if you're interested."

"Six. Let's see—it's ten-thirty now. Six might be fine. Can I let you know for sure a little later?"

Her excitement vaporized, and a hard glint came into her green eyes. "Yes, I see. For your information, Lucinda Ballenkamp is still in town, lives at the same house, runs the bank and is the prize catch of the century, relentlessly pursued by all the local bachelors."

McCoy grinned. "Thanks, Pris. Don't know what I'd do without you."

He vanished through the door and closed it. He'd arranged for hot water to be brought up since this hotel didn't have it piped in as yet to all of the rooms.

He stripped off his traveling clothes and then, naked, hurried back to the connecting door. He opened it a foot and pushed his head through.

"Oh, Pris, you better write out the usual telegram and take it down to the office and send it. Tell the general that I'm back and cleaning up my paper work here. That's all he needs to know. Thanks, Pris."

She stared at his head poking around the barely opened door, and her frown deepened. Pris opened her mouth to say something then closed it. He was about to shut the door when she held up her hand to stop him. She sat at the small desk where she was opening mail.

"Mr. McCoy, pardon me for asking, but are you stark naked?"

"Priscilla Quincy, what a perfectly outrageous thing for a proper young lady to be asking!" He couldn't hold his frown for long and grinned. "Right, Priscilla, about as naked as a newborn babe, but this is all of me you get to see or your pappy would use me for shotgun practice out on that big ranch of his."

Priscilla sighed. "Yes, you're right of course. That is, unless of course . . ."

"Pris, we've been over this before, remember? I'm not about to get myself hitched to you or any other young beautiful and wanton filly. So just be a good girl and open the mail and send that wire, so I can be officially here at my post awaiting the directions of our glorious leader."

Pris pouted for a moment, her red hair flouncing as she looked around quickly. Her eyes, almost as green as his, shot off a dozen sparks. "Of course, I could always tell the major that you overpowered me on the desk and had your way with me. Then he'd still use his shotgun, but it would be to get you to a church and a preacher."

McCoy nodded. "Good, we're back to that shotgun. You know you would never lie like that, Priscilla, and I know you would never make up a crazy story like that. So we can still be friends. Lovers are easy to find, little lady, but one good friend like you is worth a hundred lovers."

"That's what you told me six months ago the last time you were here."

"You remembered?"

"Of course. I just hope that one of these days you'll forget and open the door all the way."

"Not a chance," McCoy said with a big grin. "Now, pretty Pris, get your little bottom off that chair and send a wire to my boss. I've got hot water turning cold in here."

He closed the door firmly, threw the bolt and then stepped into the steaming water in the portable steel tub that was only half long enough for his legs.

Spur McCoy, ace agent for the United States Secret Service, had the whole western half of the country to cover until they got more men to help him. Then he'd first move his office to Denver, leave a man here and eventually move all the way to San Francisco, spotting agents along the way.

McCoy was big enough for the job. He stood six-two and weighed in at just over 185 pounds of hard muscles. He face was tanned and windburned from more time spent outdoors than in, and he usually wore a black, low-crowned, flat-topped Stetson with a wide flat brim and a row of Mexican silver coins around the headband.

He was suited to his job. He'd graduated from Harvard, spent enough time in the Civil War to come out an infantry captain and served a year in Washington D.C. as an aide to an old family friend who was a U.S. Senator from New York. When the Secret Service was formed, he rushed to join and had been with the service ever since. What he wanted now was three more agents in his area.

He stepped into the bath, got used to the near boiling water and settled down to soak. Then he opened the two scented letters and read them. Both were from Lucinda, written nearly a month apart. Both were almost the same, wishing he were back home so they could go out to the opera or to a concert.

Then there was the rest she wasn't saying. He looked over at his bed, which was freshly made each week whether he used it or not. It looked small, lumpy and uncomfortable. That nice big featherbed in Lucinda's master bedroom would be much better for his first night back in St. Louis.

Spur put the letters on the floor and soaked another five minutes before he began to wash himself.

He scrubbed away the days of train travel and even some Idaho grit and stepped from the tub clean and in need of a shave and a haircut. He gave himself a shave with some of the leftover hot water, then checked his pocket watch. 11:20 A.M.

He put on tweed town pants, a gray shirt, a black leather vest and a string tie. He pulled on his polished black, high topped cowboy boots and headed for the hall. He just had time to get to the St. Louis State Bank and invite Lucinda out to dinner—or did they call it lunch yet here in St. Louis?

He reached for the door to the hall when someone knocked on the connecting door to the office. He unlatched the bolt and opened the door.

Priscilla stood there with a big smile. "I sent the wire, and while I was there one came through for you." She handed him the envelope.

"Not an assignment already?"

"We won't know until we open the envelope, will we, Mr. McCoy?"

He tore open the end of the yellow and black envelope and read the wire:

"TO: SPUR MCCOY, CAPITAL INVESTIGATIONS, CLAYMORE HOTEL, ST. LOUIS. MO. NOTIFY ME OF YOUR ARRIVAL. AM SENDING TODAY, WEDNESDAY, 26 OCTOBER, A NEW AGENT FOR YOU TO WORK WITH ON YOUR NEXT ASSIGNMENT. TAKE TWO OR THREE DAYS TO GET TO KNOW EACH OTHER, DECIDE HOW YOU CAN BEST WORK TOGETHER. YOUR NEW ASSIGNMENT NOW BEING PUT TOGETHER. IT'S UNUSUAL. TAKE CARE OF THAT ARM WOUND. (YOU USUALLY HAVE BEEN SHOT SOMEWHERE.) DETAILS OF NEXT ASSIGNMENT COMING SPECIAL RAIL EXPRESS WITH HAND DELIVERY. SENDING: W. D. HALLECK, LT. GENERAL, US ARMY, CAPITAL INVESTIGATIONS, WASHINGTON D.C."

McCoy groaned and handed the telegram to Priscilla. "Take care of this. If the new agent comes while I'm out, show him some of our files. Try to figure out if he's a political appointee or if he's had any training. I'm going to go out to lunch."

"With Lucinda?"

"Hopefully." He turned and hurried out of the office before she could give him any more bad news. He worked alone, damnit! General Halleck knew that. Why was he sending out a second agent? Nothing said about him being permanent at least, just somebody to help him on this next assignment. Damn!

The St. Louis State Bank looked the same as it had six months ago. Solid blocks of granite had been carefully placed together into a two-story building that should stand for 200 years. He pushed through the heavy swinging door and stepped into the bank.

Five iron teller's cages were in a long counter, leaving a sizeable lobby. To the left were two closed doors and a desk with a woman sitting behind it.

When he stopped in front of her, she looked up and grinned.

"Yes, sir, and what can I do for you today?"

"I'm here to see Miss Ballenkamp in response to her letter."

"Who shall I say is calling?"

"Spur McCoy."

The woman's face fell, and she sighed. "Might have known," she mumbled as she rose and went to the first door marked "President". She knocked, then opened the door and said something. A moment later a tall blonde woman in a severely cut woman's suit rushed past her surprised secretary.

"Spur, I hoped you'd be back soon." She almost jumped into his arms, looked around the bank a moment, touched her hair and beamed, then motioned him into her office. "We better talk this over in my office, Mr. McCoy. Right this way."

The office door closed softly, and Lucinda Ballenkamp slid the bolt into its slot, making no sound. She turned and caught Spur's head and kissed him deeply, pushing hard against him and tightening her arms around his back like bands of shrinking rawhide.

When the kiss ended she sighed and leaned against his chest.

"You finally came back. It's been six months."

"About right. Looks like you're still running the bank. I hear you're fighting off the bachelors and fortune hunters."

"Yes, yes, yes—because I'm waiting for you, silly man." She kissed him again, then led him to a small couch at the side of the room.

"It's new. I sometimes have small catnaps in the afternoons. It peps me up."

"Ever have a catnap in the morning?"

"Not so close to the noon hour. I always take two hours off for what we're calling lunch now. That would seem like a better time for us to have that small nap."

"We'll lunch at your big house on the hill or your downtown apartment?" McCoy asked.

Lucinda was all a man could ask for. She was tall enough for McCoy at five-six and had long, honey-blonde hair that now fell nearly to her waist. She hadn't cut it in over a year.

Her cheekbones were high, making little round mounds when she smiled. Soft brown eyes showed under thick eyelashes.

Lucinda's face was a marvel of engineering and construction with a nose just right over a wide mouth that had nearly perfect white teeth. The top of the suit coat strained, holding in her full breasts. The pinched-in suit coat showed her figure to the best possible extent, even though the skirt of the suit hugged her hips and plunged within an inch of the floor. It was considered a business suit so it didn't have to touch the floor.

"Hey, Spur, I answered your question, but you didn't seem to have heard me."

"I was just undressing you with my eyes. When I do that with lots of enthusiasm, sometimes my ears don't work so well."

"Let's go to the apartment. It's closer and we'll have more time. In fact, it's a quarter to twelve, so let's leave right now. Yes, I want to be seen leaving with you. Maybe it'll put some pressure on you to stay at home and take care of my needs and put that little band of gold around my finger."

He kissed her hard, and she hung in his arms, eyes wide.

"Oh, God!" she breathed. "Let me get myself collected so it won't look like you made love to me on the couch, and we can get out of here."

Ten minutes later they were in a three-story apartment building which had an elevator with a steel cage.

"This thing really work?" McCoy asked.

"So far," she said, closing the door and pushing the buzzer twice. "Somebody down in the basement does something, and we go up to the third floor."

In her apartment, they went directly to the bedroom.

"Do you know how long it's been since—"

He kissed her, stopping the words, but she pulled away. "Damnit, McCoy, I'm saving myself for you. I haven't been with a man since I was with you last. I need you!"

She tore off the jacket of the suit, pulled up her white blouse under it and unbuttoned it, then pushed back her chemise so he could find her breasts.

He grinned, kissed her lips gently, then bent and kissed her surging breasts, working around one slowly until he came to the delicate pinkness of areola, then higher and higher until he licked her surging nipple. He kissed it, then bit it gently and a moment later moved to her other breast to repeat the ministrations.

"Oh, God, but that gets me moving. I want you deep inside me right now!"

She pulled up her skirt, pushed down her pink silk bloomers, kicked them off her feet, then dropped on the bed and opened her arms.

"If you take off your pants or do anything but open your fly, I'm gonna hit you in the face, Spur McCoy. Right now, dig him out and poke me about a hundred times. I'm on fire! I'm so hot I don't think I can stand it another minute without you inside my little hole!"

McCoy did as he was instructed. His fly buttons rubbed her tender flesh, but she didn't seem to notice.

"Hot and fast and hard, like you've been waiting for

me all these months, too. Now, McCoy, fuck me hard right now."

McCoy had been needing her ever since he saw her in the bank, and now he plunged into the glory of her pink slot and found they still fitted together perfectly. He drove in with long hard strokes, stimulating as much of her tender parts as he could each time.

On the fourth stroke she shivered and then wailed, and a long series of vibrations were followed at once by sharp jolting spasms that shook her to her very core.

It was two or three minutes before Lucinda's climax abated and she openned her eyes.

"Oh, God, what a good one!" Then she began humping against him. It was her signal that it was his turn, and he blasted into her hard again and soon sensed the gushing starting high up in his groin and rushing forward.

He poked harder and harder, and just as he was about to feel he had to stop to breathe, he came in a series of six jolts that he thought would put an end to the entire world.

McCoy grunted and brayed as he climaxed, then his panting became softer and softer until it gave way to his near normal breathing.

"Oh, God, I don't see how anything could ever be better—or even as good. Not with anyone else, I assure you. Yes, I've had men before you, smarty pants, but not one of them ever measured up to you." She laughed. "In fact I don't think any two of them put together ever measured up to your performance. Marvelous."

She turned her head, closed her eyes and went to sleep. This simple little action always surprised him. Somehow, what put other women on edge for a half hour acted upon Lucinda as a sleeping potion.

He knew if he moved he'd awaken her. He rested on the softness of her body, still enclosed by her and still thinking of her. A moment later he shut his eyes and dozed off. He'd never done that before. He came back to consciousness with a start and saw that she was awake and watching him.

"I was so good that it put you to sleep?"

"Better than that. You knocked me unconscious." He pulled away from her, and they both sat up on the side of the bed.

"I hope you weren't hungry. I didn't even think about having some lunch sent up."

"We can eat anytime."

"Time . . . what time is it? I have an important conference at two-thirty with some builders. I want to do the financing on a big new building they want to put up. Ten stories high almost and downtown. They haven't even suggested how much money they will need, but I want to finance it. I'll have to sell some of my other investments, but this is exactly why Daddy built up the bank—so we could help local people get ahead."

"And for the usual seven percent."

She threw an angry glance at him. "We haven't talked about the loan rate either. It could be less than that for this much money and over a ten year payback."

They stopped talking business then. It was early, and they had plenty of time. They sat near the window and looked out on St. Louis and the country beyond.

"It's a growing, wonderful town," Lucinda said. "I want to be a big part of that growth. That's why we can't spend all afternoon here in bed."

Twice more they made love, then she arrived back at the bank with ten minutes to spare.

McCoy checked in with his office, but Priscilla said no one had come and that there was nothing interesting in the mail, unless he wanted to buy some land in Arizona.

He went about his business of gathering up his affairs. There were some reports Priscilla gave him that he needed to read, initial and send back to Washington. She showed him two more interesting letters from people who knew of some gigantic fraud against the government. He had no idea how they got his name and address.

Later he went out and bought a new carpetbag, one that he could collapse and tie behind a saddle if need be or could stack full of clothes and goods and stow it on the train. He needed some new clothes and picked out two pair of town pants, two pair of jeans, a hard-wearing blue shirt for range wear and a pair of dress shirts. Then he had his hat cleaned and blocked.

He also had his Peacemaker given an overhaul by Bernard, his favorite gunsmith. He checked his backup Peacemaker, remembered that it had never been fired and took it down to Bernard's test range to be sure it was somewhat accurate.

"Low and right an inch at thirty feet," Bernard determined. "Be sure which weapon you have. Your number one Peacemaker fires high and to the right, the other one low and to the right. Could make a difference."

Spur had never carried a hidden gun, but now he bought one—a neat little derringer taking the same .45 rounds that fit his Peacemaker. When he got back to the office, he was satisfied. He had done most of the things he needed to do, had put Lucinda's charms to the test, had a dinner date with her for tonight after the bank closed, and all was right with the world.

It was after four in the afternoon when he breezed into his office and stopped short.

A woman sat in a chair next to the desk and was seemingly in an animated conversation with Priscilla. When he came in both stood up as if they were in a conspiracy against him.

The other woman was about five-five with jet black hair, cut short with bangs across the forehead and shaped tightly against her head in back. She wore a traveling dress that couldn't hide her big breasts but did dip in delightfully at the waist before it flared over her hips and hit the floor.

McCoy saw flashes of blue eyes over a turned-up nose, small mouth and firm chin. She was a pretty woman, and he figured her at about 24.

Priscilla found her voice first. "Oh, Mr. McCoy, I'd like you to meet Jessica Flanders. That's Secret Service Agent Jessica Flanders. She's the new agent sent from Washington to help you on your next assignment."

Chapter Three

Spur McCoy leaned against the wall. Never in his life had he been more surprised, and that, mixed with indignation and outrage bordering on anger, forced him to turn toward the door as he fought to control himself.

When he looked back at the women, his face had gone stiff and cold. He held out his hand. "Welcome to St. Louis, Agent Flanders."

She shook his hand briefly, a firm quick pressure, then released it.

"Agent McCoy, I know that you're angry. Priscilla told me that the general didn't warn you that I was a woman. I'm sorry. I had no idea that you were so . . . so set in your ways." Her eyes hardened, and her firm chin lifted a notch.

"However, Agent McCoy, I, too, am an agent of the United States Secret Service, and I have been assigned here to work on an upcoming case. I'm not sure what it is just yet, but I can guess that it has something to do with forgery or the counterfeiting of United States bank notes. I've spent the better part of a year in our Washington office working on such cases. Some people think that I'm an expert in the field. The general must have sent me here to help you on some upcoming forgery or counterfeiting case because of my experience."

McCoy had dropped his hand to his side and now nodded routinely.

"Yes, I understand your orders, Miss Flanders. We all get orders, and we all have to follow them—myself as well. If this new assignment is about counterfeiting, I'm sure your expertise will be invaluable."

He turned to Priscilla. "Anything new yet on those orders from the general?"

"Not a thing, Mr. McCoy."

"They'll come. Right now we'll need another desk in here for Agent Flanders."

"I've taken care of that already, Mr. McCoy. The hotel said that they'll have one up here before closing time tonight. I've laid out some supplies that Agent Flanders will need. I think all of that is well in hand."

McCoy nodded again as he tried hard not to show his emotions. "Good, good. Anything I need to look at in the mail?"

"No sir. We went over most of that before."

"Fine. I'll be checking out for today then. I'll be back tomorrow about nine."

He went out the door with a nod to both women. Agent Spur McCoy controlled himself until he was through the hallway and halfway down the steps to the first floor before he exploded. He slammed the flat of his hand against the wall twice, then hurried out the side door of the hotel into the alley where he let out a long and resounding, "No, damnit!"

McCoy took a deep breath and shook his head. Not only an associate agent, but a goddamned woman agent! Yes, he knew there were three or four now in the service, but he never figured that he'd even meet one, let alone have to work hand in glove with one.

"Damnit to hell!" McCoy growled as he walked out of the alley and down the street to the first saloon he came to—Raunchy Bill's Saloon.

Since it was the closest watering hole to the office, McCoy had been in it more than a few times. The first drink was always on the house from Raunchy Bill. He slammed through the swinging doors and pointed one finger at Willis the barkeep. The man promptly took a bottle of bourbon off the back shelf and poured a shot for McCoy, then stood there, not even corking the bottle, waiting for the first drink to vanish. It did.

"One more, Willis. I am not going to get stinking drunk, but I should. If I do, you know where I live?"

Willis nodded. He'd been through this routine with McCoy at least a dozen times, but he'd never had to pour the detective into his room at the Claymore Hotel. Willis had no idea McCoy worked for the government.

"Good. Now put the rest of that bottle on my tab and tell them painted whores to stay a half mile away from my table. Tonight I hate all women."

For an hour, McCoy sat and stared at the third shot of whiskey. All that time he was fighting with himself about whether he should refuse the assignment when it came and wire the general that he must either take the woman agent back or McCoy would resign.

"What I goddamn will not do is work a case with a goddamn woman agent," McCoy mumbled to himself. Once that was out in the open and at least spoken softly, McCoy felt a little bit mollified. He began to see small cracks of light in the total darkness, little slivers of brightness that helped illuminate his predicament.

Yes, he could do that. He would make her investigate every minutia of the case, send her on trips to Omaha and Cheyenne and Chicago to get evidence, send her on background checks on a suspect, run her pretty little ass off in first one direction and then another. When she was out of his hair, he would be able to work on the case without any interference from her and without having to protect her pretty little tits.

McCoy frowned. Yes, she did have good tits that fairly screamed to be let out. He shook his head. He was getting drunk. She was too tall. He liked short women. Today he liked short women. She was too skinny. He liked a woman with some meat on her bones so her pelvis didn't slam into his. Yeah, a little more meat on Agent Jessica Flanders' sleek and slender little ass would make her a much better roll in the hay.

He jammed the cork back in the bottle of bourbon, gave the third shot to the drunk at the next table and found himself a game of dime limit poker that already had four players. Five was just about right for good betting.

McCoy played until 2:00 A.M. In the course of the evening he had been as much as $25 ahead and $10 behind. He wound up the last hand winning on a bluff with his opener pair of jacks and crawled out of the saloon tired, no wiser, and two dollars richer.

The next morning McCoy awoke at 7:00. It had been years since he had slept in past 6:30 when he was alone in bed. He dressed, shaved, combed his longish dark hair and remembered he hadn't seen a barber yesterday as he had planned. He walked two blocks out of the way to a small café where he had a lumberjack's breakfast. He didn't want to run into Miss Pussyfoot Agent Flanders before he had to. It would be hard enough when he got to the office.

After breakfast he stopped at his usual barber who scolded him for not coming in more often for his haircut. McCoy liked his hair to hang long around his neck, just touching his collar and half-hiding his ears. No businessman's cut for him.

He arrived at the office at 8:30 and found both women already there. A new desk huddled in one corner of the room with Agent Flanders sitting behind it reading notices from the head office and recent mailings.

Her short, dark hair clung to her head like a helmet and not a strand was out of place. She looked up and smiled, then the look faded as she saw the grim expression on McCoy's face.

"Good, you're here, Flanders. What's your weapon?"

"My weapon? Oh, I have a five shot .38 caliber Smith and Wesson with a four-inch barrel. I carry it in my reticule, but I also have a gunbelt and side leather if the occasion demands it."

"Can you shoot?"

"Yes."

"Good. Let's go down to Bernard's range in back of his gunshop and see what you can do."

"Right now?"

"If you're going to back me up, I want to be sure you can use that little peashooter. Just a minute while I get my backup Peacemaker."

He barged into his room, brought back his spare .45 Colt and nodded at the door. He did not wait for her or open the door and let her go out first. McCoy marched out of the room, down the hall and let her catch up when she could.

She wore a proper dress, a matching colored sweater for the fall chill and a small hat that blended in with the color scheme. Just what every Secret Service agent should wear, he groused to himself.

Bernard wasn't open yet, so they went around to the alley directly behind his shop where the gunsmith had set up a shooting range. McCoy put five tin cans on the stack of railroad ties that Bernard had positioned to stop bullets. They fired from the alley into the barricade that was built two feet in back of the rear wall of the gunshop. That way nobody complained about stray rounds. The city told Bernard he would have to move his testing range out of the downtown area, but nobody followed up on it. That had been two years ago.

McCoy marked off a line in the dust 20 feet from the row of five cans sitting on the rail ties.

He turned to her. "Agent Flanders, you're walking down a street in a small Western town and one of the bad guys opens up on you with a handgun from thirty feet away. The bad guy is the second can on the right in that line. What will you do?"

The reticule over her shoulder flipped open, her left hand darted in and brought out the short-barreled .38. Her thumb had cocked the weapon before it cleared the reticule's side. She brought it up in a quick point and fired.

The second can from the right slammed backward off the rail tie. She fired four more times, and all five of the tin cans flew into the air.

"After that I'd duck down somewhere and reload," Agent Flanders said.

McCoy's mouth dropped open for just a moment, but long enough for her to see.

"Fine, so you can shoot. You better reload your piece now so it'll be ready in case you need it. How many rounds do you carry with you?"

"Forty. I used to carry twenty, but once I was in a shootout with four forgers and I ran dry. I promised myself never to be out of rounds again."

He watched her as she opened the cylinder, flipped out the spent brass, quickly loaded in five new rounds and closed the weapon with the hammer resting on the empty chamber.

"Put it away and try this one." He handed her his backup .45 Peacemaker, the one that fired an inch to the right and high. Then he went to the target and set up three more cans on the ties.

Back at the 20 foot line, he watched her hefting the Colt. McCoy sat down on the ground and asked her for the Colt which she handed over. He lay it beside his right hand in the alley and looked up.

"Your weapon is not available—lost, stolen, fouled. I get hit and can't fire. Those three cans up there are the bad guys ready to kill us both. What do you do? Now!"

Jessica Flanders dropped to one knee beside him, swept up his .45, held it with both hands and knocked down two of the three cans with three rounds.

McCoy stood and took the weapon from her. He replaced the three rounds and slowly nodded.

"Agent Flanders, looks like you can shoot. A damn good thing. That's what keeps agents alive out here in the West. How far west have you been?"

"Once to San Francisco, once to Denver. I didn't see much of the small town action."

"At least you're honest."

She turned and faced him with a concerned look on her countenance.

"Agent McCoy, I realize that you were stunned and angered when I reported in as your backup on this upcoming assignment. I'm sorry, but there's nothing I can do about my gender. Just let me do my job, that's all that I ask. Now if this petty little testing is over, let's get back to the office. We got a wire first thing this morning that our orders would be in on the

Railway Express which should arrive in our office a little after nine"

"About now," McCoy said.

"Yes, about now."

When they got back to the office, Priscilla handed McCoy a large envelope.

"Looks like the new orders have arrived," Priscilla said.

McCoy tore open the big envelope and let the pages slide out on Priscilla's desk. There were three groups of papers pinned together. On top was the customary careful script of the general's secretary who wrote all of the orders.

McCoy quickly scanned the first sheet. He grunted and flipped to the second group of papers, then to the pinned together third group. There he stopped. Clipped to each of four sheets of paper was one brand-new $20 bill.

"Counterfeiting case," McCoy said. "You were right." He handed her one of the sheets with the bill on it. "Is that a good note or funny money?"

She stared at it. "The plate is perfect. I can find no mistakes, no shading, no lack of detail. It looks genuine, but the final test is the paper." She lifted the edge of the bill and rubbed it between her fingers, then she folded it and slowly shook her head.

"No, it's not legal tender. I'd guess that the plate is genuine but the paper is not government issue. Not one in a thousand people can tell a bill printed like this is a counterfeit."

Spur settled down and read the orders again.

"Spur McCoy, St. Louis Office. Enclosed all material we have on the activity of one Flavian Kirby, age 61, retired engraver from the U.S. Mint here in Washington D.C. When he left he stole engraving plates of both sides of a $20 bill. They are the exact size as a $20 federal bank note.

"Copies of the bills are enclosed. He is a master printer as well and moves around the country setting up his printing plant, grinding off as much money as he needs, then moving on. He is not trying to get rich or flood the country with this bogus money, but he must be stopped.

"As Miss Flanders will tell you, these bills are extremely hard to spot as counterfeit. The best weapon we have against them is the serial number. Each of the bills has the same number, which is 338605438. This is the only sure way a nonexpert can spot the bills. We have notified all banks and financial institutions in your area to be on the lookout for such counterfeit bills.

"Our investigators here tell us that Kirby has moved to St. Louis. In a town of 200,000 people it will be easier to find him than it was in Chicago.

"The man in question is five-feet-four, bearded, unkempt, always wears a dirty, misshapen town hat, uses spectacles all the time, is not given to wild spending sprees. His one easiest spotted vice is the ladies. He is given to the use of prostitutes and has an amazing appetite for a man of his age. He enjoys the most expensive whores in town, so be on the lookout at any fancy parlors that may be open there.

"All banks are cooperating and will give you notice if they find any such bills. Some smaller banks will scan all $20 bills for this number.

"Kirby is believed to be in your city at this time. Expend all possible energy to track him down and arrest him. Is known to be armed at all times with a sword in a cane, a derringer attached to a gold watch fob and concealed in an enlarged vest pocket, and a second derringer in an ankle holster on his right leg.

"Approach with extreme caution. The government wants this man to be taken alive and put on trial to discourage other employees from stealing from the U.S Bureau of Engraving and Printing.

"Other details on the case are enclosed."

McCoy read the rest of the material which was just background on the suspect, his work record, his retirement and the subsequent discovery of the lost plate. Agent Flanders read the reports when McCoy finished with them. She then compared the new $20 bills. She took one off the paper, rubbed away the spot of glue, wadded the bill up into a ball, then spread it out. She took a $20 bill from her own reticule and did the same thing.

The counterfeit did not flatten out as well nor return to its original shape as well as the genuine one.

"The paper he's using is a little too stiff. He knows it, of course, but he can't find the same paper the government uses. It's a special formula by a company in Maine, and the firm is bound by law to sell this particular paper to no one else."

"So we have the crushability and the serial number to go by," McCoy said. "I don't see how this is going to be any big problem."

Agent Flanders still frowned. "This bill is so damned good that not even an experienced teller at a bank will be able to tell by the feel. I'd say we have a big problem, unless we get lucky. Where do we start?"

McCoy scowled and shook his head. "Damnnit, Flanders, you're the expert on counterfeiting. You're here to help, so suppose you tell me where we start."

Priscilla Quincy looked up in wonder.

Chapter Four

Agent Jessica Flanders looked at Spur McCoy to be sure he was serious. She saw that he was and picked up a pencil and a pad of paper from her desk.

"The usual procedures have been started. The Treasury Department has notified all of the bank and financial groups in this area about the chances of counterfeiting, and the banks will make random checks on twenty dollar bills.

"I'd suggest we visit the five or six biggest banks ourselves to go through their twenties and see if we can find anything."

McCoy frowned, then lifted his hand to stop her.

"What if we did find a twenty with this serial number and knew it was a fake? How would a bank know who had deposited it, and if they even found out that, how would the depositor know where he got the bill—if it was a large store, say, or even a saloon?"

"That's the next problem. First we find the bogus bills, then we try to tie down where they came from."

McCoy nodded and stood. "Sounds reasonable. Agent Flanders, you check the banks. Plenty of time to get to the six or seven largest ones before closing time. I'm going to work it from the other end."

Agent Flanders looked up and wrinkled her brow. "I don't quite understand, Mr. McCoy. Which other end are you going to investigate?"

"Specifically I'm going to look for Mr. Flavian Kirby himself and try to find out if anyone has seen him. The best way to do that is to see if he's been a customer at any one of the four or five best parlors in St. Louis. That's the end I'm going to cover, Miss Flanders."

Spots of red peppered Priscilla's face and neck as she blushed and ducked her head. Agent Flanders didn't even blink.

"Yes, good idea, and I'd say you're just the man for the job. You can come and go easily from such establishments without arousing any suspicion."

She slipped on her hat, pinned it in place and marched toward the door. "Oh, in case you wondered, I worked up a list of the biggest banks in town yesterday so I'm all ready to get started. I'll take one of these bogus bills with me to show the bankers. I'm sure you'll have no trouble finding the parlors." She swept out the door and closed it more forcefully than was needed.

Priscilla stood there with her fists on her hips. "McCoy, you certainly weren't nice to your new partner. I'm surprised she so much as speaks to you.

You didn't even make sure she had accommodations last night. Fortunately she's staying here at the hotel. You seem to forget sometimes that women are people, too. Miss Flanders has feelings just like anyone else."

McCoy grinned and chuckled. "Damn, I must have been rough on her if you're standing up and scolding me this way. All right, I'll go easy. Remember, she wasn't my idea, I didn't ask for any help, so you just keep that in mind."

He grabbed his hat and settled it on his head. "Like I told you, I'm going to check out the fancy parlors. Three or four of them popped up lately that the town fathers are not quite sure how to handle. You catch the mail today. Looks like you'll be working right here in the office for some time now, young lady."

"I'm pleased. I'll go through the mail carefully." Her pout was gone, and she grinned again. It was more like the old Pris that he knew.

McCoy started at the top. It was called the St. Louis Club, or usually just the Club, and it was a membership operation that had the best food, best bar and best whores in town. You bought a membership at the door for each visit at a $3 fee. It was not a cheap whorehouse.

He knew that most arrangements were made to use the Club in advance either by the new fancy messenger service that they had between four of the major hotels and the appointment office in the Club or simply by letter.

The Club was on a side street just two blocks from the main thoroughfare of Olive Street. It had no red lights, no big banners or signs. The only identification was the number 333 and the small brass plate on the door which read, THE CLUB.

McCoy had known the owner of the Club for over five years. She was a woman of intelligence, remarkable business sense, good taste, and above all a knack for providing a gentleman with the entertainment and amusement that he wanted most—sex, drink and fine food. She had begun as a whore, saved her money, bought her own bordello, expanded and then made enough profits to interest some investors in establishing the Club. It was a favorite of the gamblers from the river boats.

He knocked on the door. A sliding panel a foot square opened, and a man in a formal dinner jacket, shirt and black tie stared at him a moment. His name was Rhodenway. He smiled, nodded and closed the panel. The heavy oak door swung inward, and McCoy stepped inside the small lobby. It had carpeting two inches thick and expensive and fancy wallpaper. Three original oil paintings hung in prominent places. There were a half dozen luxurious sofas, settees and love seats around the sides of the room.

Rhodenway's formal clothes were immaculate as usual. His smile was warmer now. "Ah, yes, Mr. McCoy. Miss Melissa would be overjoyed to see you. I gather that you're here on business and not for pleasure?"

"Quite right, Rhodenway. I appreciate your fine memory. As I recall, I've only been inside twice before. Exceptionally kind of you to remember."

The tall, dignified man did not respond to the compliment. Instead he turned, motioned to McCoy and

led him down a short hallway to a room at the front of
the building. Rhodenway knocked on the door once,
paused and then tapped three more times.

A girl in her late teens answered the door. McCoy had
never seen her before. She smiled sweetly and wore a
dress that cost twice a month's pay for a working man.

"Right this way, sir. Miss Melissa is in her private
office. Whom should I say is calling?"

"Spur McCoy. I only need ten minutes of her time."

The girl nodded and hurried away. It gave him time
to examine the room. It was an entryway, no more than
eight feet square, yet furnished as if it were in a pal-
ace with a thick carpet and paintings on the wall that
looked like nothing he had ever seen before. One was
four feet square and had a woman with three arms and
three breasts and the body of an alligator. The man in
the picture was breathing fire and had six legs but the
torso and the head of a human. McCoy shook his head
in amazement. Either he was going crazy or some artist
was far ahead of his time.

The young girl came back and led him into a luxurious apartment. This sitting room had all sorts of upholstered furniture set in small groups as if several people were having different conversations. The room was
elegant, and at the far end on a pure white couch sat a
woman in a startling red dress.

"Yes, dear boy. I haven't seen you in some time. How
is everything going with the secret service these days?"

The woman speaking was Miss Melissa. No one
had ever known her last name. She was now in
her mid-forties but was sleek and slender as a girl
in her teens. Only her face gave her away. She

wore so little makeup that he hardly knew she had
any on.

"Come, come, don't stand there gawking like a
schoolboy. You must have business. You always have
business when you come to see me at the expense of
my sexual fantasies. What is it this time?"

Quickly he told her about the counterfeiter and his
special tastes. McCoy painted the picture much bleaker
than it actually was.

"This man could flood the town with bogus money
which will all be returned to the depositor. Every
deposit will be checked at every bank for any of
those twenties, and when they are found they will be
deducted from the total and returned. If he uses your
establishment and spends wildly, it could cost you a
thousand dollars a day if he isn't stopped."

"Dear boy, I've seen funny money before. I can spot
it, and my bookkeeper can spot it."

McCoy took out of his pocket two $20 bills. Both
were new, unused. He laid them on the couch beside
Miss Melissa.

"Which one is counterfeit?"

She looked at them, picked them up, rubbed them,
folded them, then laid them down.

"It's a trick. Neither of them is fake. Both are as good
and solid as a double gold eagle."

McCoy took out another of the bogus bills and laid
it beside the first two. "Check the serial numbers.
Have you ever seen two bank notes with the same
serial number before?"

"Of course not." She frowned, then she picked up the
two bills with the same number and stared. "But they

look so good. The engraving is perfect." She nodded. "If this guy feels like it, he can print himself up a billion dollars worth of twenties and never get caught. The only damn way to spot them would be that serial number."

She put down the bills. "What do you want me to do?"

"The man is a little over sixty, but loves to make love. We understand he utilizes the best houses in whatever town he's working. We have reason to believe he's here in St. Louis, or soon will be. I at once thought of you. Where better for a man to spend all that easily printed money than at the Club?"

She preened herself for a moment, then smiled. "Naturally. We have the best reputation, the best in decor, the best privacy, the best in drink and wine and food. Of course we also offer the most elegant, the most beautiful, the youngest and the hottest young pussies in town. Who do we watch for?"

He gave her the description of the man.

"Not a chance. He'd never get past Rhodenway."

"He would if you told Rhodenway to watch for him and to be sure to let him in. We not only want him, but we need to recover those two plates, the front and back of the twenty dollar bill. We'd be pleased if you would talk to Rhodenway, explain it to him, then send someone to my office or my hotel room when he shows up.

"We won't touch him at your place, but we will follow him back to wherever he's staying and hope we can recover the plates."

"Done. Let me go down and talk to Rhodenway for a moment then I'll be back. Can I offer you anything? Have you had your lunch yet? Yes, we call our noon meal here lunch. Be surprised how many lunches we serve along with the special desert on her backside." Miss Melissa chortled as she swept out of the room.

McCoy sat in one of the upholstered chairs and tried to figure what this master counterfeiter would do.

By now he knew that there must be dozens of law enforcement agencies and city cops after him. Chicago alone would put a fire on his tailfeathers if they ever caught him.

Hell, he would have to change something, the first of which would be his appearance—not his habits but his looks. Gone would be the beard, and he'd have the best suit of clothes his bogus money could buy, instead of his old rags. He'd go slow spending the 20s where they could be traced.

A man buys a 50 cent item and gets change for a counterfeit $20 bill. That leaves him with $19.50 of real money he can spend anywhere without leaving a trace. Say he peddled $1000 of those funny bills in Chicago and came away with $900 in U.S. currency. A man could do a heap of living on $900 without spending another of those tainted bills.

The average store clerk earned about $450 a year if he was lucky. Money went a long ways.

The more he thought about it, the more McCoy decided that Flavian Kirby wouldn't play it quite that conservative. Stealing the plates, printing up the money and fooling the government was one thing. Now he had a record of outfoxing the authorities. That would be where the fun lay for him now.

Flavian would go right on spending his bogus money and feel the thrill of getting away with it. He'd change his appearance but not his habits. That was why McCoy knew he had to get out to the three or four other top social clubs and have them keep a watch for the $20 bills. He wrote the serial number of the counterfeit $20 on a pad of paper and had it ready when Miss Melissa came back.

"Now, our staff is ready and waiting to find this counterfeiter for you. I've arranged to have a light lunch here for you and Evette, and even if you don't wish to stay after the meal, Evette will understand."

"Miss Melissa, I appreciate your kindness and hospitality, but I have a dozen more people to alert about this hombre, and I just can't take the time right now. Maybe I could take a rain check from you on that offer."

Miss Melissa cocked her head to one side as a girl stepped into the sitting room. She wore a thin, silk, pink robe that almost wasn't there. It revealed in stunning clarity surging breasts, a swatch of darkness at her crotch and a shower of dark brown hair that came just below her shoulders.

"Sorry, Evette, maybe later," McCoy said. He was sweating by the time he made it to the door, and he was sure that Evette had seen the start of a bulge behind his fly. What sacrifices he made for the good of the secret service!

McCoy talked to the owners or managers of the other three parlors. None was as flashy or as well-appointed as the Club, but each had a clientele and worked hard at providing food, drink and girls in any order that was desired. All agreed to cooperate fully in watching for Flavian Kirby and the bogus bills.

By the time he got down to the fifth name on his list he was into the bordellos, where the madams were quicker to deal with. He said he'd see to it that any of the $20 bills with the right serial number on it would be fully refunded, if he was notified about it within two or three hours after it was found.

He left the bad bill number everywhere he went and even told the café owner where he had lunch about it. By 4:00 o'clock he had covered the 23 largest whorehouses in town. He wasn't sure how many there were left. The St. Louis City Council had been trying to close up the raunchiest of them but had little success. The Mississippi River boat traffic had pegged St. Louis as a major sex capital, and it was a title hard to get rid of.

By the time McCoy made it back to the office, it was nearly five in the afternoon. Priscilla was still there.

"Not much in the mail. Another wire from the general is on your desk."

He slouched behind the unpolished oak and ripped open the wire.

"TO: SPUR MCCOY, CAPITAL INVESTIGATIONS, CLAYMORE HOTEL, ST. LOUIS, MISSOURI. TODAY RECEIVED COMPLAINT FROM JEFFERSON SPRINGS, MISSOURI, ABOUT THE JEFFERSON SPRINGS BANK ISSUING ITS OWN PAPER CURRENCY. THEY ARE IN DENOMINATIONS OF $1, $5 AND $10. NO OTHER BANK KNOWN TO BE IN THAT GENERAL AREA. STATE OF MISSOURI NO LONGER CHARTERS BANKS TO ISSUE CURRENCY. FOLLOW-UP ON THIS AS QUICK-

LY AS POSSIBLE AS TIME PERMITS ON THE MORE URGENT COUNTERFEITING ASSIGNMENT. KEEP ME INFORMED OF PROGRESS ON BOTH PROJECTS WITH REPORTS AT LEAST WEEKLY. SENDING: GEN. W. D. HALLECK, WASHINGTON, D.C."

McCoy looked up and scowled at Priscilla. "You hear of any more of those phony banks printing up their own money any more? Lots of it back in the fifties and sixties. I haven't heard of any lately."

"I saw something in one of the newspapers about it yesterday. I can try and find the article for you."

"Please do that. Any word from our lady agent?"

"We had lunch together. So far she hadn't found any of the fake twenties. She figured she would keep at it until the last bank closed at five."

"I might send her out to Jefferson City to look into this bank swindle." He gave the telegram to Priscilla. "I figured that all of these old shysters had been caught by now. Wonder how this one slipped through for so long?"

"It seems to me the newspaper said it was a new bank that seemed to be doing just fine, making loans, cashing checks, everything. I know I have the article at home."

"Bring it in tomorrow."

"How did your afternoon go in the bawdy houses?"

"I'm so tired I can hardly walk."

Priscilla looked up, those pink spots blossoming on her cheeks again.

"Don't believe it. I left that serial number at twenty-seven different establishments. If he's in town, we should have him spotted soon."

The door opened and a grinning Jessica Flanders pranced into the room holding a well-worn bank note in her hand.

"Breakthrough. I just found one of the bogus twenties at the Landowners Bank of St. Louis."

Chapter Five

Spur McCoy looked up at Agent Flanders. "You found the first bogus twenty. Good. Who deposited it?"

Jessica shook her head. "It was in the cash drawer of one of the tellers, but the young man said he'd handled thirty or forty of the twenty dollar bills today and had no idea if he took it in today or if it had been in his cash drawer for three days. That's when he took over the window and took out all new bills from the vault."

"Does he handle any big stores or industrial accounts?"

"I didn't ask."

"Tomorrow, as soon as they open, get a list of his customers for the past three days. Some banks keep records like that when drafts are cashed. See if you can find any of the bordellos on the list."

"I'll do that. I'm having a notice printed to distribute to every bank and every store in town asking them to be on the lookout for this special twenty dollar bill. If we can get everyone watching for it . . ."

McCoy shook his head. "No, not a good idea. All that will do is force Flavian to spend the real money he's taken in when he changed a fake twenty. That won't help us. It could also put him on a train or boat out of town. We need the notices but only for specific stores and banks.

"The bordellos are checking every twenty they take in before they accept it. All of the banks should be checking every twenty they get over the counter. That should be your message for them tomorrow."

Jessica nodded slowly. "Yes, I see what you mean. We don't want to scare him away now that we know he's in town."

"We don't know that for sure yet, Miss Flanders. Someone from Chicago who took in one of his bogus marks might have come through St. Louis and spent it, but I'd say the odds are that he's here.

"One more minor problem. Flavian has been passing bogus money for nearly six months now. He knows that a thousand lawmen are looking for him. If you were in his place, Miss Flanders, what would you do?"

"Change his appearance. Shave off his beard and moustache, trim his hair close, buy some conservative and well-fitting clothes. That would give him a much different look."

"I figure that's about what he's done. It's easier to change your clothes and shave off a beard than it is to change your habits. I'd say the parlors and bordellos are still our best bet of snagging him."

Agent Flanders sighed. "I guess you're right. Tomorrow I'll go see all of the banks in town and give them my flyer that has the number of the bill on it. That could improve our chances. Some of these banks might not want to be bothered to check each twenty, but most of them don't take in that many big bills."

McCoy pushed the telegram over to the new agent. "What do you make of this?"

When she read it she frowned. "Strange. Most of those fake banks were routed out of business ten years ago. How can this one pop up like this with all the new state regulations?"

"It's beyond me; that's your area. Why don't you take a run out there to Jefferson Springs tomorrow and see what you can find out?"

"But what about the counterfeiting case here?"

"Seems the general has given us two assignments that kind of overlap. Tell you what. You catch the 8:05 train west tomorrow, and I'll cover the banks for you. That way we can double up on the work and get moving on the new assignment. Could be a few days before we get anything more on our counterfeiter. This bank deal could ruin a lot of honest folks out in Jefferson Springs if it isn't dealt with quickly."

"Right. I've read about how they operate. Back in the sixties they issued money, great looking bills, some even in different colors. One of these so-called banks they ran down had as its only assets a rented room, a barrel stove and one chair."

"Sounds reasonable, so that's your assignment for tomorrow. Get some travel money from Pris and best plan to stay overnight. See if any of that outfit is left and do what needs doing. Wire us if you have any problems."

"Yes sir," Jessica said. "Oh, I had a message for you. I talked to the owner of the St. Louis State Bank. She said your account was overdue and that you should stop in for a conference as soon as possible to keep your credit rating. I'm not sure what she meant by that."

Priscilla looked away and became busy at her desk.

"Yes, thanks, I'll take care of it. Now, I'd say it's near quitting time, so if you ladies will excuse me, I'll be calling it a day."

"No night duty at the pleasure palaces?" Jessica asked with a tinge of irony in her voice.

"Later on. They don't get moving until the dinner trade after six. Evening, ladies."

Spur moved through the connecting door into his room and slid the bolt home on the inside. So, Lucinda wanted to see him again. Fine, but he probably should be working the whore houses. Hell, he didn't know how big this Flavian Kirby was on dining out. He might just utilize the parlors for the girls and the drinks. With some proper timing he could take care of both small tasks.

Spur stripped off his shirt, gave himself a sponge bath to the waist, scrubbed his face and shaved again to get things down to the pink. Then he combed his hair, slapped on a little bay rum and rose water on his face to cut the sting, then put on a pair of town pants, a matching brown shirt, a string tie and a soft brown jacket. He felt dressed up enough to haunt one or two of the parlors or Lucinda's town apartment.

He checked her bank, but everyone was gone. A short walk later he lifted the knocker on her apartment door and was rewarded with quick steps inside and the door coming open.

Lucinda stood there. "Spur, you got my message." She pulled him inside, kissed him wetly and then motioned to the table set for two. "I figured a girl has to compete with those damn parlors, so here it is—dinner, the finest bourbon in St. Louis and for desert, me."

She had brought her cook in from the other house and prepared a gourmet feast—squab, small steaks, a fish dish along with half a dozen vegetables, wine and coffee. McCoy ate until he could barely roll out of his chair. They watched the sunset outside her window, then hurried into the bedroom.

"McCoy, you're ungrateful for all I'm giving you. Do you know that? Why don't you give up and settle down and marry me and make an honest woman of me so I can join polite society again?"

He grinned. It was a little ritual they went through almost every time. He knew his lines.

"Because you really don't want to get married. Because you'd rather feel sexy and raunchy and have somebody like me grab you and kiss you like this."

He kissed her deep, his tongue almost getting lost in her throat.

When it ended she relaxed in his arms and stared up at him.

"Besides, you want somebody to rip off your blouse, fondle your fine breasts, slowly set them on fire and make your nipples throb with fresh, hot new blood."

As he said it he opened the buttons down the front of her blouse, then pushed away her chemise and attacked her breasts with both his hands and his mouth.

By now, Lucinda was gasping. She could hardly talk. When she pointed to the bed, he carried her there, putting her down gently. Her legs stretched wide, and her knees came up, billowing her skirt around her waist. She wore nothing under it.

"Yes, yes, yes, McCoy, I'll marry you for tonight, but just for tonight. Now get on with it before I melt!"

In a modest but fancy hotel halfway across town, a man of five-feet-four inches considered himself in the mirror. Yes, a fantastic change. Anyone hunting him now would have a devil of a time recognizing him. His face was clean-shaven, done in three stages by himself, so there would be no witnesses here in St. Louis. His face still stung from the razor, but the results were gratifying. He found two small brown patches on one cheek he never knew were there. Liver spots some called them. So he was 61; what did he expect? He combed his hair with care. It had been years since it had been this short, a regular business-man's haircut, short on the sides with a part down the right side.

He slipped on the pair of glasses he had bought at a variety store. They had thick hornrims on them but were pure glass inside. He polished the glass and could see as well as always. His eyesight had always been excellent. Forty years as an engraver had not dulled his vision.

Now he set a sporty soft-billed cap on his head. It was made of wool and would be warm to cover his balding spot, but it also gave him a rakish look.

Once more he checked over his clothing. The suit was new, the latest fashion from New York. He had found himself suddenly short of honest cash and had to spend one of the Kirby Twenties, as he called them, but it had been worth it. The suit was a deep blue with just the hint of a pinstripe.

His shoes were the finest leather and were black to match the suit. Satisfied with his appearance, he checked a locked valise that he had put under the bed. Inside were banded bundles of bills, Kirby Twenties. He knew exactly how much he had left— $88,380. He kept track where and when he spent the bogus bills, partly so he would know where to travel next and partly so he would know when he needed to find a spot to set up a small print shop. In Chicago he had simply bought a one-man shop that was for sale, took over the press and at night printed out his new supply of Kirby Twenties.

He looked in an envelope marked U.S. bills. In the big envelope was the legitimate Silver Certificates issued by his old boss the Bureau of Engraving and Printing. He didn't have an exact count of this cash. He had left Chicago with about $1,200, and most of it was still there.

He took out $60 and put it in his wallet which fit neatly in the back pocket of his new suit. That should be enough for an evening at one of the lavish new whorehouses he had heard about. They were the main reason he had come to St. Louis. Food, drink and sex all at the same table!

Kirby went downstairs, caught a cab and gave the address, 333 Boundary St. The cabby gave him a grin.

"Hope you got an appointment. That place has been busy as hell tonight. Must be payday or something."

At the door of the Club, the panel opened and Rhodenway stared out. He continued to look at the small man outside.

"The name is Amway. I have an appointment for 6:15 tonight."

A moment later the panel closed and the door opened. Rhodenway motioned to a young girl seated on one of the sofas.

"Mr. Amway to 604," he said sharply.

The girl nodded, hooked her hand through his arm and led him down the hallway. There was no elevator here. They climbed to the sixth floor and to room 604. She stopped and watched him for a moment.

"Business before dinner," the girl said softly. She held out a silver tray just long enough to hold paper currency. On it was a slip of paper with the figure $45. The short man reached in his pocket, took out his wallet, placed two U.S. printed twenties and a five on the tray and put away his wallet. At these prices there would be no tips. This had better be good. The girl smiled, tucked the tray and the money under her arm and knocked on the door twice.

When Flavian Kirby looked around, the winsome girl was gone. The door opened and another lovely stood there. She was an inch shorter than he was, as he had proscribed, blonde with long hair and on the chunky side just the way he liked them. The girl smiled.

"Mr. Amway, I'm Delphine. Please come in, and I'll have our dinner sent right up. You ordered the roast pheasant, wild rice and stuffing along with a fine port wine. Everything should be ready."

His eyes bulged. He'd never seen a whore who looked like this. She could have been at a society ball or at the President's inauguration. She was beautiful, hair perfect, surging breasts almost covered by a clinging silk gown. Her waist was ample and the gown was cut short, mid-thigh as he had ordered. He wanted to jump on top of her right there.

The large room had soft carpeting, finely decorated wallpaper, oil and watercolor paintings on the wall, elegant furnishings, a big open window with a river view and a small dining table to the left near the window. It was luxurious.

"I know you're anxious. Let me ring for the order, then we can get better acquainted before the meal arrives."

She went to a pull cord and tugged on it four times. A moment later she led him to a double bed, exquisitely covered with a spread with what he swore must be gold threads.

When she sat down on the bed, the gown slipped open, revealing one of her large breasts.

"My dear!"

Delphine smiled. "You just go right ahead and enjoy. Whatever you want, I want. You can have some small bites if you wish."

He bent and kissed the glowing orb. A dozen kisses later he licked the nipple and felt it surge upward.

"My goodness, you really know what you want, Mr. Amway."

A knock on the door interrupted them. She pushed her breast beneath the fabric, stood up and walked across the thick carpet to the door.

A young girl in a white tunic that was skintight rolled a cart into the room. She was dark-eyed, black-haired and slender as a reed. She pushed the cart to the dining table set for two and set out the covered dishes and the chilled bottle of wine.

Then she bowed, pushed the cart out of the room and left without a word.

Delphine went to the bed where the man slowly rubbed a lump behind his pants's fly.

"Dinnertime, Mr. Amway. Then we do whatever you want to do for the rest of the night." She paused. "You should seat me now, Mr. Amway."

He jumped to her side, pulled out a chair, let her ease into it and then pushed it forward to the table. Kirby took his place opposite her as Delphine uncovered the chafing dishes.

"Oh, roast pheasant! I just love it." She used a knife and fork and quickly carved the bird into half a dozen pieces.

"Which piece to start with? A breast or a drumstick?"

The dinner was a smashing success. Kirby proved he could hold his wine, and finally he was filled to his limit.

"A short nap," he said. "I want your tits to be my pillow."

She slipped out of the robe and, naked, led him to the bed. He kissed her breasts and nibbled at them, then positioned her slantwise across the big bed. He slid out of his shoes and jacket and lay down with his head nestled on her bountiful breasts.

"I'm in heaven," he said. His eyes closed, and a moment later he was sleeping.

He awoke with a start less than five minutes later. Something had bothered his slumber. Then he felt it again. Delicate fingers had opened his fly, worked through his underwear and had brought him to a full erection while he snoozed with his head cushioned on her breasts.

"Sonofabitch," he whispered. "Nobody's ever done me that way before. You're good, Delphine, damn good."

She undressed him, and when they sat side by side on the big featherbed, she kissed his cheek gently, then smiled sweetly at him.

"Mr. Amway, just what kind of sexy games do you want to play now?"

Chapter Six

Flavian Kirby, going by the name of Amway, faced the most beautiful woman he'd ever seen sitting stark naked on the bed beside him.

"What kind of sexy games do I want to play?" he asked. "Hell, all of them. You can start by stripping me naked. I do love to have a sexy, naked woman undress me."

"What about this big fellah down here?" Delphine asked. She stroked his stiff cock and then bent and kissed its purple head.

"Hell, he'll just have to wait his fucking turn."

Delphine moved quickly, straddling his torso and sitting on his lap. Slowly she brushed her breasts against his jacket, then slid it off his arms. Next she attacked his vest and his shirt until he was naked to the waist.

Delphine pushed him down gently to the bed and moved higher, lowering one of her breasts into his mouth.

"Glory!" was all he had a chance to say before he was overcome with a warm, marvelous tit filling his mouth. He chewed and licked it, and when he was about to yelp, she pulled that breast out and slipped the other one in.

"Some men don't like to suck tits, but I think you do. Later you can be on top and really eat my girls right down to a nub." As he mouthed her breast, she pulled his pants and long underwear down around his knees.

She stood up and took off his new town shoes, his socks, and then his trousers and long johns.

She urged him to slide up on the bed, then she began kissing his feet, playing with his toes with one hand and gently stroking his rock hard cock with the other.

"Woman, what the hell you doing?" Kirby yelped.

"Getting you ready for the best fuck you've ever had. Isn't that what you want?"

She didn't wait for an answer. She worked up his leg with her hand, massaging and kneading. She came to his balls and fingered them a moment.

Her head then went between his legs, and she licked his balls until he whimpered.

"No, no more I'm almost ready to shoot!"

She lifted her head, stroked him twice with her hand, then mouthed his cock and pumped twice more with her mouth, enveloping most of him until he screeched like a wounded mountain lion.

His hips bucked upward half a dozen times, and she accepted all he had. He panted like a two-mile-run horse and stared at her in amazement. It took him three minutes to get his breathing under control so he could talk.

"How'd you make me come so fast? I'm sixty-one years-old, for God's sakes. I ain't no quick erupting fourteen year-old never been sucked-off virgin."

She smiled and lay down beside him. "You want to use my pussy for a pillow while you get your strength back?"

He shook his head. "Tits again. Damn but you got a fine set of big tits. I'm more a tit man than a leg lover anyway."

She moved so he could lay his head on her breasts, and he sighed. "Goddamn, this is starting out good."

"Tell me, Mr. Amway, what is the one thing you wish you could do to a woman, or you'd like a woman to do to you that you've never got up nerve enough to ask for?"

"Lordy, I've done about everything."

"A stand-up fuck?"

"Done that."

"Us both eating each other at the same time, end to end?"

"Tried that, but you done your half already."

"How about fucking me when I'm standing on my head?"

"Never tried that."

She laughed, rolled off him onto her back and pulled him with her. "Good, because it won't work— the wrong angles." She spread her legs and caught his cock and worked on it until it came rock hard again.

"Inside me, quickly. If we're going to get in five fucks before midnight we have to hurry."

"Why midnight? I bought the whole night."

"Of course, Mr. Amway, but after midnight we sleep for two hours, wake up and try something new. We also get a late night dinner at two A.M. You wouldn't want to miss that would you?"

He lifted away from her, crawled between her sleek thighs, aimed for her heartland—and missed. She giggled, put down one hand and helped him find the right slot. He plunged into her twat like an arrow into water.

"Oh, yeah!" Amway shouted. "Now this is what enjoying life is all about. Great food, good cocksucking and now a fuck that won't let me quit."

Delphine brought her legs up and circled them around his torso, locking them together. Then her arms banded like steel around his back and she started humping him, grabbing him with her pussy muscles, then letting him almost slide out before capturing his prick again.

"Lord oh Lord, but are you good. Nobody ever milked me that way before. How did you learn to do that so fucking good?"

She smiled at him in the soft lamp light. "Practice, Mr. Amway. I'm the best because I do a lot of practicing."

She was bucking against him harder now, and before he realized it, he had climaxed again. When the last thrusts of his hips had finished he sagged on top of her, so exhausted he could hardly move.

It was five minutes this time before he could talk. He looked at her and rolled away. "Glory! I don't know when I've been fucked so damn wonderful."

"I'd say never, Mr. Amway. This is Delphine, and I'm the highest price girl in the stable here. Everything I do is the best. You want a full body massage?"

Without waiting for his response, she rolled him over on his stomach, and starting with his arms over his head, she worked his hands and fingers and relaxed each set of muscles before moving on. She had both arms done and went to work on his shoulders when she realized he was asleep.

At once she got up, went to the window and opened it, letting the cold October air rush in. She closed the window and stood there watching the street below. He was too old. Maybe once more and he'd be through for the night. He might even miss the two o'clock late dinner. Delphine was damn certain that she wouldn't miss it. A working girl in this business had to keep up her strength.

She watched him sleeping. He wouldn't wake up until morning if she let him snooze. She went to his trousers, checked the pockets and found more than $200 in what looked like new bills. They were under a little flap that was supposed to hide them, but she'd seen every kind of wallet ever made.

She was tempted. Delphine could use another $200 in her Oregon fund. When she had enough cash saved, she would steam out of this St. Louis so fast she'd leave it spinning. Next she'd grab the train in Omaha and be in Oregon before she knew it. Oregon! It had a magic ring to it. She'd never been there, but she knew two girls who had. They said it rained a lot, but that made the country so green it must look like the Emerald Island of Ireland.

Delphine left the window and nibbled at some of the cold pheasant. She salted the leftover drumstick and chewed all of the meat off it. Back to work.

She eased Amway over onto his back and worked on his flaccid tool. Quickly she had him hard again.

He moaned in his sleep, humped his hips once and smiled.

She woke him when the late dinner came at 2:00 A.M. He was groggy for a while, but the wine revived him, and the spicy sausages and chicken wings and little cherry cakes were more than enough to get him fully awake.

When they finished eating, she rolled the small cart out of the room and locked the door. In her most tempting naked way, Delphine swayed as she walked back to where he sat on the bed. She waltzed her fur muff right up to his chin and brushed it against his lips.

"Damn, I'd love to, but twice a night is my limit. I'm so washed out not even you could get me up for another go around. I might as well get dressed and go back to my hotel. I'm at an age where I need my sleep."

Delphine nodded. She'd been expecting as much. "Usually if a man's happy with my work, he makes a small donation to my retirement fund."

He grinned. "Delphine, you'll never retire, not with a hot little cunt like yours. But I can afford to turn a twenty your way. Will that help?"

She jumped on his lap, hugged him, kissed his cheek, then beamed at him. "That would just be ever so grand. You must promise to come back and see me tomorrow, maybe in the afternoon." She helped him dress and walked arm in arm with him to the secluded side entrance where they had a cab waiting for him.

When Delphine reported to Miss Melissa that she was available again, she said nothing about the $20 bill that Flavian Kirby had given her. He had reached in the wrong compartment and given her one of the counterfeits.

Delphine went back to her own room, eased the floorboard up and took out a small metal box in which she kept her traveling money. She put the bogus $20 bill along with the rest of her stashed loot. She didn't have to count it. She knew that with this $20 she now had $1,435. When she got to an even $2,000 she was heading for Portland.

Spur McCoy left Lucinda's apartment at 6:30 the next morning while the banker slept. It was their usual pattern. He gave his face and torso a quick sponge bath and dressed, then hurried down to a café for coffee, his first cigar and breakfast.

Today he would check all the banks again and urge them to look over every $20 bill they handled. It would be quite a task. He picked up the printed flyers and circled the bogus serial number on each of them.

He had Jessica's list from the office. There were 22 banking and financial establishments in Denver. He talked to all but three before the day was over and got back to the office just before 4:00 that afternoon.

Priscilla was on the job. "Jessica got off on the 8:05 for Jefferson City. She wired from there that she had arrived and was starting to hunt for the suspects. How did you do today with all of your banker friends?"

He told her that he had damn near talked his mouth off all day long.

"We've had no reports of fake twenty dollar bills from any of the pleasure palaces," Priscilla said. "At least none today which would be from their take last night. Either they aren't watching for the serial number on the bill or our man didn't spend any fake money yesterday."

"Or the girls and madams missed it." McCoy tossed his hat at his desk. "We don't have a damn thing to go on. Five will get you fifty that Flavian Kirby has changed his appearance, so that's a dead end. How are we going to find this man?"

Priscilla seldom saw McCoy this worried. She frowned at him. "Now don't you go getting upset, Mr. McCoy. You've whipped tougher ones than this. I'm betting that the parlors will be where our first real lead comes from. Oh, did you check that teller who handled the first fake bill?"

"That I did. He's a prissy little sonofabitch who doesn't really want to cooperate with us. His manager made him give me a list of the business firms he serviced during the past three days. That bank keeps a record, but the list I got didn't help. On it were hardware stores, cafés, a livery and even a saddle shop, but not one single bordello."

McCoy sat at his desk and looked at the new mail. Nothing from the general. He pushed it aside. "Anything here I need to look over?"

"Nothing that can't wait. A request from Washington for some more information on one of the old cases. I'll find your report on it tomorrow."

"Fair enough. Why don't you go on home. I'm about to take off myself and call it a wasted day. I'm tired of talking to bankers."

Priscilla looked up quickly and grinned.

"Yes, except for that one lady banker," he said. "Now get out of here. There's a new production at the Variety Theatre on tonight, and I sort of promised that one lady banker that I'd take her to see it."

In Jefferson Springs, Missouri, Secret Service Agent Jessica Flanders stepped off the train and first went to check in with the local lawman.

"Hey, we don't even got a town marshal no more," the man at the General Store told her. Jefferson Springs was little more than a whistle stop, with about 200 people scattered in a long row of houses along the one main street that was half a block over from the railroad tracks.

"How far away is the county sheriff?" she asked.

"Sheriff? Yep, we got one of them, but he's nigh on to twenty-five mile out west a piece. Used to have a deputy here, but nothing ever happened, so the sheriff took him back to the county seat."

"What's the name of the county seat?" Jessica asked.

"That one I know. Forest Grove, over there at the edge of Grove County. Lots of farm folks over that way."

"What was your name again, sir?"

"Me, oh, I'm Hirum Jarek. That last name is Slovakian in case you're interested."

"Good to meet you, Mr. Jarek. Is the post office here in your store?"

"Certainly is, Miss. You have something to mail or need some stamps or something?"

"Just some information. You must know about everyone in town. Can you tell me where I can find the Jefferson Springs Bank? I didn't see it as I walked here from the railroad station just now."

"Bank? Town this size don't got no bank, Miss."

"I'm certain this is the right town. It's called the Jefferson Springs Bank."

The man folded his arms across his chest. He was thin and rangy, and now his face took on a tense, defensive look about it that surprised her.

"Got to be mistaken, Miss. Never been a bank in this town for all the days I been here. I opened the store nigh on to twelve years ago. Must have us mixed up with Jefferson Springs over in Illinois. It happens all the time."

She nodded, but a gnawing doubt creeped into her mind that this wasn't going to be as easy as it first looked.

"Well, thanks for your time. The hotel, just down the street, is still open, isn't it?"

"Sure as rain. My kinfolk run it. They have a batch of nice rooms there, and the café across the street turns out a good mess of fine cooking."

She thanked him and left the store, her small valise still in hand. No bank. Amazing! She hadn't seen the actual fraudulent bank notes, but if they came from Jefferson Springs, Missouri, this was the town. Could it be possible that there was a bank here that no one knew about?

It seemed ridiculous even to consider the idea. One thing struck her as she paced along the boardwalk toward the two-story hotel. If nobody knew about a bank here, none of the local people could have lost any money in it. That was one satisfying thought.

She looked across the street and saw what appeared to her to be a typical bank building. It was solid, conservative and had newspapers pasted over the windows on the inside. From where she stood she could see just the end of some lettering that had been scraped off the window. The last letters that were not quite obliterated were "ank."

She continued to the hotel and checked in. She had a small room, clean and aired out, with sheets and a passable mattress. One chair, a scarred dresser and the usual pitcher full of water and a bowl for washing completed the picture. There was no mirror on the dresser.

She sat on the bed a moment and looked at the small watch she carried on a chain around her neck. It was just past 3:30 in the afternoon. Jessica adjusted her trim brown hat, repinned it, then checked the traveling dress. Yes, it was sufficient for dinner out in a town like this.

She walked down from her second floor room and nodded at the desk clerk but kept the key to her room in her reticule.

She walked north past the General Store, then crossed the street, pausing at every small store and business firm on the way. There were only 15 stores that she counted. She watched a woman working in a dress shop, pinning up cloth on a clothes dummy. The woman glanced up, saw her and nodded.

Two stores later Jessica was in front of the building that could only be a bank. Now it was plain that the lettering across the big front window had been scraped off, probably with a sharp knife or a razor. She could still see the outline of the lettering on the glass. Plainly it said: Jefferson Springs Bank.

Jessica heard something behind her, and when she turned around, the store owner and the woman from the dress shop were so close they hemmed her in against the building. Mr. Jarek, the General Store merchant, held a six-gun aimed at her stomach, almost touching her dress.

"Like I said, Miss, we ain't never had no bank here in Jefferson City, Missouri. You best just come along with us."

Chapter Seven

Spur McCoy had enjoyed the production of *Hamlet* at the Variety Theatre the night before, and after the play the games in the lady banker's big featherbed had been even more invigorating. But with a new morning and his first cup of coffee, he got back to business.

There was no morning telegram from Jessica in Jefferson City. This bothered him some, but he decided she could take care of herself on a little bank scam gone bad like this one. He decided that he should make a tour of the city's ten largest retail stores, tell them about the fake $20 and see if they would cooperate. He was running out of ideas on how to find this counterfeiter.

Before he left the office, a messenger came with a note that he should come to the Missouri State Bank at once. They had found one of the fake bills. He followed the messenger back to the bank where a tall, somber man ushered him into an office.

The name plate on the desk said he was H. Charles Devinger, President.

"Mr. Devinger, you found one of the counterfeit twenties?"

He shook hands with the agent and nodded. "Mr. McCoy, indeed we have. One of my bright young tellers caught it, and she even knows who deposited it." He held out the bill, and McCoy checked the serial number which he had memorized. Then he compared it with one of the counterfeit bills from an envelope in his pocket.

"It's a match, Mr. Devinger. Could I talk to that teller?"

The banker motioned, and a slender young woman came into the room. She was medium sized with boyish hips, and the fit of her dress failed to reveal any sizeable breasts. She had dark hair and brows and a faint hue of color in her skin that suggested perhaps some Indian blood. Her dark eyes danced with excitement, and her smile would light up a coal mine tunnel at midnight.

"Miss Cloud, would you tell Agent McCoy about the deposit?"

"Yes sir. The bill was the only twenty in the cash deposit from a small business I always handle— the Rathmore Clothier Shop. Mr. Rathmore comes in every morning at opening time with the receipts from the day before. I saw the twenty, and it didn't feel right. But all the twenties I've handled since we got the notice don't feel right."

She took a deep breath, and McCoy saw her breasts rise beneath the fabric. That made him feel ever so much better. They were there, just kind of hiding.

"I checked the serial number with the one I wrote down on my pad, and it matched. I showed it to the head teller who said indeed it was the same. He told me to go ahead and accept it and not upset the depositor. I did, and they sent the messenger to your office—and here I am."

"What do you know about this depositor, Miss Cloud?"

"Mr. Rathmore is a sweet man, kind and thoughtful. He's gentle and honest, and I'm sure he didn't know the bill was a fake. It's a well-made counterfeit."

"Could you give me the address of the firm?"

She recited it from memory, and the bank president nodded. "Yes, Mr. McCoy, that's the store. Is there anything else we need to do?"

"No, I'll confiscate this counterfeit bill and put it in one of your bank's envelopes to identify where it came from. You'll deduct it from the deposit, and if possible we'll compensate Mr. Rathmore."

McCoy smiled at Miss Cloud. "I may be back to ask you some more questions later." She nodded and scurried out of the room.

"Your first break in the case, Mr. McCoy?"

"No, we've picked up another bill, but we had no lead as to where it came from. This is our best lead so far." He took the envelope the banker gave him, put the $20 bill inside and shook the man's hand.

"Thanks for your help. Please alert your people to watch for any more such bills. I'm going to go buy myself a new shirt."

McCoy found the small men's clothing store right

where the banker said it would be, and when he stepped inside, he saw that it had only one clerk, probably the owner, Mr. Rathmore himself.

"Yes sir, what can I do for you today?" the man asked. He was smaller than average, dressed immaculately in a conservative mold. He wore spectacles and had thinning gray hair. McCoy figured he was about 50.

McCoy told the clothier why he was there and showed him his identification and badge and then the counterfeit bill.

"Gracious, this is terrible. I had no idea the man wasn't honest. He was dressed well. A conservative suit, good shirt, links in his cuffs, gold watch and chain. Goodness me, will I get in trouble?"

"Not if you cooperate. You do remember who gave you the twenty?"

"Yes, it was the only one I took in yesterday. He bought a new tie, and two pairs of socks and a new vest to go with the suit he wore."

"Can you describe him for me? How tall was he?"

"On the short side, five-feet-four, I'd say. Not heavy, no more than a hundred and twenty pounds. He's one of those men who get thinner as they get older instead of the other way around. My guess is that he's just over sixty years-old. He had bright, clear blue eyes. I tend to notice that sort of thing. They matched his blue suit."

"Did he have any accent?"

"No, not that I recall. Midwestern if any, although I did detect a slight twang of the Maine coast. Yes, it was down east, reminded me of my early days in Boston."

"Any facial hair?"

"Oh, no, cleanly shaven and with some bay rum or such. Quite a spiffy gentleman if you ask me."

"Shoes?"

"Best style. Bet he paid over eight dollars for them. Excellent make of shoe."

"Spiffy, dapper, about sixty, clean-shaven. Did he wear a hat?"

"Curious, he didn't. I'd have expected him to."

"White shirt, stiff collar?"

"Exactly, like he was going to a fancy party or ball or something."

"What time of the day did he come in?"

"Just before I closed at six. In fact he made me a little late getting home for my supper, and my wife was upset."

"Did he have the appearance of going to some event?"

"Yes, he seemed keyed up, excited."

Spur McCoy dug into his wallet, took out a $20 bill and handed it to the clothier. "This is to replace your loss. The bank has deducted the fake twenty from your account. We don't have to replace counterfeit bills, but in this case you've cooperated with me and given us some valuable information, so the government will replace your loss."

McCoy took the man's thanks and hurried out of the store. Now he had a description of the counterfeiter for the whorehouses. It would take him half the day to get around to them. He started with Miss Melissa at the Club.

"Talk to your top girls," McCoy suggested. "See if any of them remember such a man, sixties, five-four, good dresser, might be in a blue suit, blue eyes, gray hair thinning, spiffy dresser and no facial hair."

"Well, now, McCoy, that cuts down the field," Miss Melissa said from where she sat in her office. "Not a lot of men in their sixties visit us. Makes it a lot easier. I'll talk to the girls, and if I find any kind of a match, I'll get a messenger over to your hotel pronto."

Two of the madams refused to talk with him. They seemed to think that if anyone could stiff the government for a few fake $20 bills, so much the better. He plowed along the streets until he had covered the top 20 whorehouses.

He got back to the office foot weary and not as enthusiastic as he had been that morning.

"Nothing new has happened since you've been gone," Priscilla said.

He told her about the match on the bill and the description of the spiffy little man passing it.

"So now you have something to work with," Priscilla said. "Now I know it won't be long. He'll spend more of the bills. Maybe he's run out of his good currency."

"I hope so. Anything from Jessica?"

Priscilla frowned and shook her head. "She said she'd let us know if anything happened one way or another before she started back—at least once a day. We haven't heard anything since she arrived in that little town. It's about eighty miles west?"

"Yes." He furrowed his brow for a moment. "I'm sure she can take care of herself. She's an experienced agent. Why don't you send her a wire to be picked up at the telegraph office. Ask her for a progress report. It should bring a response."

He grabbed his hat. "What time do the banks close now?"

"Usually about four, but then they have to balance and all, so most of the workers don't get away until around five."

"Good. I want to talk to that teller again. You close up at five if I'm not back."

"No night work?" Priscilla asked wistfully.

"Not for you, Pris. You get home and get your rest. Tomorrow might be a tougher day."

He hurried out of the hotel and straight for the Missouri State Bank. It was only four blocks away, so he marched at a brisk pace and arrived just before five. Two workers were leaving the bank by the side door. Someone unlocked the door and let them out, then locked it again. He called out to the two young men.

"Pardon me, but has Miss Cloud left yet? I'm the government man who talked to her this morning."

They stopped and looked at each other, then one of them came back.

"I'm certain she's still here. Something about not balancing. Since you're a lawman I guess it's all right to let you in."

"I have some more questions for her."

The bank teller went back, rapped on the door and spoke with the guard there a moment, then waved McCoy forward.

"Yes, she's still here. We have to sign in and out these days. The guard, Percy, will take you to her window."

Moments later McCoy found Miss Cloud with her chin in her hand. Before she looked up she let out a little cry of joy. "I found it! I found that miserable two dollar mistake!"

"I'm quite glad you found it," McCoy said. She looked up startled and smiled.

"Well, Mr. McCoy. You said you might have some questions for me, but you didn't come back."

"If you can finish up your work here, I'd be delighted to ask the questions over a bit of dinner, if that's all right with you."

Her smile lit up the place. "Yes, I would enjoy that. It'll take me about a minute and a half."

They were the last ones out of the bank. The guard signed them out, and then he, too, left making sure all the doors were locked up tight.

"We have good roundsmen here in St. Louis," he told McCoy. "Not hardly any trouble with nighttime pranksters or robbers. Fact, we've never been robbed, but keep your elbows crossed so we don't."

McCoy took her to a small nearby restaurant run by some Italian immigrants whose style of cooking had caught his taste buds by surprise more than once. They settled at a table for two toward the back of the eatery, and she put her hands under her chin and watched him.

"You really don't have any questions for me, do you, Mr. McCoy?"

"Of course I do. I already asked you one. Now for the second question, what's your first name, or do I have to go on calling you Miss Cloud?"

She laughed, and it brought a smile to his face.

"My parents named me Feather, but when my mother died, Daddy insisted that I have more of a white name, so we decided on Esther. That's a Persian name that means star. Also it's Biblical. It's the Persian name of the captive Hadassahk, whom Ahesuerus made his queen."

"Your mother was Sioux?"

"No, she was half Osage. My father is all white."

"Your parents created a beautiful combination in you," he said.

"Thank you. I'm not used to compliments. Some people don't like it when they find out that I'm part Indian."

"That's a stupid problem that is entirely their fault. As for me, I'm fascinated. Will it be all right to call you Feather?"

For a moment she was quiet, her face showing surprise, then she smiled. "That would please me. May I call you Spur?"

"That would please me."

When the waiter came McCoy ordered for both of them. There were three dishes, all with a lot of meat and cheese and spices. Feather said she had never tasted anything like it in her life.

They had small cakes in a sauce for dessert, and when the candle flickered on the table, McCoy realized that they had spent two hours in the restaurant. The waiter hovered. McCoy paid the bill, and they walked out into the early evening.

"I'll see you home," he said.

"Not necessary. I don't live far away."

"I want to see that you get home safely."

She nodded, and they strolled down the dark street. They had talked of everything during their meal.

McCoy was strangely moved. He'd told this sweet young girl things about his youth he had never told anyone. In response she had shared with him things that had happened to her family and her before they had come here.

He was moved and mystified. How had this happened? She was only another woman. She did not hold his hand nor catch his arm. They walked along together, yet separately. Spur McCoy grinned in the darkness.

In two hours Feather Cloud had become a special friend. He knew that he would never touch her, except perhaps a good night handshake. She was one of those women he met from time to time, maybe once every five years. He knew that here was a woman he could settle down with, who he could spend the rest of his life getting to know and understand and love.

He also knew that it would not happen. He wasn't ready. Hell, he might never be ready. She said something, and he turned toward her.

"Excuse me, Feather, I missed what you said."

"I was only remarking that I've never seen the moon so huge. It looks twice as big here as it does out on the plains or on the coast. Do you think men will ever get to the moon?"

McCoy chuckled. "Doubt if we'll find a bird that big to carry a man all that way. Men have tried to fly for centuries. One over in Europe somewhere glued feathers on his arms and jumped off a high place flapping like crazy. Killed himself. I reckon we'll just have to wait a while until somebody figures out how we can fly.

"What about balloons? Men fly in them."

"True. I saw one once. First one I ever heard of was back in 1830 by a man named Charles Durant in New York City. Went all the way across the Hudson River to New Jersey."

"Some day I want to fly in a balloon," Feather said.

"I hope you do." McCoy shook his head at the glowing orb above them. "That full moon sure can do strange things to people. I haven't thought about that balloon flight for ten years."

They came to her place, an apartment on the second floor of a big building. At the door she turned and held out her hand.

"Mr. Spur McCoy, I thank you for the delightful dinner and the talk. I haven't talked that way for years. I wish you good fortune in finding that counterfeiter. Now I must go up. Father will be worried about me."

He shook her hand.

"Miss Feather Cloud, I have been delighted myself with this evening. I'll remember it for a long time. Perhaps I'll see you again."

She smiled in the half-darkness of the glowing gas lamp on the porch. "Perhaps, Mr. McCoy, but probably not. Good night."

She went through the door, and McCoy turned and walked away. Tonight he would stay in his room at the hotel and wonder what might have been.

Chapter Eight

Agent Jessica Flanders stared at the six-gun almost touching her stomach.

"Mr. Jarek, I want you to consider carefully what you're doing. You are committing assault and battery against me, and you are threatening my life with a firearm. If you move me one foot from where I stand, you will be subject to kidnapping charges. All of these counts could put you in state prison for the rest of your natural life."

"Yeah, yeah, I've heard you lawyers talk before. Just come with us and I won't have to shoot you."

"Have you ever shot a person before, Mr. Jarek?"

He frowned, and he pushed the muzzle against her stomach. "Not as such. Shot at a robber once, but I missed him. I ain't about to miss this close. Now just come around the corner of this building and down the alley a ways. We got somebody mighty anxious to meet you."

"Do you know who I am?"

"Don't know, don't care," the woman beside Jarek said. "Know you're here to cause us a powerful batch of trouble, and we don't aim to see that happen."

"I didn't catch your name, Madam."

"I didn't throw it. Fact is I'm Nan Lattimer, case it'll do you a pea picking batch of good. This misbegotten gent is my brother. You best come along now. He ain't got a whole lot of patience left in him."

The gun jabbed harder now, and Jessica decided to hold her identity secret for a while longer. She'd see what they had in mind for the moment. She turned, with both of them close behind her, walked along the front of the former bank building, turned into the alley and went down it about 30 feet.

Nan Lattimer hurried ahead and opened a door at the back of what Jessica still figured was a bank. She stepped inside and saw two lamps glowing in a dim room without windows.

"Who the hell's there? Who the hell's disturbing me at my work?" The angry bellow came from somewhere ahead.

Jessica's eyes adjusted to the gloom, and soon she saw a towering hulk of a figure bent over some kind of machinery.

"Not to worry, Ed. Just me and some friends."

"Jarek, damn your eyes! Never sneak up on me again that way. Had my blunderbuss out here and half-trigger pulled." The figure had not turned around but simply went on working over the machine that Jessica now saw was a printing press. On a table nearby she spotted dozens of pieces of paper slightly larger than a bank note.

They looked about seven by three inches, the same size as the federal bank notes and silver certificates.

As the trio moved forward slowly, the figure turned around. He wore a dark cape that had a hood on it, so she couldn't really see his face now that his back was to the light.

"Ed, got a new friend for you here. Don't know her name, but she's a pretty little thing. She was getting nosy about the bank."

A roaring bellow of disapproval gushed from the man, and Jessica took a step backward, bumping into Nan Lattimer who snorted.

"What are you doing here in the bank, Ed?" Jessica asked. She knew what he was doing; she wondered if he did.

"Printing. I'm the best damn printer in the state of Missouri."

"What are you printing?"

"Fancy bank notes for the Jefferson City Bank."

"Is that a good thing to do, Ed?"

The hood fell back from his head, and she saw his face from a side lamp. It was scarred and hairless, disfigured so badly it was hard to determine where his features were.

A gaping hole opened again, and he spoke normally.

"Uh, good to print? Yeah, I print all the time. Not much left for me to do. My other press got burned up in the . . . the mess."

"Was it a fire, Ed?"

He flew at her with surprising speed. She had no idea how old he was. The charge lasted only two steps before he faltered, out of breath and out of energy. He stumbled, and only Jarek's rush forward to catch him stopped him from falling.

"Don't . . . never . . . not a good word. Ed don't like it," the hulking figure snarled. He turned then, and the robe fell off his back and dropped down from his arms. The flames had seared all of his torso and his upper arms. Scar tissue showed a deep flame red. He growled and pulled up the robe, fitting it over his head. Jessica saw that either his forearms and hands had not been touched by the fire or the burns had healed naturally.

"What do you do with the bills you print, Ed?" Jessica asked in a pleasant, soft voice.

She was sure he heard her, but he only stood at the press and shook his head.

Nan Lattimer went to the workbench and brought back some of the printed material. In the lamplight she showed the bills to Jessica. These were on oversized paper and still needed to be cut and trimmed to the correct length and width.

"This is professional work, Ed," Jessica said. "Did you make the engraving plates as well?"

His only response was a nod.

Jarek touched Jessica's shoulders, and they moved away from the hulking man toward a small room that had a table, three chairs and a bed which was rumpled and unmade. A small wood burning stove with a smoke pipe out through the wall stood against the brick interior.

Jarek no longer held the gun. He let Jessica and Nan sit down, then he poured them hot coffee from a pot on the stove.

"Now, I ask you, Miss, what else could we do? This is his life. He's a printer. For years he worked on those plates, making them just like the ones they had in Kansas City and over in Nebraska. He was a real printer then, a damn good one. Provided all the work here in town and in three or four other spots along the rail line."

"Then the fire hit his print shop," Nan said taking over the story. "He tried to save it. Jarek and two others had to pull him out of it just before the roof crashed in. Might have been better to leave him there. Took him more than two years to heal. We tried everything we knew. Kept him in a tub of cool water most of the time. It kept him from screaming. Now he's healed, but his mind wanders. How old do you guess he might be?"

Jessica shook her head.

"He was eighty-two last November. Everyone in town takes turns caring for him, bringing in his meals. He lives in this building. Sun hurts his eyes, so he seldom goes outside."

"So what he's really printing is play money?" Jessica said.

"Absolutely. Until about six months ago when some young no goods broke into the bank one night and stole about a gunnysack full of the notes. They're the ones who have been doing the damage. They spent those fives and tens from here to Chicago. Most folks accepted them, 'cause they are printed so well. Most folks don't know towns and banks can't print their own bills anymore like they did back in the late fifties.

"Right after all them bills got stolen was when we scraped the name of the Jefferson City Bank off the front of the window. Didn't want no more bank robbers. Ain't heard nothing from nobody until you showed up."

"Now you've got to stop him," Jessica said. "You'll have to gather up all of those worthless bills and burn them."

Jarek snorted. "Hell, woman, we can't do that. Just suggesting it to Ed would kill him. You want to kill that poor old man?"

"More than ten thousand dollars worth of these bills have shown up at banks across Missouri, Kansas and Illinois. People are going bankrupt when they are proved worthless. One man killed himself when he was ruined. You've got to stop this."

"Just who are you to be ordering us around, Missie?" Nan demanded.

Jessica slowly reached in her reticule and brought out her badge and her identification.

"I'm from Washington and the United States Secret Service. One of our jobs is to stop counterfeiting. Technically that's what Ed is doing here. I could arrest him and both of you and everyone in town who knows about it."

Jarek had his six-gun out again. "No, ma'am, don't reckon we can let you do that. See, Ed is my granddad, and I can't let you or any other federal lawman come in here and do harm to my kin."

"That gun won't stop it from happening. There's a better way. Just change the plates; let him print something else. We can distract him, or maybe when he sleeps, change the plates and destroy the ones that make the bills and put something else in the press. Wouldn't there be a good chance that he wouldn't even notice?"

Nan Lattimer laughed and shook her head. "Not Gramps. He's too sharp for that. The fire didn't hurt one of his eyes. He sees good as ever out of it."

Jarek motioned with the gun. "Sorry, Miss Flanders, but I guess you're going to have to spend the next few days with us until we figure out some way to get Grand-dad moved to some other small town. We can't have him hurt none, no sir. He's kin, my granddad, and you ain't gonna hurt him."

Jessica looked at the revolver and saw the hammer was cocked. She wouldn't have a chance drawing her own weapon. She put her identification back in her reticule and shrugged as if giving up. Jessica closed the handbag and held it by the foot-long strings. She stood when Jarek motioned for her to do so and turned slightly away from him.

Then she spun back, her reticule with the heavy .38 in it slamming forward toward Jarek's own six-gun like a ten pound hammer.

Spur McCoy found it hard to believe. It was the following morning after he'd walked Feather Cloud home, and now he stared at Priscilla.

"You mean there isn't a single message from Jessica Flanders? Nothing in response to your wire of yesterday morning?"

"Not a thing, Mr. McCoy. I walked past the telegraph office on my way to work this morning. They said the message went out yesterday morning, but there is no record of any reply from Jefferson City."

McCoy made up his mind fast as he always did. "When's the next train west? I've missed the eight-oh-five. Is there one at nine? It's eight-thirty now. I can make a nine o'clock."

Priscilla checked the train schedule. "Yes, nine-ten, westbound. It's a combination train, freight and passengers, so it'll stop at every place along the way. Gets in at Jefferson City a little after noon."

"I'm on it." He gathered up his hat and took two long steps to the connecting door. "I'll take a small bag with my spare weapon and a change of clothes. I hope there's nothing wrong out there in Jefferson City."

Slightly before noon, 80 miles to the west of St. Louis, Secret Service Agent Spur McCoy stepped down from the train at the Jefferson City Station. They had missed three flag stops and two mail stops because no bags were out to be picked up.

He stared down the one-street town. It looked about as he had figured it would—mostly farming and a little ranching this far west in Missouri. He headed for the biggest store in town, the General Store, and had just stepped inside when a thin, rangy man came up to him.

"Just off the train I see. What can I do for you this morning?"

"Like some cigars, two for a nickel if'n you have any."

"Certainly. One of my most popular items among smokers. How many today?"

"A dozen."

McCoy paid for the cheroots, put eleven of them in his shirt pocket and lit the other one. Then he lifted his small carpetbag and left the store. The man was not friendly, but not hostile either.

The agent took a slow walk down one side of the main street and up the other. One building in the middle of town looked like it could have been a bank, but the front window was washed clean and then probably whitewashed from the inside. There were no letters of any kind showing through the whiteness. Still it could have been a bank at one time.

No other building in town remotely resembled the rock solid edifice that a financial institution should be, nor was there any structure that claimed to be a bank now or that had once been one.

He saw only two saloons, not many for a town of this size. Must be a stay-at-home, churchgoing crowd. He tried the larger of the two and stepped through the door into a dark, smoky interior.

He went to the bar and asked for a beer.

"Warm all right? Our ice house ran dry last month."

"Set a case or two outside come sundown and it'll stay chilled all day."

The barkeep was probably also the owner. Only two other men in the place worked on mugs of beer, and he could see no girls. Figured. He accepted the warm mug of suds and tossed the barkeep a dime. He got half that back in change.

"Lively looking little town," McCoy said. "I just got off the noon train out of St. Louis."

The barkeep nodded and wiped the clean mahogany again.

"You here selling?" he asked.

McCoy knew it was a shot in the dark. He wasn't dressed in the white shirt and dark suit that was the trademark of the drummer.

"No, thankfully. Just looking around with the idea of setting up a business. Anything this town needs? How about a good bordello with about six girls out of Chicago?"

The barkeep snorted. "City council ran the last of the whores out of town ten years ago. Not about to get any more set up here. Them five old men come down hard on anything they don't like. Damn tough for me to make a living here with no tits around, but I manage."

"Town fathers that tough?"

"Damn site tougher—straight and Baptist most of them. Me and Old Ben got the only saloons in town, and they keep rooting at us, but we got the damn U.S. Constitution backing us up and we're staying in business."

"Yeah, it's a free country."

"Damn right."

"One thing bothers me. Somebody said there wasn't no bank in town. Mean I'd have to get on the train and go down the tracks to the county seat for some banking services?"

"About the size of it. Had a bank here ten, twelve years ago, but it went bust. Roiled a bunch of good folks. Now most everyone banks for hisself. Oh, there is Mr. Jarek who owns the General Store. He does some lending at interest now and again."

"But not a business loan or a line of credit, I'd imagine," McCoy said.

"You got that right."

"Think a hardware store would go here?"

"Get most of that kind of goods from the General Store."

"But I'd carry a lot of things he can't. All sorts of hinges and maybe roofing and even some lumber."

"Might work. Might not. Tougher in this town. Half the folks here are related."

"You're talking me into getting back on the train."

"Might be the best move you made all day. We got another westbound long about three o'clock."

McCoy finished his beer, waved his thanks and strode out the door. A scattering of clouds shaded the sun.

He moved down to the hotel, a two-story affair. Inside it was clean enough. A middle-aged woman smiled at him from behind the desk.

"You been looking over our town, so what do you think? Nice clean community, church-minded, plenty of business. You looking to settle or to go into business?"

"Maybe a little of both. Figure first I'll get a room and rest up a little. You have one left?"

"Matter-of-fact, I do." She turned a register book around to him, and he dipped the pen in the ink bottle and scratched down his moniker. He scanned the rest of the page and saw that Jessica's name was not on that sheet. Some entry two lines above his had been marked out completely so it couldn't be read.

He flipped the book around.

"Say I was scouting for a new business. What about law and order? A town marshal, sheriff, policeman? What do we have here?"

"Not much of any right now. Sheriff called the deputy back since he had nothing to do here. We take care of ourselves just fine. Anything happen we wire the sheriff and he comes in."

"I hear the old bank is closed up. How would I get change, cash checks, have an account to pay my bills if I was running a business? What do you do?"

"Mostly cash here. I manage to keep enough change around. Not a real problem. The merchants help each other out. They got two banks over in the county seat about twenty-five miles west."

"Oh, then it sounds like I couldn't run to the bank every morning."

"Not likely. You're in room eight. That's ground floor and to the right down there that-a-way."

"Thanks for your help. I may want to talk some new business ideas with you later on."

"Always use new money in a town this size."

He found the room which was sparse, clean and simple with a bed, chair, wash bowl and pitcher of water on a small stand. He tried the bed. Better than sleeping on the ground, but not much.

McCoy stood behind the thin white curtains and stared out the window. It opened on the front of the hotel and looked across the street at the building he thought once could have been the bank.

As he watched he saw a man turn down the alley beside the building, pause, look around a moment, then vanish into a door of the old bank building. Interesting.

It was a place to start, but not until after dark. He made up his mind quickly. Jarek, the General Store, was the rich man in town. If there was any counterfeiting here, he'd know about it. Telling might be a different thing.

Spur left his bag under the bed and made certain that a small string linked through the two handles. If anyone opened it, they wouldn't see the string which would be on the floor when he returned.

He adjusted his six-gun on his hip and left the hotel with a wave to the owner. McCoy made no wasted moves. He marched directly to the General Store and entered. Jarek had just finished waiting on someone. The customer looked at McCoy curiously and then left by the front door.

"Ah, yes, the cheroot man. Smoked those twelve up already?"

"No, I'm a United States Secret Serviceman here to inspect the Jefferson City Bank. You know about it, and you know what happened to Agent Jessica Flanders." McCoy drew his Peacemaker .45 Colt and held the muzzle toward the floor.

"You have about thirty seconds to start talking, then I'm putting handcuffs on you and taking you back to St. Louis with me. Now, where is Jessica and where is the damned Jefferson City Bank?"

Chapter Nine

Hirum Jarek stared at the six-gun and the handcuffs that Agent McCoy had just pulled from his pocket as he threatened to arrest the store owner. His eyes bulged for a moment, and his hands came up in denial.

"Now hold on there, Agent McCoy, or whoever you are. We got laws in this country, and they don't allow anyone running around with a fancy title and a gun and then stomping all over us. Fact is, I don't know nothing of what you're talking about. There is no Jefferson City Bank."

McCoy pulled one of the spurious Jefferson City Bank $5 notes from his pocket and pushed in front of Jarek's face.

"You can see, can't you? You can read. It says the Jefferson City Bank of Jefferson City, Missouri. A note payable in gold by the Jefferson City Bank."

"I've never seen that note before in my life," Jarek said. McCoy spun him around, whipped his hands behind his long, lean body and fastened the cuffs on him. Then he grabbed his shoulder and marched the man toward the front door.

"No, not a step farther!" A woman's voice rang out from the rear of the store. McCoy stopped, looked back and saw the twin barrels of a Greener aimed over the counter near the cash drawer. He could see only the top of a gray-haired head on the other side of the counter.

"Lay down your weapon, Mr. Lawman, and then take them infernal manacles off my brother."

McCoy spun around, grabbed Jarek and pulled him in front of his body, facing the shotgun.

"Don't reckon you'll gun down your own kin to get at me, whoever you are. Stand up and put your hands on top of your head or I'm going to start putting slugs through that thin counter front and punch some nasty, bloody holes in your body."

"Oh, dear." The woman's head vanished for a moment, then a hand pushed the shotgun out of reach on top of the counter. Slowly the woman stood up. She looked to be in her early forties, dressed plain and proper.

"Your name, please," McCoy said, his Peacemaker still covering her.

"Nan Standish," the woman said. "Don't hurt my brother."

"We won't hurt him. He'll have a nice comfortable jail cell in St. Louis, probably all to himself. Judge probably will send him to prison for a year and a day."

"Oh, no, not that!" the woman wailed.

"Then suppose you tell me about the Jefferson City Bank and where Miss Jessica Flanders is."

"Well, about the bank. Never was one really. Our grandfather—we call him Gramps—used to have this print shop." She told him about the fire, the innocent printing of the fake play money, and the robbery.

"So it ain't our fault 'tall. Some robbing owlhoot stole them bills thinking they were real."

"Over ten thousand dollars worth are in circulation," McCoy said. "When banks get them, they refuse to honor them and send them to us. More than one small business has gone bankrupt because of your grandfather's little game. Now where is Agent Jessica Flanders?"

"She's at my place in a locked room," Mrs. Standish said. "No chance she can get out. I'll trade you her for leaving Gramps alone."

"Not a chance, Mrs. Standish. Right now you take me to Jessica, or I'm going to arrest your brother and charge him with counterfeiting."

"Oh, dear, it wasn't supposed to happen this way."

"It never is. Do you want to see Jarek here in jail, or will you take me to Miss Flanders?"

"I'll lock the front door and then take you to my place out the back. Reckon Jarek will have to come, too."

"I reckon."

Five minutes later McCoy pushed Jarek, still cuffed, through the front door of his sister's modest two-story house. It was only a block off Main Street. They went up the stairs, and the woman nodded at a door at the end of the hall.

"It was a small room for storage. No windows but plenty of light. I even put a mattress on the floor for her to sleep on."

"Thoughtful of you. Now open the door." McCoy raised his voice. "Jessica, if you're in there don't do anything rash. Everything is under control."

Mrs. Standish opened a half-inch steel bolt and pushed the door inward. Jessica stood in the middle of the room waiting for them. She was fully dressed and held her reticule in one hand, the small brown hat in the other.

"About time you got here, McCoy. Make Jarek give me back my .38, then I'll show you the counterfeiting setup."

McCoy chuckled. "You're welcome for your thanks for my rescuing you. You all right?"

"Only a slight bruise on my shoulder. I got it when I knocked Jarek's gun away with my purse and he tackled me. They tell you about the crazy old man?"

"He is not crazy," Mrs. Standish said. "He just needs a little care. After all, he's eighty-two now."

It was ten minutes later before Jessica had her .38 revolver back in her purse and she led the four of them to the side door of the old bank building. Jarek was still in handcuffs, and several of the locals stared at the strange scene.

"They set it up right in here," Jessica said. "Even humored the old man by painting the name on the window saying Jefferson City Bank." She pushed open the alley door and stepped into the dark interior.

McCoy struck a kitchen match and looked around. He spotted an oil lamp on a big wooden box and lit the wick, then put the glass chimney back in place.

"Before the press was right over here," Jessica said.

The entire room was bare except for the one wooden box.

"They moved him," Jessica said. "Mrs. Standish there said that's what they would have to do. First I need to find just one of those bills in this room to prove that the printing was done here."

Jarek laughed. "Kind of hard to prove who did the printing, ain't it, McCoy? You best undo my cuffs here before I bring an unjust arrest charge against you."

"You're just in custody, not under arrest, Jarek. You've got no case. You might have when I formally arrest you and take you east on the next train. What time does it leave?"

"Four-thirty," Mrs. Standish replied without thinking. Then she frowned, berating herself silently.

"Good," McCoy said. "That gives us a few more minutes for one of you to tell us where Gramps and his printing press are. Otherwise, Jarek here goes in handcuffs, under arrest, all the way back to St. Louis."

Mrs. Standish crossed her arms over her ample chest and scowled. "Leastwise the government will have to buy his ticket. He'll enjoy seeing the big town. He's never been there. Besides, you don't got no charges that's gonna stick.

"I sure do," Jessica said. "Pointing a weapon at a federal officer, assault and battery, kidnapping . . ."

"Just who do you have for witnesses to all of those terrible crimes?" Mrs. Standish asked.

"You were there, Mrs. Standish. I'll call you as a witness."

"I never seen nothing. Fact is, I was in my dress shop all that afternoon."

McCoy cleared his throat. "Afraid what the lady says is right, Jessica. We don't have enough witnesses. But then neither do they. Why don't you take Mrs. Standish outside for about five minutes, and I'll see how much persuasion I can use on Mr. Jarek here. He doesn't look like he can stand pain too well. Mr. Jarek, have you ever had both of your thumbs broken at the same time?"

Jarek began to edge away from McCoy and shook his head.

"No cause to get violent here," Jarek said. "We made a deal. You get the girl back, and you don't fool with Gramps."

"That was *your* deal. I never agreed to it. Now Jessica, you just hustle that little gray-haired lady out into the alley. You can leave the alley door open in case she wants to listen to her kin in here taking some punishment."

"Right, McCoy. I can do that." She grabbed Mrs. Standish and propelled her towards the alley door. They were almost there when Mrs. Standish stopped.

"No, don't hurt him. Fact is, he don't know where Gramps is. Me and three lady friends moved him last night."

"Is he at your house?"

"No, he won't stay with me. Tried to get him to stay there time and again."

"Let's see," McCoy said. "Jarek, I'd figure that you should take in forty, maybe fifty dollars a day at your store. With you in custody for, say two weeks before a judge releases you in St. Louis—that would mean you could be out as much as seven hundred dollars. Sounds like one pile of money to me. You have a spare seven hundred to throw away like that?"

Jarek shook his head. "You know I don't, McCoy. You also know that Gramps ain't no criminal. It can't be a crime to print fake money if you don't spend any of it. I bet any fair judge would say that Gramps is not guilty of anything but bad luck, that damn fire, and some owlhoots who did the passing of the play money. The man is eighty-two years old, for God's sake."

McCoy took another tactic. "Let's say, just for the sake of argument, that your Grandfather is not guilty of passing any money. Printing it is also a crime, but we could show that he had no intent to pass the bills. I'm sure that would go well with any judge in the land. Then, knowing his physical and emotional condition, I'm sure the judge would be lenient. So instead of all that trouble, why don't we settle this right here and now without the help of a federal judge or a trip to St. Louis."

"Now you're talking more sense," Jarek said. "What kind of a bargain can we arrange here? We already gave you back the lady agent."

"That's something else we'll have to talk about. First, Gramps. You've moved him somewhere here in town. The way half the town is interrelated, you could probably go on moving him every day or so for a year and we'd never find him. We don't have the time for that."

"We'll promise that no more of the fake bills will ever get outside of the room where he's working," Mrs. Standish said.

"Not good enough," McCoy countered. "I have to go back to my boss with those plates."

"He worked ten years on those plates as an engraver," Jarek said. "They are his pride and his life. Without them he'd wither up and die in a week."

"Then let's have him do some more engraving," McCoy said. He held up one of the five dollar bills. "See this big circle in red on the left. Across it in quarter inch letters, I want him to engrave at an angle: PLAY MONEY. Then below that: NOT NEGOTIABLE."

"He'll know what that means," Mrs. Standish said.

"He also knows about the robbers," McCoy said. "All you have to do is convince him that he must do this. Then he can print all the money that he wants to, and he might even be able to sell it to a game company."

Jarek nodded slowly. "Yes, it might work. He has three sets of plates, the ones, fives and tens. He'd have to engrave on all of them. That would keep him busy for two months."

"What else?" Mrs. Standish asked.

"We'll have to gather up all of the printed bills, save a few representative ones, then burn everything else," Jessica said.

Mrs. Standish took a deep breath and then sighed. "I guess we can convince him that we're sending the money to a bank that wants it. He won't like it, but then he'll have to print up some more of the new bills with the play money words across them."

McCoy reached over and tapped Jarek on the shoulder. "Does this sound possible to you, Mr. Jarek?"

He nodded. "Yes, but it'll take some doing, probably the rest of today and tonight. We'll give you our answer first thing in the morning."

McCoy looked at Jessica. "That sound reasonable to you, Jess?"

She said it did. "I'll go wire a report to Pris and to the general."

McCoy took the handcuffs off Jarek's wrists. "Looks like we have a deal. I'll print up on a bill the size of the letters and the spelling so there's no mistake. I want it black ink on the red, so it will stand out."

"Yes, yes," Jarek said rubbing his wrists. "I used to help him in his print shop years ago. That can be done easily. Now all I have to do is convince him to do as you say."

"Be persuasive. If you can't, we'll have to take some action against him for printing those bills."

Jessica and Spur went to the telegraph office at the small depot and sent the wires.

They had an early dinner at a pleasant cafe and were pleased with the food. Then they headed for the hotel. Jessica's bag was waiting for them.

The woman behind the desk nodded. "Hear you'll be wanting a room, Miss. My sister says you're working with the lawman there, so I'll put you in number seven, right down the hall, first floor."

Jessica said that would be fine and signed the register. When McCoy walked her down to the room, she motioned him inside, then closed the door and locked it.

When she turned around and faced him, Jessica Flanders had a secret smile. She stepped over to

McCoy, reached up and kissed his lips. Then she found his right hand and placed it over her breast. She kissed him again, and a moment later their tongues were fighting each other.

When the hot kiss ended, she smiled even sweeter. "McCoy, I've heard that you're a devil with the women on your cases. Everyone talks about you. Now I think it's time I see if all of those stories and wild rumors are true." She stepped back and began to unbutton the top of her dress, and McCoy grinned right back at her and helped with the buttons.

Chapter Ten

Jennifer caught his hands at her buttons and watched him until he looked down at her.

"Don't you even want to know why?"

"I'm not the curious type, but since I started out being so angry with you, I guess I do want to know why."

"Good." She let him undo the buttons until she could lift the dress off over her head. She wore three petticoats under the dress and a chemise.

He lifted the petticoats off one by one until she had on only the chemise, silk underpants and high white stockings that came halfway up her delightful thighs.

She began working on his clothing then, insisting that she do it all herself. By the time she had his shirt off and his longjohns unbuttoned to show his hairy chest, she told him.

"I promised myself that I had come on too strong with you back in St. Louis. Then when I got caught here in

Jefferson City by Jarek, I promised myself that if you ever rescued me, I'd undress and do you proper the way a thankful female should."

"Just gratitude? No desire? This is just a reward for saving your fancy little bottom from being kidnapped and locked up in a stuffy room?"

She pulled the chemise off and let him stare at her breasts. They were fuller than he had imagined, with rosebuds for nipples and wide pink areolas that seemed to darken even as he watched them.

He bent and kissed each breast, heard her quick gasps of pleasure or surprise and looked up at her.

"Mr. McCoy . . ."

"I'd like you to call me Spur, whether we're here in bed fucking up a storm or at the office."

She grinned at the naughty word.

"Don't try to shock me. My father was a cop and a good one and had a vocabulary that could make a long-shoreman blush. Fine, I'll call you Spur, and as far as desire goes . . ." She pulled his face down toward her breasts again.

"Desire? I learned about making love when I was seventeen. He was the boy next door, and he never had made love before either, except with the pleasures of his hand. We tore off each other's clothes and romped around in the sunshine and petted and experimented.

"We both had talked to older siblings and knew how it was done, no big secret there, but at first he couldn't get into me. I used some saliva on his penis, and it slid right in. We made love seven times in just a little over an hour. He couldn't get enough, and neither could I."

She moved and eased her other pulsating breast into his mouth. "I was lucky that day that I didn't get pregnant. He came back for more, but I told him never again until I was married, and he ran so fast I thought he had a rocket in his pants.

"I had heard about you and the ladies when I was in Washington D.C. As soon as I checked in with Priscilla, I asked her if the rumors were anywhere near true, and she told me yes but that she had never even seen your body with your shirt off, let alone made love to you."

He lifted himself off of her breasts, slid out of his boots, pants and longjohns, then hooked his thumbs in the silk underpants she wore. Her hands caught his.

"In a moment. You talked about desire, about passion. I really need to get warmed up a little more first."

He picked her up, kissed her and eased her down gently on the bed. Her eyes came open, and he slipped down beside her, his hands working on her breasts. He left her lips and kissed her cheek, then pushed back her dark short hair and licked her ear.

"Oh, glory!" she whispered. He licked it again, and she caught him with her arms and held him tightly.

"That . . . that is so delightfully sexy!"

He licked the crook of her neck under her chin, and her hands moved to find his crotch and found him only half-aroused. She looked at him in surprise.

"Don't I excite you? You aren't even hard yet."

"Sometimes I need a little warming up as well."

"Oh, Lord! I was thinking only of myself." She sat up, pushed him down and fondled his balls and limp penis. She bent down and kissed the soft head, and McCoy felt a surge of desire.

She laughed softly. "He likes that."

"Most do," McCoy said. He got his hands back on her breasts and kneaded and petted them. He could feel her nipples harden and flush with hot blood. She kissed his manhood again and licked it until it was fully erect.

She caught his hands as she lay beside him and moved them to her underpants. "Please now, Spur, take them off and touch me down there. I'm getting so hot I want to scream."

He pulled down the soft garment and tossed it to the floor. Slowly she spread her legs. His hand came up her leg gently, petting, caressing, warming the inside of her thigh. Her breathing came faster now. She opened her eyes and watched him. His finger circled the damp spot at her crotch, and she cried out in excitement. Then he brushed his hand across her small hard node and she gasped. He set up a rhythm, rubbing the node back and forth, playing it like a banjo.

"Oh, God!" she whispered, then her hips bounced upwards and her whole body shook in a grinding, climax that made her gasp and cry out in delight. When the last of the spasms had torn through her, Jessica opened her eyes in amazement.

"Nobody in the world ever did that for me before," she said, her eyes wide, her breath still coming in gasps. "Lordy, but that was fine, just ever so fine."

She pulled him over her then, and he found her slot. Though it was wet with her own juices, he added some of his own, then looked down at her.

"You sure this is all right with you, Jess?"

"Dear Lord, yes. Now hurry or I know that I'll just burst."

He slid into her, and she sighed and then yelped in delight, her small hips pounding upward to gain as much penetration as possible.

"Oh!" she cried out in sudden pain. "You . . . you touched something in there that nobody's ever even come close to before. You must be so big!"

He eased off a little, then began to stroke slowly all the way in and all the way out until she yelped in wonder and her hips began to buck again.

This time he beat her to it, kicking in fast and hard, slamming into her and nudging her higher and higher on the bed. He pounded seven hard strokes more before he climaxed and eased down on top of her.

Her arms went around his shoulders, and they lay there for five minutes before she let him go. He eased away from her, dropping beside her on his back, his hand reaching to find hers.

"You're two ahead of me," he said.

She smiled at him. "I know. I've never been so sensitive before. I guess it was just wanting you so much and knowing how good you were going to be. I'm glad we had this time. Promise me that you never, ever will tell Pris."

Spur grinned. "I won't have to tell her. She'll look at you when we get back to the office and she'll give me an angry stare and she'll know. Don't ask me how she does it, but she can always tell."

"She wants you, Spur."

"I know, but that would ruin our business relationship. I keep the two strictly separate, then she doesn't get hurt."

Jessica leaned up on one elbow and watched him. "You've never been married?"

"Ours isn't the kind of a job a wife or a husband would understand or put up with. I'm better off this way."

"You don't ever want to settle down?"

"Someday, when I get tired of the field work. The general said he's got a spot for me in Washington working at a desk. Reckon that won't be for a few years yet. Maybe then, I'll find a winsome widow and settle down."

"More likely your bride will be some sexy and shapely sweet young thing half your age, and before you get out of bed, you'll have six kids." They both laughed.

"Again," she said reaching for him.

It was a long but rewarding night. Five times they satisfied each other, the last just before 4:00 A.M. when they drifted off to sleep.

The next morning, they had breakfast at the café across the street and met Jarek at his store shortly after he opened at 8:00 o'clock. The thin, tall man nodded curtly.

"Well, I done it. He didn't want to do it, said it would spoil the new bills, but I promised him they would work just as well. I convinced him at last. Wasn't easy, but I guess it'll be worth it."

"What about the already printed bills?" Jessica asked.

He shot her an angry glance, then sighed. "Hell, I had to buy them from him. He said he'd sell the whole print batch for twenty dollars. I paid him in brand new one dollar federal bank notes so it looked like more. Got all the Jefferson City Bank bills in a cardboard box in back."

"Let's see them," McCoy said.

Jarek led them past a curtain into the storeroom. It was stacked with boxes that almost reached the ceiling. It smelled of old leather and new saddles. Jarek stopped at a carton sitting on a small workbench, opened it and stepped away.

Jessica looked inside and cried out in surprise. "So many of them. How long has he been printing these?"

"Going on two years now. Does a few every day, but they stack up. Most of these aren't cut to size even. He doesn't like to do that. The stolen ones weren't cut either."

"You're sure this is all of them?" Jessica asked.

"Absolutely. My sister moved him to a vacant house near her place so she can help take care of him. She said she picked up every one at the old bank and around his new print shop in one of the bedrooms. They're all here. We find any more I'll promise to burn them soon as I see them."

McCoy nodded. "That's good enough for me. You have a stove back here to keep this place warm in the winter?"

He did, and the two agents took turns tossing hand-fuls of the spurious Jefferson City Bank paper money into the stove. It took them almost a half hour.

By then, Mrs. Standish had come to the store. Jessica had saved three of each denomination, put them in an envelope and tucked it into her reticule.

Spur McCoy took a pen and a bottle of black ink and printed the word he wanted across the red circle: PLAY MONEY and NOT NEGOTIABLE. He gave the bill to Mrs. Standish.

"Lord, he was upset about adding these words to his engravings. Kept asking me why he needed to put this on them. I told him it was the new banking laws and he had to follow them just as any other bank or he'd get us all in trouble. That convinced him."

"How long will it take him to do the engravings on both sides of the plates for the three bills?" McCoy asked.

"He said about a week. A week means nothing to him. I'll see to it that he does it proper."

Jessica listened and nodded. "Mrs. Standish, as soon as he has the first plate done on both sides, have him print me five of the bills and mail them to me at our St. Louis address. That way we'll be sure that everything is as it should be and we won't have to come back out here. Do that with the next two fake bills as well."

Mrs. Standish gave a sigh and nodded. "Lordy, I'm so thankful this is at last cleared up. Half the town's been holding its breath since them sidewinders stole all them paper money bills from the old bank. Now we can relax a little. Not sure if Gramps knew he was doing anything wrong or not."

"Either way, I think that the Secret Service will be satisfied," McCoy said. He looked at Jessica who seemed to have a small secret smile this morning. "When does the next eastbound train leave?"

Jessica looked at Mrs. Standish.

"There's a train through at a quarter of eleven. If you

hurry, you should be able to catch it."

"I don't think I can be ready in that time," Jessica said. "When's the next one?"

"One-thirty or so," Jarek said.

They shook hands all around, then the two agents headed for the hotel.

"Curious why you didn't think you could be ready to leave on the earlier train," McCoy said.

She grinned at him. "I'll bet you can think of the reason, if you'll really put your mind to it." She caught his arm and pulled it against her so it brushed her breast. "At least I hope you can figure out what we might do for another couple of hours in your hotel room."

He figured it out.

They made the 1:30 train with only half a minute to spare and laughed all the way to their seats. Jessica was still flushed from the power of the last roaring climax in the hotel room just before they dressed and ran for the train.

It was a three and a half hour train ride to St. Louis and they sat close together and talked. By the time they got to St. Louis they both knew most of what was important about each other and a lot that would be of no value at all.

As they got off in St. Louis and hailed a cab, he cautioned her again about Priscilla. "Don't be surprised if she asks you point blank. I've had Pris do it before. Just take it casually, but don't go into any details, for God's sake. I don't want any more trouble with Pris. She's the best helper I've ever had in the office, and I don't want to lose her."

When they walked into the office with their overnight carpetbags, Priscilla jumped up from her desk and ran to meet them. She grinned at McCoy, said the general had replied to his solution to the Jefferson City Bank swindle and agreed with his actions.

She looked at Jessica. "We were so worried about you. Were you in any danger? I want to take you to dinner tonight and have you tell me all about it. I wonder if I could ever be a female agent? You're a person I really respect and look up to."

McCoy went to his desk, looked at the stack of mail and discarded the obviously nonessential items. He read the wire from the general first, then scanned his mail and found nothing that would sidetrack him from the problem of the $20 bill counterfeiter.

He tried to get Priscilla's eye twice, then called out. "Miss Quincy, might I have a word with you?"

She came directly with a notebook and a pencil. "Yes, Mr. McCoy. A letter?"

"No. Anything new on the Flavian Kirby counterfeiting case?"

"Oh, yes, there is something. A note came for you sometime last night from a Mr. Rhodenway. He says our suspect was there but no one found out where he was staying. He said you might contact him at your convenience."

"Damnit, Pris, why didn't you tell me that the second I got in the door?" He grabbed his hat, adjusted his gunbelt and marched out the door.

Chapter Eleven

It was a little after 5:30 when Spur McCoy rang the bell at the Club and waited for the sliding panel to open. Rhodenway saw him and opened the door at once.

"Miss Melissa wants to talk to you. I understand you were out of town for a time." The tall, dignified man motioned, and a pretty young girl came and took McCoy's arm and led him up one flight and down the hall to Melissa's suite. The girl knocked on the door, then opened it and ushered McCoy inside.

Melissa came through a curtain that warded off her office area. She nodded at McCoy and showed him four $20 bills.

"All fakes, all with the number you gave us. We know who the little bastard is, but we kept accepting his money until you got here. Where the hell were you last night?"

McCoy explained, and she was somewhat mollified.

"The little man has an appointment for six-thirty for dinner first. This is four nights in a row. I'd guess the old man may only have dinner and a little messing around tonight. His wad is about shot for a week or so."

"Anywhere I can observe him coming and then leaving?"

She led him down the hall to a small room near the front of the building. It had an intricate lattice work front to it, and through the slats he could see most of the entryway and the front door. Rhodenway stood beside the door, stiff and formal, waiting for the next knock or ring.

"Six-thirty, you said. Is he on time?"

"Usually. You know that no one leaves by our front door but uses the side door on Whatley Street. I'd suggest you be there waiting with a buggy. He's latched on to Delphine again. I'll have her walk him to the back door and give you some kind of a signal when he leaves."

The madam of the most expensive parlor in town watched him. "Anything else?"

"That seems to cover it. We won't arrest him here, of course, as we promised. We want to follow him back to wherever he's staying and try to get the plates back."

"Yes. Fine." She looked at him closely. "You want some company up here while you wait? The door locks. It's on the house, of course. Any of the ladies except Delphine. She's getting ready. The little joker demands a freshly bathed girl."

"The man lives well. No one for me tonight, thanks. Not that I don't appreciate the offer, but I better wait alone and tend to business."

"You're a good cop, Spur. Hope you catch the little bastard tonight. I'm tired of fooling around with him."

"We should do it tonight. I need to go out and make some arrangements, but I'll be back here well before six-thirty."

Once outside, McCoy hurried to Jessica's hotel room in the Claymore and knocked.

She came to the door and opened it a crack, with the muzzle of her .38 showing along with a slice of her face.

"Oh, McCoy."

"We've got a lead on Flavian Kirby. Tonight at the Club. I need you to rent a cab and wait by the side door with me so we can tail him when he leaves."

Jessica opened the door and waved him inside. She stood there in her chemise and petticoats.

"See how much easier this is after last night? Wait until I get into a dress and some better shoes, and I'll be ready."

McCoy watched with a touch of sadness as the dress covered up her sleek body, then he remembered it all naked and writhing and humping.

On the street they rented a cab at the livery, then drove to the side entrance to the Club.

"Now, you wait here, and I'll go inside and try to identify him on his way in at six-thirty. Then when he's upstairs, I'll come out here and wait with you. He usually takes one of that line of cabs waiting over there across the street near the side door. A good stand for those cabbies, I've heard."

Jessica shook her pretty head. "What a business! It's just a whorehouse with a bar and a kitchen. Evidently a lot of men go nuts over the place. It must be well furnished."

He told her from what he had seen of it, that it was expensive and in good taste.

"Hey, maybe I should apply for a job. Those girls are living a lot fancier than I am."

"They also work harder. Most of them are on a half hour schedule, unless it's an all-nighter."

She looked at him curiously and grinned. "You ever had an all-nighter at a whorehouse?"

"Never paid for making love in my life."

"That's not answering the question."

He laughed softly. "I've had a few good friends who just happened to be fancy ladies, and they invited me to spend the night. But no money changed hands."

"Ah hah!" Jessica said.

He stepped out of the cab, then walked around the block to the front door of the Club.

One minute before 6:30, Flavian Kirby, going by the name of Mr. Amway, stepped into the entryway of the Club, was greeted formally by Rhodenway and had a young girl escort him down the hallway and out of sight. McCoy wondered where the money changed hands—perhaps with the escorts to the room or maybe with the whores themselves. He went down the stairs and out the side door.

That way no one going out saw anyone coming in. It was all extremely private without even a central dining room. He waved away a cabby who hurried forward and walked down a block until he came to the buggy they had rented.

Jessica sat in the rig with one hand in her reticule, gripping her .38. She had brought a jacket which was tucked around her to ward off the October night breeze. She made room for McCoy to step into the rig.

"We have our quarry in the nest. Now when he comes out, we'll be ready."

"How long? Half the night?"

"No, this is his fourth night in a row, Miss Melissa said. She guessed it would be dinner and a little messing around and that he would pull out before eight o'clock."

"Let's hope so," Jessica said. "I'm cold and I'm hungry and I was wishing that we were up in my hotel room tearing our clothes off."

McCoy put his arm around her and drew her close. "I can help you stay a little warmer." His left hand slid under her jacket, worked through two buttons, then closed around one of her trembling breasts.

"Oh, glory! You do know how to warm up a girl. That feels ever so much better."

"Nothing serious here," he said kissing her cheek. "Just a little warming up for a lovely lady."

She snuggled against him and sighed. "Oh, yes, now this is what detective work should be all about. If we have to wait for someone, we can at least be comfortable." Jessica grinned, reached up and kissed his lips. Then she settled down against him.

More than a dozen men came out the well-lighted side door and hailed cabs. None of them was short enough to be their target. By 8:00 o'clock they wondered aloud if Miss Melissa had misjudged her customer.

"He could have more sexual stamina that we figured," Morgan said softly. Jessica sighed and moved his hand from one breast to the other.

"Another candidate," McCoy said. A woman stood momentarily in the doorway and waved—Delphine, the signal. "Yes, he's the right size, and he has that silly black derby hat on tonight. He wore it when he came. Not a lot of them around this town. And that's Delphine making sure we know that's him." McCoy retrieved his hand from her breast and both sat up straighter. Their rig was pointing the same way as the hacks across the street. They watched Kirby take the second hack in line. It swung out and rolled down the street.

In the gloom of the pale moon and only an occasional gas street lamp, McCoy followed the hack half a block behind. He held back when the small man got out of the rig in front of the Mayflower Hotel.

"This is a natural place for him to stay. Expensive, elegant and exclusive." He parked three doors down at the curb and walked along the concrete sidewalk with Jessica.

"Trying to figure out how to handle this. The hotel has a doorman. Might even be hard to get in without showing our badges, but we don't want to tip him off. I'll show my badge as a last resort."

He had to. The doorman didn't know their names, had never heard of a Mr. Amyway or a Mr. Kirby and wouldn't let them inside until they showed their badges.

At the desk McCoy took a harder attitude.

"A man just came in here two minutes ago. He has called himself Mr. Amway. You saw him. How is he registered and what's his room number?"

"I'm sorry, but I can't give out—"

"You'll tell me now, or I'll put handcuffs on you and

arrest you for interfering with a law officer. Which will
it be?"

The clerk was older than McCoy and knew how
the police and lawmen could operate. He nodded and
handed a small card to McCoy.

It listed the man in room 303 as J.A. Archibald, for-
merly of New York City, in town on a vacation.

McCoy gave the card back. "Don't warn him in any
way that we're on our way to see him, or you'll really
get in trouble."

The clerk nodded, and McCoy and Jessica hurried to
the stairs and up to room 303. They stood on each side of
the door as McCoy knocked three times. Nothing happened. McCoy knocked again, but no one answered the
door.

McCoy fumbled in his pocket and came up with a
ring of skeleton keys. The fourth key he tried worked,
and he edged the door open.

Down the hall at room 308, the door silently opened
a narrow crack and a solitary eye watched the pair at
room 303. The man watching smiled, then scowled.
Someone was after him. Somehow he had been identified. Perhaps at that damn Club. He'd spent enough
of the counterfeit bills there.

His mind whirled. What to do now? He had left a
valise, clothes and personal items in the room so it
would look occupied. He had even rumpled the bed
to make it look as if he had taken an afternoon nap.
But none of the money was in the room nor any
identification.

What next? They would watch the room and wait
for him to come back. Evidently they had followed

him from the Club and browbeat the room clerk for his room number. The clerk knew nothing about 308. He had bribed one of the bellboys to mark the room occupied under another name and even enter room payments.

Now he had to get out of this hotel, out of St. Louis. Damnit, Delphine! He knew he was spending too much time with her. She had been the best woman he had ever known or fucked. Damnit! Now where would he go? He had plenty of good money left. It was hard to spend more than one of the brand new bills at a time. He had crumpled them and spilled sand and dirt over them to make them look worn, but some clerks had sharp eyes.

He continued to watch room 303. It took them just five minutes to search the room, then ease out the door. A man and a woman? Must be federal lawmen. He wasn't worried about them, but they were a complication. He had taken the precaution of getting this room that opened on a fire escape that ran down the side of the building.

Then what? The bellboy he bribed to get this room was off duty now. They would have no way of checking which room he was in except by a room to room search, and the management here wouldn't allow that. He had enough money, but he needed to pass some more and get change. St. Louis was getting too hot for him. He had to move on. A boat! He'd grab a river boat and go downstream. New Orleans!

Quickly he gathered up all his belongings. He heard noises in the hall and watched again as the two detectives came out of his room, each walking to opposite ends of the hallway. By the time the woman came to his door he had eased it fully closed. She passed, and he breathed easier.

It took him another five minutes to pack the rest of his clothes and goods in his big traveling bag. The smaller valise held the plates and a stack of blank paper as well as his store of $88,000 in $20 bills. He could afford to drop the heavy bag but never the valise.

He waited another half hour, then checked the hall but could spot neither of the detectives. They were somewhere, waiting for him.

He went to the window, unlocked it, then edged it upward. It moved without a sound. Just outside, the steel bands of the fire escape came down from the sixth floor. There was a small landing outside his window and then a stairway down the side to the alley.

Once out of the window and on the fire escape, he moved quickly down to the ground. He paused for a moment, watching both ends of the alley. For a moment he frowned, thinking that he saw movement at the farthest end. He shook his head. He was starting to imagine things. Before he left the room, he had taken out the .38 caliber revolver he carried now for emergencies and pushed the barrel down inside his belt. It felt secure there and would be easy to draw.

He turned and walked toward the near end of the alley where the feeble street lamp glowed. He would soon be away and out on another adventure. Kirby loved the chase, but not when it came as close as it had today. He would never let that happen again.

Twenty yards from the street he stopped and leaned against the building and rested a moment. The clothes bag was heavier than he remembered. He studied the shadows at the end of the alley but could see no lurking detective. They both must be in the hall waiting for him to return to room 303. What a good move that had been getting a second room!

He picked up the bags and hurried ahead. He would not take a cab, since drivers sometimes had good memories. He would walk to the waterfront. It wasn't much over a mile. He could do that, find the right ship that would sail with the dawn and be on board and fast asleep before midnight. Yes!

He came to the mouth of the alley and paused.

"Hold it right there. We're the police. Don't move!"

The words came out of the blackness like a lightning bolt, catching him by total surprise. A woman's voice! So they hadn't stayed in the hallway. They had tricked him.

Kirby dropped his heavy clothing bag, drew his revolver and fired at where he figured the voice was. A shot came in return, digging into his left arm. He cried out in pain but held on the valise and began running. Another shot came after him but missed. He saw a shadow chasing him. He stopped and fired at the shadow. He saw the woman grunt in pain and fall. He turned and raced into the darkness along the unlit street, his feet pounding the sidewalk as fast as they could.

Behind him he again heard someone running. This would be the man; the woman was down. Good. Now it was one to one at least.

He darted up an alley and ran as softly as he could, but his new leather shoes still slapped the ground. He'd have to walk if he wanted to move quietly.

Flavian Kirby knew he couldn't afford to walk. Not now. Not with that lawman following him. He hurried again toward a faint light at the end of the alley. The waterfront had to be in this direction. He ran on.

Chapter Twelve

Flavian Kirby clutched the valise to his chest with both hands as he ran. He was fast losing his breath. The years were catching up with him. He could hear someone behind him. No matter how many alleys he went down or streets he followed, the gent behind seemed to be back there and getting closer. Kirby thought of hiding the valise and giving up. He had no more of the bogus bills in his wallet. There would be no proof against him. But he discarded the idea as stupid. Delphine would identify him as the man who gave her the bogus bills. The lawmen would scour every alley he had used until they found the plates. No, he had to keep running.

At last he could smell the river ahead. Was it still practical or possible to get on a steamer? That could take some time—buying a ticket and finding a cabin. Where would the lawman be?

He had to stop. His lungs burned like the inside of a red-hot stove. His breath came in short gasps and gulps. He backed into a narrow space between two buildings in a dank and dark alley and tried to hold his breath as he heard the running steps come closer.

Then they were past, and he forced himself out of the small space and walked back the way he had just come. He was almost at the end of the long alley when he heard the footsteps coming toward him once more. The lawman had not been fooled.

Just ahead was a pier with a stern wheeler tied up. Flavian raced across the street, walked calmly up the gangplank and vanished in the structure of the big Mississippi river boat.

Spur McCoy had just cleared the edge of the building facing the street when he saw a shadow rush up the gangplank of a boat tied at the dock just across the way. It had to be his man. Where else could he go?

The big boat was preparing to get underway. McCoy raced across the street and jumped over two feet of muddy water, landing on the gangplank as the steamer slowly edged away from the dock.

"You just made it, mate," the gangway man shouted. "You need a ticket. See the purser on deck B."

McCoy hurried to Deck B, up one level, and found the purser's office. He showed his badge.

"I'm chasing a man who just got on board. Did anyone buy a ticket not more than two or three minutes ago?"

The man shook his head. "No sir. Ain't sold a ticket now in an hour."

"You didn't see a small man, about five-four, well-dressed, carrying one valise?"

"Afraid not. You don't need a ticket, you being a government man and all. Good luck in finding him. Just don't disturb any of our cabin passengers."

"Then he didn't rent a cabin?"

"Couldn't. We're full up on both A and B decks."

McCoy thanked him and felt the steamer's big wheel turn faster as they started to plow upstream on the mighty Mississippi. He toured B deck, watching for the dapper little man and the valise. The ship had plenty of lights but there were dark recesses where he could see nothing. He worked the whole deck, saw dozens of strolling passengers, a pair of lovers locked in a kiss, and a man and woman screaming at each other in a good fight.

But no Kirby.

McCoy walked down to A deck, which was nearer water level, and prowled over most of it. Nothing. He went into the big gambling hall midships and worked the crowd there. At least 50 people crowded around gambling tables of all kinds from dice to poker to roulette.

For one fleeting glance he saw a man he thought could be Kirby, but when the man turned around it wasn't. Again he prowled the decks, staring at each cabin as he passed, wondering where the counterfeiter might be. They were out in the channel now, at least a quarter of a mile to shore.

The only thing certain was that Kirby was still on the ship. He hadn't jumped in the Mississippi and swam to shore, not with all of that valuable fake money.

A movement in the shadows ahead caught McCoy's attention. He paused, turned away, then spun around and looked closer. Beside one of the big funnels he saw a person crouched in the shadows.

McCoy drew his six-gun, darted to the spot and grabbed an arm. He pulled out a ten year-old boy who was shivering with fear.

"Don't shoot. Don't shoot me. I know I ain't got no ticket, but I just had to get away from my pa. He beat me something fierce. Figured he'd kill me before I grew up so I sneaked on board and . . ."

McCoy dropped his arm, gave the boy two dollars and returned to the search. Far down along A deck he heard a scream and ran that way. A moment later a cabin door in front of him flew open, and a large man tumbled out and skidded to a stop on his belly. The man tried to get up, but looked back in the cabin and didn't move.

"Close the door," he heard a voice inside order. "Close the door, and I won't kill that no-good husband of yours."

A woman's hand reached out for the door. It had swung outward and automatically latched against the bulkhead. When she leaned around to grab the door, she saw McCoy flat against the bulkhead on the other side of the door.

Instead of grabbing the door, the woman dove out of the room, hit the deck and rolled away out of sight of the person in the cabin.

McCoy edged his six-gun around the door without showing himself. "It's all over, Kirby. Give it up. There's no way out of that cabin, and I'm not moving until you throw out your gun."

For several moments there was a strained silence, then a revolver fired from inside the cabin, and the bullet grazed McCoy's wrist just under the butt of his Peacemaker. Instinctively he fired in return.

Before he could fire again, a flash of white roared past McCoy, ran the eight feet to the rail and dove overboard into the Mississippi.

"Man overboard!" McCoy bellowed. The big paddle behind the boat ran slower and slower. McCoy darted into the room and saw the valise sitting on the bunk. He opened it to be sure it was what he wanted, saw the fake bills and a carefully wrapped bundle and carried the bag out to the deck.

The captain ran up and asked who had called man overboard. McCoy showed him his credentials and said the man was a wanted criminal. The captain ordered two sailors to put a small boat over the side. McCoy, carrying the valise, demanded that he go on the search.

"The man is a federal prisoner and in my control," he told them. They didn't argue. The big boat's blades turned just enough to hold it against the downstream current. A moment later the rowboat was caught by the power of the Mississippi and swept downstream. The big river boat blasted its steam whistle, the huge blades churned the water, and the boat moved on upstream. As the small rowboat drifted downstream, one of the sailors on the oars looked at McCoy.

"You're the captain here, but I'd guess he'd try for the near shore, less than two hundred yards here, but the current would wash him half a mile downstream before he could make it."

"Look where you think we might find him," Spur ordered.

The two sailors pulled for the shore as they drifted down with the current. The night was black as thick smoke. In the distance now he could still see the brightly lighted river boat plowing against the current.

It was some time before McCoy could see the near shoreline, lined with trees and brush.

"Man must have been a good swimmer or he wouldn't have jumped in," the sailor said.

"Don't know," McCoy answered, "but he was over sixty years old. Don't see how he could swim far."

They pulled hard on the oars then and soon came close to the shallows.

"He could walk on in from here," the other sailor said.

"Put me on shore quietly, and I'll look for him along there. You keep working the riverbank. If you find either him or his body, shoot off that flare gun you have in the bow."

McCoy only got wet to his ankles when he stepped into the edge of the Mississippi and walked on to dry land. He jogged along a path by the river for five minutes but found no sign of the counterfeiter.

Put yourself in the other guy's shoes, McCoy told himself. He had the valise, sure now that he had the bulk of the bogus bills and the plates, but not the wanted man. Either he or his drowned body would close the case.

What would he do if he was Kirby and had just managed to swim to shore? He'd have no matches that would work. He'd look for the first light and ask for help. McCoy wondered if the water was so cold the man would die before he could get ashore.

McCoy remembered how the little man had ran. He was fast on his feet. McCoy thought he would be able to chase him down after a block or two, but he hadn't. The little man must be tougher than he looked.

McCoy carried the valise and jogged downstream another 100 yards. This time when he came from behind some trees, he saw lights ahead. There was a cluster of three or four buildings. He approached the first one quietly but saw no muddy or wet footprints on the wooden porch.

He went on and checked all four houses but saw no obvious place where Kirby could have entered.

Next he went to all four houses and peeked in the lighted windows. In the first three he saw nothing out of the ordinary. In one a family of four played dominoes on the kitchen table. In another two older folks sat and rocked and read.

In the third house he found only a mother and a small child breast feeding.

At the last one he saw something strange. The man of the house lay on his stomach on the floor with his hands tied behind his back.

A woman put more wood into an already hot fire in the open fireplace. She seemed ill-at-ease, nervous. McCoy listened but could hear nothing unusual. Then someone coughed, a deep racking sound that sounded like Mississippi river water in a lung.

The woman came back into view with a wet pair of pants and a shirt. She hung them over the backs of wooden chairs and pushed them toward the fireplace.

Had to be Kirby. Did Kirby still have his .38? With the new solid cartridges they would fire just as well wet as dry. Surprise was his best weapon.

McCoy went to the far window, but it did not look in on the living room. The kitchen was dark. He went back to the door, set the valise under the edge of the porch where it couldn't be seen and eased up on the boards.

He moved slowly to the door, making no sound. Thank God this family didn't have a dog. He touched the door knob, praying that it wouldn't be locked. Most of these houses probably didn't even have locks on the doors.

He turned the knob gently with his left hand, unlatching the door. Now he squared with the door and with his right hand lifted his six-gun out of leather and cocked the hammer. Then he rammed the door inward and jumped into the room.

"Don't anyone move!" he bellowed. Everyone froze. He took in the little tableau in a fraction of a second. The woman had just wrung out some underwear in a pan on the living room table. Her husband lay tied at the far end of the room.

Flavian Kirby sat in a chair at the end of the kitchen table wearing the woman's flannel robe. A girl about three sat on his lap, and Kirby's .38 revolver had it's muzzle against the side of her head.

"Welcome to our little group, lawman," Kirby said with a wry smile. "Now don't do anything stupid or this little one never lives to see four years of age. You wouldn't want that on your conscience, would you?"

Spur McCoy growled but slowly lowered his six-gun.

"That's right. Now you just lay that fancy .45 shooter on the floor right beside your foot. First, take it off cock, so it won't go off by accident."

McCoy scowled as he did it. There was nothing else to do right now.

Kirby had combed his wet hair and evidently cleaned the Mississippi mud off of himself. He nodded to the woman. "Alice, you just go right ahead there and get my underdrawers dry so I can be nice and comfortable when I ride out of here. Go on, woman."

She finished wringing out the longjohns and draped them over a chair near the fire.

"Now, suppose you tell me your name, lawman."

"Spur McCoy."

"Good, always fine to know names. This here is Alice. Ain't she a fine one? Look at that saucy little bottom and them good tits. We gonna have play time after a while. Over there all tied up on the floor is George who's a mite testy right now. This little one is Cindy. So, now we know each other.

"Alice, you get some more of that twine and tie Mr. McCoy's hands behind his back. Do that for me, darling."

She frowned but took twine from the table. McCoy moved his hands behind him. He was outsmarted for the moment, but that didn't mean any of these innocent folks had to die.

When McCoy was tied, the shorter man came up to him and snorted.

"You don't look so fucking good now, lawman. What bunch you with in Washington?"

"Secret Service."

"Ha, protector of the currency. Suppose you know I slaved in that Bureau of Engraving and Printing for damn near thirty years. Left me damn near broke."

He held the .38 by the handle and slashed the barrel into McCoy's belly, making him gasp for breath.

"Yeah, McCoy, not a bigshot Secret Service agent now, are you? Lay down over there besides good old George."

McCoy did. At least his feet weren't tied. He turned so he could look at George and nodded. "Give me some time," he whispered.

Kirby stared at the group. He pulled the chairs back a little from the fire so his clothes wouldn't burn, then he carried the small girl and pushed Alice ahead of him into another room. "Time for bed for little Cindy here. We'll lock her door from the outside so she don't bother us none."

He and Alice were back a moment later. "Now, Alice, you're being a good girl. Suppose you go right on being good and I won't have to shoot old George over there, right?"

Alice was in her late twenties, a little thick at the waist with large breasts and a small saucy bottom as Kirby had described her.

"You'll do whatever I tell you to do so old George over there doesn't get shot, right?"

"Yes," she said softly.

"Good, strip yourself down to your waist. I want to see them good-looking tits you got."

Her face registered surprise and shock. "You never said I'd have to do nothing like that."

Kirby cocked the .38 revolver and aimed it at George. Quickly the woman unbuttoned her blouse and tore it off, then took off a chemise and unwound a wrapper that held her big breasts in place. They fell out like two sacks of spilled watermelons.

"My God, what big tits!" Kirby said. "Bring them over here, Alice. Nothing a husband hates more than to see another man at his wife. Sit down here on the table and let me play with them suckers. Them is really a fine pair."

McCoy had turned slightly and pushed his hands toward George.

"Try and untie them," McCoy whispered.

George moved his hands a little and touched the twine. This had to work. McCoy figured if it didn't, all of them except little Cindy had about a half hour to live.

Chapter Thirteen

"Alice didn't tie you tight," George whispered. "Making progress."

"Shut up, you two," Flavian Kirby said. "You're interrupting my gnawing on these big tits. Damn they are fine ones."

"Don't think about it," McCoy whispered. "If you don't get me free, we're both dead men and Alice along with us."

Kirby had settled in to devouring the woman. He sucked and chewed and licked on her breasts as he pulled down her dress and the rest of her clothing. Soon she was naked, and he grinned.

"Hell, not bad for a quick one. Hey, George, you got some hot pussy of a woman here. She's cunt damp already."

George stopped working on Spur's hands when he saw Flavian look over his shoulder.

"Don't hurt her," George pleaded.

"Hell, a couple of pokings never hurt any little gal. Get yourself down on the floor, woman. I like it rough once in a while."

George tugged on the twine, and McCoy pulled and twisted his hands and wrists to help matters. He looked over and saw the woman flat on her back and Kirby trying to get her legs spread. McCoy felt one of the loops give.

"Yes, that's it, faster," McCoy whispered.

Kirby yelped in delight as he spread Alice's legs apart and knelt between them. He fumbled at his crotch as he whipped the robe away and went down on her.

"Oh, yes, you are ready, Alice. You hot little cunt. You'd take on any man who got you naked. Admit it now, wouldn't you?"

She didn't answer but just turned her head away. McCoy could see that her eyes were closed.

Another strand of twine loosened. McCoy tugged and pulled at his hands until his arms ached. Slowly his right hand slid past the twine and more of the loops loosened.

Kirby drove forward and gave a big yelp of pleasure.

"Damn, but you're tight. Don't he ever get into you? Hell, I'd have you twice a day if'n I was his age."

McCoy could see Kirby's rear end under the robe pumping back and forth. At his age it should take him a few minutes to get his pleasure fulfilled.

McCoy gave one more pull and his right hand came free. Quickly he undid the rest of the twine, then reached over and untied George's hands.

"Now," McCoy whispered. Both men lunged up from the floor and charged Kirby. When he saw them coming he pulled out and rolled away from them. His right hand grabbed his six-gun and he got off one shot before Alice clubbed his wrist with both of her fisted hands and the gun flew to the floor.

It was too far away for him to reach. Alice kicked it away with her bare foot, and it skittered toward the two charging men.

Faster than McCoy figured possible, Kirby bolted for the door, opened it and charged into the night.

George went to his wife, kissed her and held her in his arms. McCoy grabbed his own six-gun, then the one from the floor and rushed out the door after the counterfeiter. He couldn't get far. He was barefooted and in a woman's pink robe.

McCoy stopped and listened and heard soft sounds as if running bare feet were heading toward the next house. McCoy fired a shot into the air in that direction, then raced after the fugitive.

He saw no door open on the next house, so he ran past it. Then he stopped and listened again. Ahead at the next house he saw a sliver of light break up the night, then vanish. A door had opened. Was it a coincidence, or had Kirby rushed inside?

McCoy sprinted to the house and looked in the window. It was a couple and two children still playing dominoes at the kitchen table.

Standing in front of them was Flavian Kirby pretending he had a gun under his robe. As McCoy watched the man inside stood, bellowed in anger and swung at the smaller man. Kirby ducked and raced out of the room to the rear of the house. McCoy tore around the side of the house but could see nothing in the moonless night.

He listened.

Soft footsteps moved away into a grove of trees and brush toward the river. McCoy fired once in that direction and charged ahead. He reached the spot where he figured Kirby should be, but no one was there. The thick brush along the Mississippi was hard enough to work through in daylight; now at night it would be nearly impossible to make good time or try to find someone inside it.

McCoy tried the outside approach. He listened to the sounds of Kirby working through the brush. A stick snapped now and then, and the branch of a tree creaked and groaned as it was pushed aside.

McCoy moved along the open stretch just outside the brush, listening and waiting.

The sounds of movement in the brush continued for half an hour, then stopped, and McCoy decided that Kirby had stopped to get a little rest, maybe some sleep. He had no idea what time it was, but he wasn't about to light a match to check his watch. He tried to see the stars but there was enough scattering of clouds to block out the North Star so he couldn't judge the time by the position of the Big Dipper that moved around the North Star every night.

He sat on the ground and waited.

Twice he nodded off but came awake the moment he started to roll to the ground.

It was a long night. He saw the stars fade and then a false dawn with streaks of light from the east. At last the darkness was eaten up by the rising sun, and McCoy moved behind a large maple tree on the fringes of the brush. Now he could see a quarter mile stretch of the brushline and not be spotted himself.

McCoy figured if he was Kirby, he'd have had enough of the brush with no shoes on and would strike out for the trail along the river, watching for an unsuspecting household where he could get some clothes, a gun and maybe a hostage or two.

McCoy waited another half hour, then he took a stroll along the trail, listening for any sounds. There were no indications that Kirby was moving through the brush. Maybe there was a dirt flat where he could run without any noise.

McCoy walked downstream faster. He saw a rider coming along the road a quarter of a mile ahead. Realizing the danger the horse presented, McCoy sprinted forward, but his move came too late.

A figure in a pink robe darted out from some brush and caught the bridle of the horse. A moment later the young woman had been pulled down, and Kirby mounted the animal, turned it and raced away.

McCoy ran up to the girl on the ground.

"Miss, I'm a law officer. Is there another horse nearby? That man is a wanted felon. I'm trying to capture him."

She was not yet 20, plain with long dark hair. She wiped her eyes, jumped up and nodded.

"Back there at my Pa's place. He's got two horses all saddled. They were gonna follow me."

100 yards around a bend and past some brush was a small house, barn and corral. Two saddled mounts stood at a rail in front of the house.

McCoy jumped into the saddle and called to the girl. "I'll bring your horses back, promise." Then he raced after the fleeing Kirby. He couldn't do much without clothes or shoes, except run and hide. If he came to a town he'd be at a disadvantage.

But there was no town. McCoy galloped his mount for a quarter of a mile, then eased her down, picked up the hoofprints of the horse ahead of him and walked the mare for a quarter of a mile. He couldn't see any horseman ahead.

He could track at a lope. The ground along the river was soft, even wet in spots, and Kirby was pushing the horse too fast. It couldn't last long.

After another half mile the trail wound around a curve in the river, and on a slight downhill stretch McCoy saw the fugitive. His horse had broken down, and Kirby was standing beside it. When he looked back and saw a rider coming, he ran into the brush along the Mississippi.

McCoy rode to the spot and saw that there was a small stream that emptied into the mighty river here. He rode along it and stared in surprise. Just across the stream was a small fishing shack. A black man lay on the porch trying to stand up.

Kirby sat in a rowboat 50 feet into the Mississippi, rowing farther into the current that swept him downstream.

There was no other boat there.

He'd have to follow him on land. In a heartbeat McCoy knew that was all he could do. If he had a rifle he could shoot the little boat into kindling. If he came to a house, he'd try to borrow a rifle.

McCoy found it easy to follow the progress of the rowboat. At this point the water slowed and the river widened. Sometimes the current carried Kirby toward the far shore, sometimes to the near one. McCoy tried to stay out of sight as much as possible.

He didn't want the counterfeiter to get the idea of going to the other side of the wide river and escaping that way.

Another mile down the river speeded up. The current swung toward McCoy's shore, and he saw Kirby fighting to stay away from the shoreline. He lost the fight.

McCoy saw his chance. The current would swing the little boat within 50 feet of the shoreline. He loaded a sixth round in his Peacemaker, rode for the point of land ahead where the small craft would sweep by and waded ten feet into the shallow shore ledge.

The rowboat swept toward him, and he spotted the hump of the pink robe. When the boat came closest to the shore, McCoy fired. He aimed not at the man but at the waterline of the small boat. The big .45 shells whacked into the dry wood of the boat and tore open holes. Five of the six rounds ripped into the side of the boat, and he heard a yelp of surprise from Kirby.

McCoy fired the rest of the rounds from the .38 but he wasn't sure any of them hit the boat. He saw Kirby sit up in the boat and shake his fist at McCoy, then he began scooping water out of the craft with his hands.

"Good, it's leaking," McCoy said out loud. He ran back to his horse and followed the shoreline as close as possible. Now he could see the boat settling lower in the Mississippi. He had to go around a patch of brush, and when he came back he didn't see anyone in the boat.

Where did he go?

Then a head popped up for a look. Kirby had to be lying in the water. McCoy had reloaded his six-gun and fired six more times at the boat, but it was beyond his range.

The boat sank lower in the water. Five minutes later McCoy paced the boat as it last sank under the muddy flow. Kirby flopped out of it like a dead fish, then began to swim for shore. He was an expert swimmer, and even with the current moving him downstream he made good progress. Less than a quarter of a mile down the river, Kirby staggered up from the mud flats along the shore and fell on the hard ground.

He looked up at McCoy and snorted. "Big win for you, McCoy. So you captured me. What's so earth-shattering here? Was I going to rip apart the economy with my $88,000."

"You were hurting a lot of good people. Did you ever think of that?"

Spur made Kirby walk. He had lost the robe in the water and walked naked as a bluejay along the country road. In the distance, McCoy saw a small town. The agent took off his shirt and let Kirby wrap it around his waist to cover his privates.

A half hour later, McCoy had Kirby deposited in the small town's one jail cell in the police station. The town marshal swore on a stack of beer bottles that he would guard the man with his life. There was only one key to the cell.

McCoy asked to see it, then put it in his pocket.

"Hey, what if the jail catches fire? How do we get this man out?"

"Put out the fire," McCoy said and went to a café for a solid meal.

An hour and a half later he was back where he had borrowed the horse. He told them what had happened to the first horse. "Looked like she foundered, but I didn't see her on the road, so she may have recovered and be down along the river about a mile." He thanked them and moved north.

He walked on back to the home of George and Alice and little Cindy where he had first found Kirby.

They all sat at the kitchen table eating a noon meal. George went to the door and invited him in. Right away Alice blushed and rushed into another room.

"She's still touchy about your seeing her naked and all," George said.

McCoy said that he understood and that he had just come back to get something he left under the steps. He went back outside and looked, but the valise wasn't there.

George held up his hands before McCoy could accuse him.

"We figured all that money was that Kirby guy's and that he owed us plenty for what he did to us—raping Alice and all."

"Where is it?" McCoy asked, his voice low and level and deadly.

"Oh, we got it. We don't want all of it, but we figure fair is fair. We'll split with that Mr. Kirby. We'll keep half, and he can have half of it back."

McCoy told him the bills were all counterfeit and not worth the paper it cost to print them.

"No, can't be!" George thundered. "I seen lots of paper money. This is genuine as rain."

"Notice the serial numbers on the bills?"

George shook his head.

"They are all the same. They were all printed from the same plate stolen from the mint in Washington D.C. Bring out the valise and I'll show you."

George brought the valise out of another room.

"Still say it's good as gold."

McCoy broke one of the bands around the bills and laid six of them out so the serial numbers showed one after another. The numbers were identical.

"You ever see two pieces of paper money with the same number on them before," McCoy asked.

"Oh, shit!"

"Afraid so. Now if you have any of these bills, you best bring them and put them back in the valise. Otherwise you'll be breaking the law by passing counterfeit money. That would put you in federal prison for ten long years."

"Oh, damn!"

Alice came through the door with a handful of the bills. "We was just aiming to go into the city and spend us some money." She scowled. "Reckon now that we can't.

"But look how we helped you," George said. "I untied your hands, and Alice there slammed Kirby's hand when he was shooting and got the gun away from him. That's got to be worth something."

McCoy took a deep breath. He'd figure out some way to cover it. He dug into his pocket, took out his wallet and lifted three good $20 bills out. He handed them to Alice.

"Here, Alice. You go to town and buy yourself something pretty. Get a new shirt for George, maybe."

She grinned. "I thank you, sir."

McCoy looked back in the valise. He better check to be sure the missing engraving plates were there as well. He found the small wrapped package and opened it. It wasn't the plates but rather a packet of what must be family pictures. He identified one of the people as Kirby.

So where the hell were the engraving plates that Flavian Kirby had stolen?

Chapter Fourteen

By the time McCoy rented a horse and rode back to the small town of Cloverville where he had left the counterfeiter, the town marshal had rustled up a pair of pants, a shirt and some shoes for the prisoner.

They weren't near as fancy as those Flavian Kirby usually wore. He sat in the corner of the cell with his eyes closed.

"Now's the time to tell me, Kirby. What did you do with the plates?"

"I eat off plates."

"You know what I mean—the engraving plates front and back of the twenty dollar bill you stole from the mint."

"You'll never find them."

"Neither will you, Kirby. You'll be in jail for forty years, if you live that long."

"Don't matter. I had my time. I had my fun. I proved that a man who was smart enough could outwit

150

the whole United States government."

"For a while, that is, Kirby. So why not give us the plates?"

"Never can tell where they might be. Maybe I sent them to Paris where some of the best counterfeiters in the world can turn out a billion dollars in twenties and flood the world market and collapse the U.S. economy."

"The bills won't pass that well in large numbers, Kirby. You know that. Not with the same serial number."

"Sure I know, but that don't put you no closer to getting the plates."

"You can talk here or back in St. Louis or in Washington. It's up to you."

By the time McCoy decided that Kirby wasn't going to talk in the jail cell, it was after suppertime. The town marshal allowed as how there wasn't a hotel in their small town, McCoy was more than welcome to have supper at his house and sleep in the spare room.

The next morning, McCoy handcuffed Kirby to the side of a rented carriage and drove back to St. Louis. He deposited Kirby in the city jail and then wired Washington D.C. with the fact that Kirby was in custody and most of the $88,000 in bogus bills had been recovered. The problem was that the engraving plates were missing.

A return wire came almost before McCoy got out of the telegraph office.

"TO MCCOY. CAPITAL INVESTIGATIONS, ST.

LOUIS. MO. MUST RECOVER THE MISSING $20 ENGRAVINGS. DON'T WANT THIS TO HAPPEN AGAIN. REPEAT. MUST RECOVER THE PLATES. SENDING. W.D. HALLECK. WASHINGTON."

Back at the office he found Jessica. Her wound on her upper arm was slight and was bandaged. She wanted all the details about Kirby's capture which he told her. Then McCoy and Jessica went back to Kirby's room in the hotel. It was the only bet they had. Maybe they could find a lead in the counterfeiter's room which had been sealed by the St. Louis police.

It took them three hours to go over the room inch by inch. They looked on the bottom of the dresser drawers, under a picture on the wall and even inside the water pitcher.

They sat on the unmade bed and pondered.

"What if he didn't have the plates with him?" McCoy suggested. "Say this was just a swing around the country to build up his supply of good money by passing bills."

"So where did he live in Chicago and Washington?" Jessica asked.

"When we're through here, I'll have someone check."

"Are we through here?" Jessica asked. She looked at the bed and grinned. "We don't have to be through. I mean, we could close the door and lock it and make some use of this bed."

He kissed her lips gently. "Later. Something has to be here to lead us to those damn plates."

"Maybe he hid them somewhere and memorized the spot," she said.

"Possible. Maybe he stored them with some of his books and furniture."

"Possible," Jessica said.

McCoy stood and slammed his hand against the side of the dresser. "Hell, the plates could be anywhere."

"What was that?" Jessica asked.

"What was what?"

"Something just fell down from behind the dresser."

McCoy went to his knees and saw a crumpled piece of paper.

"It must have been wedged behind the dresser. When you moved it, the paper fell."

They spread out the paper slowly. The handwriting was neat and perfectly formed, the way an engraver would write. It took McCoy a moment to figure out what it said.

"Mr. Lance Whitmore, 124 Chesterton Lain." Then there were some random marks.

"What in the world?" Jessica asked.

"The name will be easy enough to trace, especially with the address. Are you familiar with Chesterton Lane near Washington? It's a fine residential street. A lot of government people live there. Evidently Kirby started to write a letter to this Whitmore. Remember Kirby is an engraver, an expert at perfection. When he misspelled the word "lane", he was angry, wadded up the paper and threw it away."

He grabbed her hand, and they hurried out of the room. McCoy led them straight to the telegraph office and sent a wire to the general.

"TO GEN. HALLECK. CAPITAL INVESTIGA-TIONS, WASHINGTON, D.C. CHECK BACK-

GROUND AND OCCUPATION OF LANCE WHITMORE, 124 CHESTERTON LANE, D.C. A DISCREET INQUIRY. MAY BE SOME CONNECTION WITH FLAVIAN KIRBY CASE. REPLY SOONEST. SENDING. MCCOY."

"I still don't understand," Priscilla said when they got back to the office and showed her the paper. "Why should a part of an address and a name be so important?"

Jessica explained. "If you were in a strange town and had something extremely valuable that you didn't want to carry with you any more, what might you do with it? You have no home address to mail it to, but you could wrap it up and mail it to a good friend or someone who would keep it for you until you asked for it without any questions."

"Another member of the gang?"

"Could be," McCoy said. "Until we learn something from Washington about who this man is, we won't know."

"How long will that take?" Jessica asked.

"An hour, a day—who knows?" McCoy said. "But I've a hunch the general is worried enough about those plates that he'll get a check made as fast as he can."

By that time it was nearing 5:00 o'clock. They told Priscilla she could go on home and take care of her father. Jessica and Spur ate that evening in the hotel dining room which wasn't known for it's excellent food but had fast service.

Just after 7:00 o'clock they went back to her room, and Jessica locked the door. McCoy slid a chair back under the knob and wedged it in solidly.

"Why, Mr. McCoy, it appears that you have some sort of wild and crazy plans for the rest of the evening."

"Just trying to protect you from the lawless outsiders," he said with a grin.

She grabbed him and kissed him, and they fell on the bed laughing. He undressed her gently and slowly, kissing away every article of clothing until she was squirming naked and excited on the big bed.

Then she sat up and undressed him, teasing him along the way until by the time she had his pants off, his erection was full and throbbing.

"Right now!" she cried and went to her hands and knees and looked back over her shoulder. McCoy grinned, knelt behind her tight little bottom and spread her cheeks to find the right slot. He nudged into her gently, slowly, listening to her moaning in front of him.

When he was fully entered, he caught the right angle of her hip and her belly and held on as he thrust back and fourth.

"More, more," she wailed. "Faster, you slowpoke, or I'll beat you to home plate again." Then she writhed under him, her body shattered by a thousand vibrations as spasm after spasm racked her frame until she nearly collapsed. He held her up and continued to drive into her. His own satisfaction came quickly but not before she was spurred into another wild series of climaxes that overshadowed his own brief leap into ecstacy.

Then slowly she eased forward until she lay on her stomach with him still in her.

"Don't move or I'll kill you," she said from where her head nearly vanished in the soft pillow.

Neither of them said a word for three or four minutes, then he withdrew from her and lay beside her on the bed.

"So how did you like your first case working with a woman agent?" she asked.

"Better than I expected. Although I did have to rescue you once."

"True, but I saw the vital piece of evidence fall from behind the dresser."

"Right, but I would have . . ."

She put her fingers over his lips to quiet him.

"Let's not get into any arguments. This case is probably about over for me. I have a feeling that the plates won't be that hard to find."

"Why, Jessica?"

"If you owned those plates, who would you send them to for safekeeping?"

"A good friend or an accomplice."

"Right. You said good friend first. My guess is that this Mr. Whitmore is exactly that—a good friend. I'd address the letter to him, enclose the plates all wrapped up and put in the letter that this was something special that I wanted Whitmore to save for me until I could get back to D.C. to pick it up."

"You might be right. If so, that means that the government people in Washington should have the plates by tonight," McCoy said."

"If this Whitmore cooperates. It could take a search warrant from a federal judge to get into his house. By that time, Whitmore might check out what was in that secret envelope and decide to do something with it on his own."

"Guess why we came to your room tonight?"

She grinned, sat up and pushed one breast into his mouth. "Could it be because a telegram marked urgent would be delivered directly to your room even if it comes late at night, and it could disturb something important going on inside your room?"

"Close enough," he said after he came away from her breast which showed delicate teeth marks.

A sudden knocking on the door brought them both upright. He motioned for her to answer it. She walked naked to the door.

"Yes, what is it?"

A voice shouted something, but neither of them could understand the words. Carefully, Jessica took the chair away, unlocked the door and edged it open an inch.

"Yes, what do you want?"

The door burst open as a shoulder hit it, bouncing Jessica back a step. Priscilla marched into the room, nodded at both of them, closed the door, locked it and replaced the chair.

She reached for the buttons at the front of her blouse and began undoing them.

"I've had about enough of being ignored. I mean, here I am a bright young person with a rather good body and full breasts and I am ignored by the sexiest man I know. I won't stand for it any longer. I'm here to say that if you don't want me, then tell me that after I get my clothes off."

McCoy sat on the bed, staring at her. He couldn't find anything to say.

Jessica watched with her mouth open as Priscilla stripped off her blouse and her chemise and thrust out her bare breasts at them.

"I can go naked, too," Priscilla said.

McCoy chuckled, and it broke the tension in the room. "Priscilla, little darling, long as you made such a bold first move, the game is wide open. Welcome aboard."

Jessica laughed, too. "Honey, I'm glad you came. We can have a great party the rest of the night. We'll worry about the damn counterfeiting plates tomorrow."

By then, Priscilla had shucked out of the rest of her clothes, and for a minute as she stood there naked, she became shy. She turned away from them, hiding herself, then took a deep breath and spun around.

"I don't want you to think I'm a virgin or anything like that. I've had sex with a man before."

McCoy grinned. "Exactly how many times, Pris?"

"How many?" She went over to the bed and sat down beside McCoy. Jessica sat close to him on the other side. Both women reached for his growing erection.

"How many men have you fucked, Pris?" Jessica asked.

"Well, you want to know exactly?"

"If you can remember," McCoy said.

She watched them, and then her chin tilted up a little as McCoy had seen so many times. "Once, one time when I was fifteen and neither of us knew what we were trying to do."

Spur chuckled, reached over and kissed her cheek. Jessica kissed her cheek, too. Pris shook her red hair, turned to McCoy and kissed him on the lips, then she pushed him down on the bed and lay on top of him.

"Oh, gracious! You'll never guess how many times I've dreamed of doing this."

Jessica sat on one side of the bed and watched. "Looks like it's your turn right now, little Pris. Enjoy."

Priscilla rolled off McCoy and lay huddled on the bed. When he reached over and kissed her lips, she responded shyly. Then he bent and kissed one breast, and she trembled. He kissed the other orb, then licked around her nipple and bit it tenderly.

Priscilla trembled, then her whole body vibrated with a storm of spasms drilling through her small frame.

"Oh, glory! Oh, God! Oh, McCoy!" She pulled him on top of her, and he cushioned her until it was over. Her eyes were wide as she stared up at him.

"Never felt anything like that before," Priscilla said. She pulled him down. "Now, put it inside me. I want to see what that feels like. I hardly remember from before."

Gently he entered her. She yelped in sudden pain, then her smile broke through and her arms encircled him and she cried for joy.

"So wonderful! Why didn't you tell me it would be this good? Why haven't I been doing this before? Oh, damn, I'm going to do it again!"

She climaxed again with the same array of moans and vibrations, and her little bottom danced on the bed, pounding upward a dozen times toward the end.

"Wonderful! That's just the most marvelous feeling that I can ever remember having. It's absolutely pure heaven!"

McCoy knew that Jessica had moved. Now he could feel her finger searching for his tight little bung. She found it at about the same time he started his climax and he finished with her watching every stroke he made.

Below them, Priscilla lay there with her arms at her sides. She smiled at them in a way neither had ever seen before. "Shame on you, Spur McCoy, for not sharing this joy, this wonder, this marvelous fucking with me before. I know that we're just getting started and that I'm new to this, but I think this is the most wonderful and marvelous and tremendous night of my life!"

They came apart, and the three of them lay on the bed.

"This is pleasant," Jessica said. "The three of us sharing together this way. Everyone has to promise that by morning we'll still be the best of friends. Whether this ever happens again is something we don't need to think about right now."

"I'll say amen to that," McCoy chimed in.

"Oh, me too, me too," Priscilla said, reaching for Spur McCoy's limp privates, trying to get him hard again.

McCoy's mind was distracted for a moment. He knew that they shouldn't be here. The office should be covered. Right at that moment he was sure that a night letter had been slipped under his door two floors below. He wondered what it said, but he was damned if he was going to go get it until morning.

Chapter Fifteen

Spur McCoy unlocked his hotel room door beside the office at 6:30 the next morning and saw the yellow and black envelope where it had been slid under his door sometime during the night. He picked it up and tore it open.

"TO SPUR MCCOY, CAPITAL INVESTIGATIONS, CLAYMORE HOTEL, ST. LOUIS, MISSOURI. RUSH TO WASHINGTON ON NEXT AVAILABLE TRAIN. BRING PRISONER IN CUFFS AND UNDER GUARD. AGENT FLANDERS TO TRAVEL WITH YOU. DEVELOPMENTS HERE RE YOUR LAST WIRE. NEED YOU HERE FOR THE WRAP-UP. REPLY SOONEST. GENERAL WILTON D. HALLECK. WASHINGTON DC SENDING."

McCoy studied the wire, then went back to the third floor where he had spent the night and knocked on the door. A sleepy, frowsy-headed Jessica answered.

"Oh, I was hoping it was you."

He waved the telegram at her. "Night letter from the general. Get dressed to travel and pack. Both of us and Kirby have been ordered to come to Washington on the next train. I'll go wire the general and make arrangements to get Kirby out of the jail. You be ready in an hour."

He turned and walked down the hall, leaving Jessica in momentary confusion.

It took them two hours to make connections for a train heading for Washington, to get their bags on board and to get the St. Louis police to bring Kirby in handcuffs and make sure he was secure in the hands of the federal officers. McCoy signed the prisoner transfer notice and handed it back to the St. Louis roundsman just as the train started to move.

They settled into two compartments, one for the two men and one for Jessica. The train was the Atlantic Flyer, a passengers-only train that had been listed as an express which stopped at selected terminals along the line.

McCoy handcuffed Kirby to the berth, made sure there was no possible means he could use to get away and settled down to read a fresh copy of the *New York Times*. It would be over 800 miles to the nation's capital. Even on this express it would take nearly a day and a half. Jessica came into the compartment shortly, and they played poker for matches, at last allowing Kirby to play, but minus the matches.

"Our job is to deliver you safely to my boss in Washington, Kirby. Nothing you can do will stop me from getting you there. So just relax and accept it. Your fun and games are over."

They left St. Louis shortly before ten o'clock and wired ahead their expected arrival time.

It still took the full day and a half they had been told. They spent the time in a dozen ways, none of them sexual, and at last turned a grousing Flavian Kirby over to Secret Service agents at the Washington central depot shortly after four in the afternoon.

General Halleck and two of his men were there to greet the prisoner and the two agents. It had been three years since Spur McCoy had seen the general who was in his late sixties now, ramrod straight and with a full beard and moustache neatly trimmed and turning gray. His dark brown eyes snapped as he looked at Kirby, then waved him away. General Halleck was a little over five-feet-ten, wore a somber black suit and a stiff collar and tie with his white shirt. His black shoes were polished to a military sheen.

"Good job, McCoy, Flanders. We wanted Kirby here to try to question him. This thing has grown a little out of bounds. Do you have any idea who the man is you had us investigate?"

"No sir," both agents said almost in unison.

"For your information, Lance Whitmore is one of the President's fair-haired boys. He was appointed to the number three post in the Bureau of Engraving and Printing. I have a sheaf of material on the man, but he seems to be on vacation right now somewhere in the Blue Mountains of Virginia."

"Convenient," McCoy murmured.

"Damned lot more than convenient. We've con-

sulted with the president who's given us approval
to get a search warrant to the Whitmore house and
grounds. I wanted you here to help us work on Kirby
and, if needed, go into the mountains."

"I've done my best on Kirby. He isn't going to say
a word. He didn't even flinch when we mentioned the
Whitmore name."

They walked to a large closed coach and the three
of them got in. A driver whipped the rig away without
instructions.

"It seems that this Whitmore used to work at one
time with Kirby. Both of them are about the same
age. Whitmore's work records are being scrutinized.
He had no firm control where he could have stolen
anything, but still it's a worry."

"Bet the president is a bit grim," Jessica said.

"He's angry, wants it settled quickly one way or the
other," the general said.

"How long has Whitmore been on his vacation,"
McCoy asked.

The general looked at his notes a moment. "About
two weeks. He's due back in six days."

McCoy nodded. To him it didn't make sense that
Whitmore could be a conspirator. If he'd been gone
two weeks, that meant he had left long before Kirby
had showed up in St. Louis and probably before Kirby
could have mailed the plates to him—if that's what he
did mail. They were riding the tails of several assump-
tions here. He kept this all to himself. Time enough to
bring it up later.

They rumbled up to the headquarters of the Secret
Service, a small granite building just a block and a half

from the White House. The carriage rolled through a guarded gate at the back of the building and stopped.

They got out, and McCoy looked around. The place hadn't changed much.

"Come inside and I'll show you what we've found out about this Whitmore. Not too encouraging, I'm afraid."

In a meeting room with a blackboard, McCoy and Jessica looked at what had been written in chalk on the board. It was a work history of Lance Whitmore.

The general took over the briefing. "He came with the Bureau of Engraving and Printing about fifteen years ago. Worked in the same department as Kirby.

"Later promoted to junior engraver, and two years later promoted again into management at a junior level. Then he quit for five years and worked for a big bank here in Washington and got shoulder deep into the political whirl.

"Two years ago he was appointed to the post of number three man at the bureau with wide-ranging powers, yet still with several checks on him."

A knock sounded on the door. It opened discreetly. The general glanced that way and nodded. "That's all the time we have for your briefing. We're on our way to serve the papers and search the Whitmore place on Chesterton Lane. Interesting how you came on this whole connection. Let's hope it pays off for us."

Jessica and McCoy followed the general out of the room and were soon back in the same plush coach. This time there were four more rigs that followed them out of the yard behind the building. Half of the men carried shotguns. All were armed in some way.

"I assume both of you have your weapons," the general said. They nodded. "Good. Probably won't need them, but never can tell."

Ten minutes later they pulled up in front of 124 Chesterton Lane. The general sat in his coach and glanced out. Four men drifted from the carriages into the shrubbery and to the rear of the house. Two more men went to each side. Then someone tapped the general's door.

"Let's find out what this is all about," General Halleck said.

He held an envelope in his gloved hand as they marched up the sidewalk, through a fancy iron gate and up the steps to a three-story house that was well-painted with carefully trimmed grounds.

The general rang a twist bell that set up a clatter somewhere in the house. A moment later a maid in uniform answered the door.

"I'm sorry but Mr. and Mrs. Whitmore are vacationing in the mountains. I can take a message for them."

"I'm General Halleck of the United States Secret Service. This is a search warrant granted by the federal district court allowing us to search the premises and adjoining area."

The girl took the envelope and nodded. "Well, I've heard of you. I guess you can go ahead and search."

"Girl, where is the mail that has arrived for the Whitmores since they've been away?"

"Oh, it's all in a safe box. I'm to put it in there every

day when it comes and lock it."

"Would you show us, please?" Jessica asked the frightened girl. She looked at Jessica, shivered and led them into a study on the first floor.

The place was furnished in good taste with a few expensive pieces but nothing lavish, McCoy noticed. The study was lined with books and was a little ostentatious. Probably painting a better picture of the man of the house.

The maid pointed to a lock box, a kind of home safe that sat to one side. It had a wide door and a combination lock.

"I'll ask you to open the safe," General Halleck said. "You'll be in no trouble with your employer for doing so. I'll see to that myself."

The girl turned the knobs. McCoy looked away so he wouldn't remember the combination. A moment later he heard the lock click, and the girl opened the wide door. Inside was a box a foot square half-filled with letters, larger envelopes, a flyer or two and one newspaper.

The general pulled the box from the safe and set it on the walnut desk top. He sorted through the material, scanning each item, then putting it to one side on the desk.

About half way into the pile he smiled and showed an envelope to McCoy.

"It has a St. Louis postmark on it from six days ago, it has six cents in postage, and it's heavy."

He gathered McCoy, Jessica and two other agents who had come in with them.

"You're my witnesses that I'm opening this mail addressed to one Lance Whitmore of 124 Chesterton

Lane." He tore off the top end of the envelope and let the contents fall out on the desk. When one item hit with a heavy clunk, they all smiled.

There was a letter and another item wrapped in several pieces of paper. The general opened the sealing tape on the heavy paper around the wrapped item. He unfolded the paper and smiled. He had them, the front and back engraved plates of the U.S. $20 treasury note.

McCoy picked up the letter that lay to one side, read it and passed it quickly to the general.

"St. Louis, October 12. You'll probably be surprised to hear from me, but I'm traveling again. Remember how we used to dream about seeing the West? I'm on my way to San Francisco.

"Enclosed are some items I want you to keep for me. Nowhere in the West does it seem safe to keep things in a person's room on in a poor excuse for a hotel vault. The items are sealed in heavy paper inside the outer envelope, so you won't need to be concerned with what they are. If you could put them in your safe I'd appreciate it.

"Next time that I'm in town, I'll stop by for dinner on me and we'll talk about old times. Hope all is well with your growing political career. Stay healthy. Sincerely, Flavian Kirby."

The general finished reading it and stared at McCoy. "So, Agent McCoy, what's your evaluation of the letter?"

"I'd say it's just what it appears to be. Whitmore was a friend, a trusted friend he could count on doing as asked without peeking in the envelope. I'd say

Mr. Whitmore has no connection whatsoever with the counterfeiting."

"You may be right. On the other hand the letter could be loaded with coded words and secret instructions. I want Whitmore picked up and brought back to my office as quickly as possible."

He turned to the open-mouthed maid who still stood by the door.

"Miss, do you have an address where your employer can be located in case of a problem here at the house?

She nodded, reached in her pocket, took out a folded piece of paper and handed it to the general. He opened it, read it and handed it to McCoy.

"Here's is your next assignment. Go get him and bring him back without a word what this is all about. I want to question him myself before he knows anything about any of this. Whatever you do, don't discuss the counterfeiting or Kirby."

"Why shall I say he needs to return to Washington at once?" McCoy asked.

"Tell him we have a small crisis in his department and his chief asked me to locate him and have him return."

"Shall I take Agent Flanders with me?"

"You feel you need backup on a peaceful messenger service job such as this?"

"No sir."

McCoy turned and strode out of the room, winking at Jessica as he passed her.

It took McCoy a day and a half to find Whitmore. He took a stage to Fort Royal and rented a horse for the last

20 miles. When he reached the rustic cabin, Whitmore was cleaning fish on the bench near a small lake.

"A crisis in my department! Enough said. I'll be dressed to travel in fifteen minutes. My wife and children can stay the rest of the time and then come back. My wife is most resourceful. Can you tell me anything more about this problem?"

McCoy said his only instructions were to tell Mr. Whitmore of the crisis and ask him to return as quickly as possible.

They rented a buggy at a nearby village and soon were on the stage heading for Washington. McCoy watched the man, but he seemed no more upset than anyone would be who had received such news about his department. They spoke little as the coach sped along.

The third day after he left, McCoy reported to the Secret Service office with Lance Whitmore in tow.

General Halleck greeted him at the door of his big office and asked Whitmore to sit down.

"I don't understand, General Halleck. I was told there is a crisis in my department at the Bureau."

"Indeed there is, Mr. Whitmore. That's exactly what we need to talk about. First a little background. I understand that you know a man named Flavian Kirby."

"Kirby, Kirby. Yes. I've known him for some years. Flavian was what threw me. We always called him Flav. As I recall, he retired a few years ago from the Bureau."

"Do you keep in touch with him?"

"No, not really. I got one card from him when he

was in Chicago some months ago. He gave no return address."

"You haven't seen him or talked to him in how long?"

"Not since he retired about three years ago. I was at the small ceremony. He seemed unhappy about having to quit, but his eyes just wouldn't hold up to the daily engraving work. Too bad, he's a fine engraver."

"Is there any reason he might send you something for safekeeping?"

"No. We weren't good friends, just acquaintances."

The general placed the letter to him on the table. It had been trimmed and reglued where it had been opened.

"This letter came to you recently and we believe it is from Mr. Kirby. Would you be so kind as to open it for us."

"You violated my privacy and my U.S. mail privacy . . ."

"We had a search warrant, Mr. Whitmore. Please open the letter."

He tore open the envelope, anger showing in his eyes. "Why could you get a search warrant? I don't understand."

"Read the letter, and tell us about it," the general purred.

Whitmore read the letter and shook his head. "I can see nothing unusual and certainly not illegal with this note. How could you get a search warrant?"

"What else is in the letter? What does he want you to keep for him?"

"I don't know. Let's look."

He unwrapped the heavy paper from around the thin package and gasped when the plates for a $20 bill fell out.

"What in the world?" Whitmore looked at both men in shock and surprise.

"Oh, my God! I knew that we had a report that one of the old plates had been tampered with and that a front and back of the twenty had been cut off, but I had no idea . . ."

General Halleck stood and held out his hand.

"Mr. Whitmore, we apologize for putting you though this minor ordeal, but it was important to us to know if you were working with Flavian Kirby on this counterfeiting. We have him in custody. He's the one who stole the plates. He also printed up $88,000 worth of the bills, but all had the same serial number. We recovered most of the fake bills. Now we have the plates and the case is wrapped up."

Whitmore stood and shook his head. "Kirby. I knew he wasn't happy about having to retire, but I never thought he'd go this far. The bills must have been terribly hard to detect. I swear, I never would have guessed that about Kirby."

They shook hands all around and Whitmore was taken by cab to his home where he said he needed to check some things before he went back to the mountains to finish his vacation.

When Whitmore was gone, the General shook McCoy's hand.

"Well done, as usual, McCoy. Now tell me, working with Agent Flanders wasn't really so difficult after all, was it?"

"No sir. She more than pulled her weight on both cases."

"Good. The next time I feel an expert could help you in solving a case, I hope you don't have a nervous fit when I send one along, male or female. Now, as far as I'm concerned, you're free to head back to St. Louis in the morning. I'll be in touch with you about a pair of new cases in your area that we're putting together right now. Take off a day or two and at least catch up on your laundry."

McCoy grinned, went out of the office and along the hall to the stairs. Jessica was waiting for him there. She linked her arm through his, and they went down the steps.

"I hear you're to go back to St. Louis tomorrow," she said.

"Yep."

"So that means we have until the eight o'clock train in the morning, right?"

"Yep."

"Any ideas?"

"Yep." He chuckled. "Now that you mention it, I'm in the mood for a good big steak dinner and then some soft and tender ministrations through the evening and far into the night."

Jessica pressed his arm tightly against her breast. She looked up at him, her eyes brimming with desire.

"I think we better go to my apartment rather than some stuffy old hotel room. I've got just all sorts of plans for you until the wee hours of the morning."

McCoy laughed softly and kissed her cheek. Already

he was thinking about the long night that stretched ahead of them.

"Oh, yes, Jessica," he said, and they hurried down the street.

SPUR

FREE PRESS
FILLY

Chapter One

Andrew Weston Pinnick stood outside his office and bellowed at a pair of ruffians who had just shot two holes in the door of the *Clarion* newspaper building.

"Be off, you scallywags. You don't scare me none. I eat your kind for breakfast and belch garlic all afternoon. Be gone. Go tell your boss he doesn't scare me either. Nobody on God's green earth is going to stop me from printing the truth and from expressing my opinions about the way this town and county are run. Just a damn shame more people in this county don't stand up to them bastards."

He whirled and marched back into his office. The front window remained boarded up after it had been shot out four times in two months. A small fire had singed the back storage room, but luckily he quickly had put it out. He even had time to take a shot at the two yahoos who must have started the fire.

He knew he was hurting them, exposing to the public what they were doing. They had vandalized his type cases two weeks ago when he had lost two days as he and Gypsy got the mixed-up fonts and sizes and letters all back in the right print trays. He didn't even think how many thousands of individual letters there were in each tray. That day he had wanted to quit—but he didn't.

He wouldn't stop exposing them until they killed him, but he gambled that they wouldn't go that far. They were not that secure, that strong yet. But if their gigantic swindle went through, they just might be strong enough to have him killed.

He had to prevent that swindle and protect the damned public and the Territory of Arizona, even if they didn't seem to know what he was doing— or maybe didn't care. Since Wednesday was press day, the louts always came after him then. So far they hadn't hurt either him or Gypsy. If they touched his daughter he'd forget himself, take his shotgun and start killing them. He would take any abuse they could throw at him, but he wouldn't allow even a scratch on his perfect, gracious, lovely daughter. He had sworn that promise to his Lilly as she lay on her death bed three years ago.

"Hey, sourpuss," Gypsy said. "Smile, Papa, we ain't beaten yet. I have just one more column to proofread and correct, and we'll be ready to print the first page. I like that front page editorial. I set it in ten point bold like you said, and it looks fine.

"That's going to cause a lot of comment. Should get some reaction from the territorial capital, if anything will."

Gypsy Pinnick smiled at her father. She was 19, slender and shapely like her mother had been, with sleek black hair that hung like a dark river to well below her waist.

Gypsy had a rosebud mouth, even white teeth, a great smile, and cheek bones so high they almost touched her eyes. He smile dazzled, and right now she stepped over to her father and rubbed the back of his neck and his shoulders.

"You're tense again. Why don't you have a nap? You'll need it before we get tonight's last page printed."

"Work to do."

"Nonsense, your work is coming tonight. I'll clean up this last column, make the corrections and pull one more proof for you to double-check. Now stretch out on that cot in back and relax for a while even if you can't sleep."

Andrew Pinnick stretched. Three or four places in his body didn't hurt him at all today. That was progress. "Maybe just for ten minutes. Anybody comes bothering, you blow that whistle like I showed you."

Gypsy's face broke into a grin, and she nodded. "Right, Papa, and I've got that .22 pistol in my desk drawer. Now get out of here."

He tried to get one more look at the front page proof, but his daughter covered it up and shooed him toward the back room.

Gypsy watched him go, then settled down to proofreading the last story on the front page, about a logger who had been killed when a tree he cut down ricocheted on its many large limbs and shot back at him ten feet beyond the stump.

She found two mistakes and marked them, then took the sheet to the composing table where she selected the correct letters from the type tray.

It took her 15 minutes to locate all the errors and correct them. Then she tightened the type in the heavy form and tapped it all down with a wooden mallet and a leather-covered block of wood to be sure all the letters were level. That done, she put the heavy page on the small proof press and inked the top thoroughly with a rubber roller.

Gypsy placed a sheet of proof paper over the form and pulled the heavy roller over the page, transferring the ink onto the paper.

When the roller stopped at the end, she peeled the page away from the type and studied it. Yes, the corrections were in place. She would let her father take one more look at it, but by then it would be too late to make any more changes.

Gypsy marveled at how her father had stood up to the richest man in town, J. Lawton Benscoter, who owned the six biggest stores in town and controlled the county politics with a choking grip. During the past five years the tension between the two men had increased to the point where they never spoke to each other except at Pine Grove Town Council meetings and other official functions.

Gypsy wondered if J. Lawton was behind the violence aimed at the newspaper over the past six months. She wasn't sure but he was certainly one candidate.

She saw that her father had fallen asleep. Good, he needed it. It was late Wednesday afternoon, and they would be working until midnight to get everything printed. There were 340 papers to print this week, a few more than last week. She tried to get more into circulation each time so they could at least pretend they were making progress.

As it was, they were barely scraping by. Advertising was what they needed, and with so few stores in town . . . She frowned. No, there were enough stores in Pine Grove to produce at least six pages a week. That is, there would be if the six largest stores in town would advertise but they didn't since they were all owned by J. Lawton Benscoter, who ran the whole town. Her father and Benscoter had been fighting for two years now about everything.

Her father was right, and Mr. Benscoter was plain stubborn. Gypsy shook her head, not understanding the whole thing, and went to wake up her father. They had to start printing or they'd be there all night.

An hour later, they had the first two pages finished. Running their old press was twice the work it would be if they had a newer one, but that was out of the question.

As she did every Wednesday night about six o'clock, Gypsy went across the street to the Home Café. Terri would have their dinners all ready to take out. His specialty Wednesday was beef stew, and he put up two bowls along with bread and coffee and all the trimmings. He had it in a cardboard box, ready and waiting.

Gypsy stopped to talk a minute. She'd known Terri for over three years now, ever since he opened the café.

"How many pages this week, big newspaper writer?" Terri asked, a twinkle in his eye.

"Six, but it should have been four. I wish you could afford to advertise. We'll almost break even this week."

They talked for five minutes, then Gypsy realized the stew was getting cold. She paid Terri, thanked him and went out the front door.

"Fire!" somebody down the block yelled. Gypsy looked down the street and saw ugly black smoke rising over some stores across the way.

Three stores were attached, wall to wall, then after an empty lot was her father's building. She ran down the boardwalk and soon saw smoke pouring from the front of the *Clarion* building.

Gypsy dropped the box of supper, raced across the street and stopped in front of the building. Flames roared out the door and through the cracks between the boards where the windows had been.

A man looked in the door, then darted back, choking from the smoke.

"My father's still in there!" Gypsy screamed and lunged toward the door. Strong hands caught her and stopped her.

"Try around back," somebody shouted.

A bucket brigade raced up, drawing water from the pump at the horse trough. The lead man threw the half-filled buckets of water through the front door, but it had little effect on the fire.

A man came around from the rear of the building, shaking his head. "Not a chance. Back door is one mass of flames. Looks like the fire started back there."

"Do something!" Gypsy screamed. "Do something to help my father."

Terri came up beside her, put his arm around her and held her tightly.

"Gypsy, they're trying. Looks like the fire had a big head start. Them buckets of water ain't gonna put out the fire. Maybe your pa got out the back door."

Terri turned to the crowd that had gathered. "Has anyone seen Mr. Pinnick, the newspaper man?" he yelled. Nobody answered, but Gypsy saw some heads shake.

Mrs. Natterson, a widow who ran the Ladies Wear shop three doors down, hurried up and put her arm around Gypsy.

"Dear girl, I know your pa is safe somewhere. A body doesn't stay inside a building like that when it's burning up. He's here somewhere, you can bet on it."

Mrs. Natterson led Gypsy away from the heat of the flames. Now the bucket brigade threw its water on the building 40 feet away to keep it from catching.

Gypsy could hear Terri calling through the crowd, asking if anyone had seen Mr. Pinnick. Slowly the truth came to her. Someone had set fire at the front door and at the back door at the same moment. This time the people trying to silence the paper had done it. They had counted on trapping her father inside and had waited until she went for their supper.

It had become an established pattern. Most folks in town knew they worked Wednesday night printing the paper. After watching for two weeks, anyone would know about when she went to the café to bring back their supper.

They had torched the building from both ends on purpose. They wanted to kill the paper and at the same time kill her father.

J. Lawton Benscoter had to be the one. He was the only man in town rich enough and powerful enough to hire men to do something like this. The two arsonists were probably on their horses and five miles out of town by now with their blood money in their pockets.

J. Lawton Benscoter! She would bring him down if it was the last thing she did. But how?

Mrs. Natterson turned and looked Gypsy in the eye.

"I can't keep up hope for you, Gypsy. We've looked everywhere. Nobody has seen your father since the fire started. There's a chance he was inside and couldn't get out."

Gypsy nodded. "I know, Mrs. Natterson. J. Lawton Benscoter hired someone to burn down the *Clarion*. He told them to torch both the front door and the back. He deliberately murdered my father, and I intend to make him pay."

Mrs. Benscoter frowned. "Gypsy, I understand your anguish, but don't just jump to conclusions. Lots of things could have happened. A can of paint could have exploded, and your Pa could have been knocked unconscious. Something might have fallen on him. Don't go putting any blame, leastwise until it can be proved. I know your Pa and Benscoter didn't get on too well."

They walked to the back of the shell of the building. The roof caved in, showering the darkening sky with a million sparks. Soon there were only a few timbers left where the 50 foot-long building had stood.

Gypsy watched it and shook her head.

"Everything is ruined, lost, burned up. All of the equipment and the type destroyed. I have to start over. We don't have much money in the bank, but I have my dowry. Pa was old fashioned about that."

"You come home with me for tonight, Gypsy," Mrs. Natterson said. "Things will look a little better in the morning. I know you've lost a lot tonight, but something will turn up tomorrow."

"No, Mrs. Natterson, nothing will be different tomorrow. I've got to do myself whatever needs to be done, and I'm going to start tonight. Do you have some paper and envelopes? I want to write some letters. I wrote a news article once telling people they had to take matters into their own hands sometimes. If the territorial officials were crooked, they had to write to the territorial attorney general and tell him. Write to the governor or a United States senator or even the president. Tell everybody what's wrong, and you stand a good chance that somebody will do something about it.

"That's what I'm going to do tonight, start writing letters. This is a blow against freedom of the press. It's in the constitution, in the bill of rights. I'll write to the *New York* Times and tell them what happened here. They'll listen. Somebody will listen. Somebody has to listen."

Gypsy sagged against Mrs. Natterson and only then did the tears come. She cried it all out in the next two hours. Mrs. Natterson took her home, fixed her a bath and then settled her down in a featherbed.

Ten minutes later, Gypsy was up asking for pen, paper and envelopes. That night she wrote ten letters to everyone she could think of who might help.

The first one went to the President of the United States, then to two senators, then the Justice Department. After that she wrote to three national newspapers. Next came the territorial officials right there in Arizona.

*   *   *

The next morning at daylight, Gypsy walked through the cooling ashes of the *Clarion* building. She would rebuild in the same spot and that meant saving what equipment she could. The case of type had not been tipped over during the fire, and only the font on the top had been harmed. Most of it was half-melted together. The rest of the cases of type were in good shape so, she had a start. Even the proof press could be salvaged. An hour later Sheriff Ben Willard came. He held his hat in his hand as he spoke to her.

"Miss Pinnick, I'm sorry about the fire. Best if you stand aside so we can search to see if your pa really was inside here last night."

She walked down to Terri's cafe and waited. A half hour later a soot-blackened Sheriff Willard came to see her. He was a medium-sized man with pot belly and a pinched face.

"Miss Pinnick, I'm sorry to report that we did find your father's remains. He must have crawled under the heavy metal of the press. The smoke and fumes probably caused his death since he ain't burned any. We took him down to the undertaker."

Gypsy thanked him and went to say good-bye to her father.

The funeral was that afternoon with half the people in town attending at the Methodist church. When it was over Gypsy went directly to the bank.

Mr. Gleason told her the newspaper account, which she now controlled, had a balance of $67.53. Her own dowry account had an even $1,000 plus interest coming up for the quarter.

When she got back to the *Clarion* shell, she saw Terri waiting for her. Nearby were 20 men with shovels, saws, hammers and other tools.

"Figured we could get a start on raising an office for you, Gypsy," Terri said. "Hear you want to rebuild. First we'll put up a tent to store what you can save. Then we figure to load up and haul off all the trash and burned timbers and such."

A tear squeezed out of Gypsy Pinnick's eye and worked slowly down her cheek. When she reached up and kissed Terri on the cheek, somebody in the crowd cheered.

She turned and smiled at them.

"Thank you, everyone. Now, let's get to work!"

Chapter Two

Spur McCoy had finished a case in Los Angeles and wired his boss in Washington D.C. for instructions. Should he return to his home base in St. Louis, or was there another problem on the coast he should look into while he was there?

The return wire came before he had finished his lunch. He opened the yellow envelope and read:

"TO: SPUR MCCOY, COAST HOTEL, LOS ANGELES, CALIFORNIA. LEAVE AT ONCE FOR ARIZONA. SMALL TOWN OF PINE GROVE SOUTH OF FLAGSTAFF ABOUT 30 MILES. POSSIBLE (VIOLATION OF FREEDOM OF THE PRESS AND) MURDER OF NEWSPAPER'S EDITOR/PUBLISHER. CONTACT GYPSY PINNICK. REPORT EXTENT OF CASE AND YOUR PROGRESS. EXPENSE

FUNDS WIRED TODAY. GENERAL WILTON D.
HALLECK SENDING."

An hour later, Spur McCoy sat on a southbound
train, heading for San Diego. From there he would
take another train to Phoenix and, that was as far
as the rail lines had been laid. To get further north,
he'd take a stagecoach to Pine Grove. Freedom of
the press was always a touchy problem. Often it
was a clash between a young, poor newspaperman and a wealthy, older businessman involved
in some kind of skullduggery. Money and power
often had its own way in spite of a crusading newspaperman, often with tragic results.

He read the wire again. Gypsy Pinnick? Could be
either a man or a woman, widow or son or daughter of the dead man. He'd find out. He had nearly
two hours before he changed trains in San Diego.

McCoy pulled his black flat-brimmed hat down
over his eyes and relaxed. He was a Secret Service
agent, one of the few federal lawmen who had
jurisdiction in all of the states and territories.
From his office in St. Louis, he prowled the western half of the nation at the bidding of General
Halleck in Washington D.C.

The agency had been started by President
Lincoln specifically to protect the currency. In
the years since then, the Secret Service had
taken on many other duties, including the protection of the president himself. William Wood
was director of the Secret Service, having been
appointed by the president. He then selected
a small group of agents to work directly for
the federal government in any aspect of law
enforcement where federal regulations had been
violated or local law authorities had asked for
help.

McCoy was in his thirties, with dark hair and intense green eyes. He stood just shy of six-two and weighed 195 pounds. He had graduated from Harvard University in Boston, served in the Civil War reaching the rank of captain, and joined the Secret Service not long after it was organized.

McCoy's father owned several large retail and import companies in New York, but McCoy had decided he didn't want to follow in his father's footsteps in the business world. Since he could shoot and ride better than any other Secret Service agent, he was assigned to the western section of the nation.

McCoy felt someone sit down beside him, but he left his hat over his eyes.

"I beg your pardon?"

The voice was female and youthful. He took a chance, raised the brim of his hat and looked into a pair of soft blue eyes surrounded by a pretty face and billows of long, curly blonde hair. He pushed back his hat and nodded.

"You were speaking to me?"

"You're the only person in this seat and I'm looking directly at you, so I'd have to at least suppose that I must be talking to you."

"So?"

"I was wondering if you knew when we get to San Diego."

"Scheduled for two-forty-six this afternoon. That should be not quite two hours yet."

"Oh!" Her pretty face clouded. "That doesn't leave much time."

McCoy grinned. "Depends on time to do what. If you need time to breathe, we have plenty. Time for a short nap, the same. Time to write a symphony or build a bridge over a great body of water would be a little short."

"True." She looked away, then bit her lip and stared back at him. "It was a childish, stupid thing to do."

McCoy enjoyed watching this pretty girl. He figured she was not much over 18, dressed well, no rings on her left hand.

"Just what was this stupid thing you did?" he asked.

"I made a bet with Madelyn, my former best friend over there on the other side of the train."

"Former best friend. That sounds serious."

"Serious for me, probably not for you. You see the bet I made with Madelyn was—"

The girl stopped, closed her eyes and sighed. Her mouth set in a firm line, and her chin came up a little.

"I bet Madelyn that I could get you to kiss me on the lips before we got to San Diego."

McCoy laughed softly. "You make bets like that often?"

"First one ever. We saw you get on, and one word led to another, and we both remarked what a . . . what a great body you had. Then I impulsively made the bet. Do you hate me?"

McCoy chuckled and looked at her. She sat tall in the seat, slender, well-formed, a long white neck and now defiant blue eyes.

"No, I don't hate you. What did you bet for?"

"I can't say."

McCoy tilted up her head by touching under her chin. He looked over at Madelyn who stared at them. McCoy reached down and kissed the blonde on the lips, came away, then when he saw her eyes still closed, he kissed her again, harder this time and brushing his tongue against her lips.

Her face blossomed into a beautiful smile, and she nodded.

"Thanks, maybe I'll see you in San Diego."

"I'm going on through to Phoenix."

He saw the relief in her eyes. "Now, if you don't mind, I want to continue the nap you interrupted."

"Yes. I get to go collect on my bet. Thanks." She hesitated, then sat on the edge of the seat.

"Why did you kiss me?"

"Why? You're a beautiful lady and spunky enough to do what you did. I like women like that. Of course, you do have quite a bit more growing up to do."

"I know, but it's going to be fun." She touched his shoulder, stood and scurried across the aisle and up one seat to Madelyn, the look of astonished surprise still on the losing girl's face.

McCoy settled back, brought his hat down over his eyes and caught a small nap to the click-click of the steel wheels going over the track sections every 30 feet.

Much later, he made his change of trains in San Diego, had to wait three hours to get moving again and arrived in Phoenix sometime during the night.

McCoy felt the heat of the day still contained in the vaulted ceiling of the railroad station. Phoenix was a firebox in the summer, and this was summer.

He caught the stage that left at six A.M. and arrived in Pine Grove, after three delays, at a little before four in the afternoon. At once he checked into the Pine Grove Hotel, ordered bath water and tried to become halfway human again. McCoy didn't hate to travel; it was that it simply took up so much time and sapped his energy.

After a solid meal in the Home Café, he looked up Gypsy Pinnick.

He knocked on a modest house a block from Main Street and two blocks down from the center of town. Moments later a curious young woman stared at him through a screen door that appeared to be locked.

"Miss Pinnick?"

"Yes."

"I'm Spur McCoy, United States Secret Service agent. I've come in response to your several letters about what happened to your father and your newspaper here."

Gypsy let out a small cry of wonder, unlocked the screen door and opened it. "Thank the Lord! Won't you come in. I've been praying that somebody would come and help us. So far we don't have any clues as to who might have set the fire. We found kerosene cans at both doors of the building where the *Clarion* was published, but we can't prove who used it to start the deadly blaze."

She led him into the small house, offered him a seat on the couch and curled into a chair nearby. "Oh, could I offer you some coffee or tea?"

"I just ate, thank you. Could I ask you to show me the site of the fire before it gets dark?"

"Good idea," Gypsy said. "I should have thought of that." Her smile made the task of trying to find the cold trail of an arsonist a little more interesting.

They poked through what was left of the rubble of the building. Most of the smaller debris had been carted off. A tent with a plank floor contained what had been salvaged from the fire.

"Not much we can use," Gypsy said. "We got the proof press working, so I turned out an extra edition a week ago. Just two pages and the same size as the letterhead paper we found in the rubble. I made only a hundred copies, but posted them around town. I offered a reward for anyone finding my father's killer. I made it a regular edition, just smaller. Don't want to break the paper's reputation of publishing every week since Papa founded it back fourteen years ago."

"Most of the type came through?"

"Almost all but the top case, some circus wood type, two inches tall. We seldom used it anyway except in a few ads."

"All of your back issues must have been lost."

"Not true, Mr. McCoy. I made sure of that. After the first small fire we had, I took a complete historical file of our fourteen years of issues home and put them in a steamer trunk. They're all safe and sound.

"Good, I'll want to look over those for the past two years. I want to know exactly who your father was fighting and why. It all should be in the papers."

"Should be, but isn't. I can tell you right now he had a running fight with the town's richest man, J. Lawton Benscoter. He's got enough money to hire men to burn down our building and then get out of town so fast they'll never be found."

"One suspect. Who else did your father pick a fight with?"

Gypsy wrinkled her forehead as she thought. The slight frown even looked attractive on her.

"I guess he didn't have any other real enemies. Oh, he took shots at anyone who he thought stepped out of line on the town council or in the legislature. He told me once he thought something really big was brewing, but evidently it simmered down. He never mentioned it again, and he certainly didn't write any big banner headlines about it or do an editorial. Papa liked to do hard-driving editorials. He shamed the town council into starting our public library and also rode them so hard they decided to buy one of those new pumper fire engines, just as soon as they get enough money. I'm not sure how they work, but they throw a stream of water from a hose. Bet that new fire engine pumper would have saved our building."

"Pine Grove is the county seat of Pine County, right?" Spur asked.

Gypsy nodded.

"Means you have a county sheriff in town. How did your father get along with the lawman?"

"Not real well. Pa was critical of him at times. Pa said that Sheriff Ben Willard was about as much good as an udder on a bull." She laughed to cover up her embarrassment.

"He go after the sheriff in print lately?"

"Not that I remember. He did write an editorial for the front page about the sale of some timber rights just outside of town for what Pa called a scandalously low price."

"Who bought the timber rights?" Spur asked.

"Oh, a man here in town we call Loophole Larson. He's a lawyer, one of only three in town and the best one. He claims he can find a loophole for his client in any lawsuit or any contract or bill of sale that was ever written. Usually he does."

"What does a lawyer want with timber rights?"

"Pa said it was to sell the rights to a third party who did not want to bid publicly on them."

"Nothing illegal about that. Is there a sawmill in town or nearby?"

"That's what Pa said was strange. There isn't a sawmill here. One up at Flagstaff, but that's thirty-two miles due north of us. Pa said wouldn't be economically feasible to haul the logs up there to saw them."

"I agree. Any talk of the railroad coming up this way from Phoenix?"

"A little talk, but no action. Nothing up here the rails can help. Some timber, but not enough to pay for it. Don't figure us or Flag will ever get railroad service."

"Bet there are a bunch of teamsters who are happy about that," Spur said.

"Deed they are. A young teamster came sparking me for a time, but he left town to work out of Phoenix. Said there was more work down there. I wasn't about to leave Pa and the paper. Anyway he never down-on-his-knee proposed to me."

"The young man was a fool," Spur said.

"Mr. McCoy, you shouldn't be talking that way." She grinned. "I do like to hear it, but right now we got to concentrate on Pa and who set those fires and who paid them."

The afternoon turned to dusk.

"Miss Pinnick, I have a room at the hotel, but I would like to bother you for a few minutes first to look over some of the past few issues of your paper. There may be something in there to give me a hint about what your father was fighting."

"That's easy. I might even boil us a pot of coffee to go with the cinnamon rolls I made this morning."

It was nearly nine that evening when Spur turned the last page of the weekly newspaper and put it back on the stack. The coffee and cinnamon rolls were all gone. He had four issues to go. He had checked every story for the past two months.

"That's enough for me tonight, Miss Pinnick. I've had a long day. I'll come tomorrow morning and check these last four issues if it's all right."

"Yes, of course—and please call me Gypsy. Everyone in town does."

He said he would, told her to call him Spur and headed down toward Main and the Pine Grove Hotel. Spur made it a habit of keeping his hotel key in his pocket, not advertising to one and all that he was not in his room when his key was in the box. He walked past the room clerk's desk and looked at the spot labeled room 212. No messages.

He hurried up to his second floor room and inserted the key into the simple door lock. He turned the handle and, keeping behind the wall, pushed the door in hard so it would swing all the way to the wall.

It did and made a klunking sound when the knob hit the wall. No one behind the door. He edged around the doorjamb and peered into the room, dimly lighted by the hallway coal oil lamp. He saw no one.

Spur stepped into the room, struck a match, flamed the coal oil lamp, turned up the wick and put the glass chimney back in place.

Something moved in the far corner of the room, and before he could reach for his colt .45, a woman walked out of the shadows toward him.

"Spur McCoy, I've got a present for you—me." She was pretty, red-headed, beautifully sculptured—and naked.

Chapter Three

The naked girl who smiled at Spur McCoy looked a bit shopworn around the edges, but she was there and she was willing. Even as his eyes feasted on her delicious body, he wondered what kind of a price or consequence went along with the obvious delights.

She walked up to him, making everything move and wiggle and bounce. Even her modest breasts did an enticing dance.

"Naked Flo is here to make you feel good. I specialize in relieving tensions and making swellings go down. Does that get your blood boiling?"

"Might. Depends why you're here, who sent you and who paid you."

Flo turned away from him. "The very idea! Nobody paid me and nobody sent me. I saw you come in a couple of hours ago and knew I

26

had to get a good poking from you or I couldn't sleep tonight. I'm not a whore, if that's what you're thinking."

"Just a part-time paid pussy, I understand. Now who sent you up here?"

She turned and watched him, but he could read nothing in her angry stare. Then her face softened as the anger faded.

"Nobody. I sleep only with those I want to, and nobody orders me around. If you're not interested in a wild night in bed, we'll just forget it."

"You'll put your clothes on and go home to your husband."

"I didn't say that, but I am married. He's not what you'd call a responsive man. Sometimes I like to get a little sexy with a stranger. Anything wrong with that?"

"Probably. I'm no expert on deviant personalities, but I had a professor who was." As Spur watched her naked form he couldn't hold back the erection that was building at his crotch. She was long and lean, flat-bellied, with slender thighs and delicious legs. Her breasts were still slightly upthrust with youth, and he guessed she was no more than 22 or 23. She might talk more in bed with him and let something slip if she was working for somebody. It might be worth a try.

He motioned her over to the bed and sat down. She slid down beside him, her thigh touching his.

"Let's talk about this in a friendly way. Any objections?"

She shook her head and leaned toward him, and when he didn't move away, she reached up and kissed his lips. Her tongue darted between his lips and into his mouth.

"Sometimes I feel so damn sexy I don't know what to do," she said when the steamy kiss ended. Her arms went around his neck, and she pulled him into another kiss. When she broke it off, her breath came faster.

"Pine Grove is a small town, so it's hard to have an affair that everyone in the county doesn't know about. But a traveling man in the hotel is another matter. No one to watch, no one checking our house, and the man is here today and tonight, makes his calls tomorrow and takes the afternoon stage for Flagstaff."

She placed one hand on his crotch and felt his erection. Her eyes glistened and a smile enlivened her face.

"So you do like me. Good. Let's get you out of your pants. Hell, I don't care about making you naked. I just want to get to your cock and play with him."

"What's your name?" Spur asked.

"Flo, Florence. I'm Florence Benscoter, Mrs. Florence Benscoter. Now, that's enough. You'll be leaving on the train tomorrow?"

"We can talk about that later." From what Gypsy had told him Benscoter was a middle-aged man in his fifties. This girl wasn't 25 yet. Was she J. Lawton's wife? She caught him around the neck and fell backwards, pulling him with her flat on the bed.

He lay on top of her and gave a little yelp of delight.

She rolled them over so she was on top and pounded her hips against his hips three times. "Just a sample. I've got the wildest ass in town." She slid off him and undid his belt buckle, then his gunbelt buckle and worked on the buttons at his fly. He started to help, but she kissed his hands away.

"Hey, make me earn it. I want your prick so bad that I'll tear these fucking buttons off if I have to." She looked up with a little girl face to spice the sexy talk.

With the buttons open, she stood and pulled off his boots, then snaked down his pants and stripped them off him. She hung the gunbelt on the head of the bed and smiled down at him.

"Oh, yes, that's how I like to see a man, laying on his back with his big cock just making a tent out of his underwear."

Spur wore some of the new, short, cotton underwear, and she pulled them down until his erection popped into sight.

"My gawd!" she yelped. "This must be heaven!" She knelt on the bed and kissed his purple-headed shaft. "My gawd but he's gorgeous, and he's all mine for all night."

Her kisses flowed down from the point along the shaft to his pubic hair. Her fingers toyed gently with his scrotum and the heavy balls inside.

"My gawd, what a man! How come no woman hog-tied you and kept you in her bedroom? You don't wear a wedding band."

"Still looking for the right woman," he said. It was his standard reply and came with no thought on his part.

"Benscoter. Didn't I see a sign with that name, Benscoter Merchandiser and General Store?"

"You did. I'm married to J. Lawton Benscoter, richest damn man in town. Yes, he's old enough to be my father. No, he don't fuck worth a shit. Yes, he still tries, but I need some poking more than once a fucking month." She sighed. "There now, I've told you all about me and my miseries. You want a good poking, or are you all talk?"

Spur pulled her down on top of him and moved her higher until he could drop one of her breasts into his mouth. He chewed a while, nibbling at her already erect nipple, then moved to the other orb. As he worked on that one he felt her blood pressure soar and her breathing quicken.

He reached one hand between her legs, found her hard clit and twanged it four times.

Flo exploded into a grunting, wailing climax that made her pound her hips against his a dozen times. Then the spasms hit her, and she shook and trembled and vibrated until he thought she'd shake herself into pieces.

"Oh, gawd! Oh, gawd! Oh, gawd!" she whispered. Then a long wailing moan came from her mouth and the vibrations tailed off. Then before she got a good breath a new set of spasms hit her, and she pounded her hips against him again and shuddered through three more climaxes before she trembled one last time and let out a long sigh of wonder.

Her eyes opened slowly. "Gawd damn! I almost never cum that way before I get poked once or twice. Gawd damn, but you are a sexy smooth one. What the fuck is it gonna be like once you get into my little pussy and start whanging away at me?"

"Better, I hope," Spur said. He was holding back with a lot of effort. Now he rolled her off him, spread her legs and slid between them. He lifted her knees and pushed them apart.

"Hurry, you big fucker, hurry. I can't keep this up all night. I want your prick inside me right now."

He bent, probed a moment, then daggered home into her wonderland. Flo's eyes went wide, then she gasped and shrilled a long high wail as he penetrated to the roots of his sword.

"Oh, damn!" Flo said with an expression of rapture and wonder. "Now . . . this . . . is . . . what . . . it always damn should be."

Spur knew there would be more than one fuck, so he wanted this one for himself. He pulled up his knees, thrust the deepest he could, and then pounded forward, pistoning into her as fast and hard as he could.

She wailed and humped back at him but couldn't match his speed. At that rate it wouldn't take him long, Spur knew, and he panted and gasped, then roared as he plunged into her, planting his load.

When he finally relaxed and sagged against her, he felt her arms pin him in place so she could enjoy the afterglow longer.

When she at last let go, she pushed him off her and turned on her side so she could see him. Tears brimmed in her eyes.

"I never cry after making love. Almost never. Why are you so damn good and my husband so damn bad in bed? Why am I so lucky? Sure, I married the richest man in town, but what the hell has that to do with making it a good marriage? He don't want no kids. Says they just get in the way. Says he had two already by his first wife and they are nothing but trouble. He waits until I bleed and gets me then so I can't have a kid. He's terrible."

Spur kept quiet. He had nothing to offer. Advice was the last thing she wanted. At first he figured she was a tempting bit of fluff sent by someone to find out who he was and why he was here. He decided that someone controlled this town right down to the bedrooms.

Looked like Flo was on the other side, but she didn't know it. He figured if what she said had any truth in it at all, she was in no way trying to pump him for information. She probably didn't even go through his luggage.

She reached over and kissed his forehead with a feather touch. "Oh, gawd, but that was fine. You know while you were getting it off, I had three more orgasms. Three more! Damn but you are a wonder."

Flo watched him a moment. "I didn't see no sample cases. Maybe you ain't a drummer, after all. You gonna be in town for long?"

"Not sure, Flo. I'm not a drummer. Sorry."

"Oh, no, I'm glad. Maybe you'll be here a week, and I can get good poking like this every night. That would be pure heaven to me, Spur McCoy. Oh, I checked the register downstairs. The night clerk and I have a little arrangement going. He lets me know when a great stud comes into the hotel. For that he gets his way with me once a month. He's not a good lover, but I'm training him. He's only twenty-one and has more energy and sperm than he can use."

They both sat up.

"Now I've offended you. Gawd damn. Didn't want to do that. I can get us a late supper sent up from the kitchen if you want. You hungry? Young men get hungry after a fine poking, but old men get sleepy. Damn, you don't look sleepy to me."

Spur laughed. "You are some woman, Flo Benscoter. No late supper. Give me ten minutes and we'll see what else we can cook up between us that's good to eat."

Her eyes widened and she grinned. "I'm getting hungry already."

As he sat there, Spur wondered if there was some way he could utilize this windfall. Would Flo know anything about her husband's dealings? Would she know about any big operation he was working on, something big enough to kill a newspaper publisher to keep it quiet? He would try to find out, but it might take several nights like this. Spur grinned. Somehow he'd have to bear up under the rugged working conditions.

Sometime around three in the morning they came up for air, and he probed gently about her husband.

"Your man, he's a big gun in this town, I'd guess?"

"Yeah, thinks he is. Wants to be governor he says. Big deal."

"How can a man in a town this size ever be territorial governor?"

"Oh, J. Lawton has all sorts of big plans. Says he's working on a deal right now that will shake up the whole damn territory. That's J. Lawton—big talker, quick fucker."

It was a bite, a start. At last they got to sleep about four in the morning, and Spur didn't wake up until nearly seven. That was late for him. He slid out of bed before she woke up and shaved and dressed. He wasn't ready for any morning pokings.

He had a big day ahead—more research on the back issues. He wondered how to handle this case. Maybe he should get a job with Benscoter and work it from the inside. No, that wouldn't work. Benscoter would be suspicious. Spur knew people had seen him at the paper's burned-out building and going into Gypsy's house. Even the walls have eyes in a small town like this.

Flo woke up and grinned. "Now that was a night to remember. Can I come back tonight?"

"What will J. Lawton think?

"He's used to it. He knows I fuck around."

"We'll see about tonight later. I've got some work to do today first. Got to earn my pay or I'll get fired."

"What work?"

"I'm with some people who buy property and then develop it and sell it again. Not sure what's in town worth considering, but that's my job. Oh, don't tell Benscoter. He'd jack the price up on anything we wanted."

"Last thing I'd do," she said.

"Good." He hesitated. "You going to get dressed and come have breakfast?"

"Yes, but at a different restaurant. The prying eyes of a small town, you know."

He had breakfast at the Home Café, then caught Gypsy at her place just before she left for the office. She picked out the four issues he hadn't read and took them along.

"I figure you can read them at the office—my tent, that is—and then ask me any questions."

As they walked along, he tried to figure out what could be of tremendous value around this section of the country. They were in the mountains. The San Francisco mountains were north of Flagstaff and the Mazatzal mountains to the south. The Mogollon rim and its plateau lay to the east.

The village of Pine Grove lay in a small pocket with an elevation of 7,419 feet, one of the highest towns in Arizona. You can't buy and sell mountains. Maybe there were some mineral deposits, but so far nothing much had been discovered. There wasn't much so far for anyone to get worked up enough about to kill a newspaper publisher. Spur hoped that there was a story somewhere in the last few issues of the *Clarion* that would give him a lead—some hint, some smell was all he hoped for.

It had to be something that the general public didn't know about yet. What else was there? Grazing rights maybe, a railroad coming through which always made a lucky few rich, but there didn't seem to be any reason to bring in the rails. No coal, no minerals, nothing the railroad could make money on hauling back out.

As they walked to the newspaper, Spur compared Gypsy Pinnick with the woman he just spent the night with. Gypsy was much prettier and younger, just as sleekly built and with what he guessed were much larger breasts. It was a winning combination.

"Oh, I got a letter yesterday from a man in Phoenix. He's a pressman, says he's rebuilt burned-out presses before. I hired him to come up and see what we need to get the press running and to tell me how much it will cost for parts. Most of it's metal. I can't see how it was hurt much, but right now it won't work."

"Can you afford it?"

She sighed. "For a few months. I have some money, not a lot, but if I can get the paper going again I'll get some advertising and the legal ads the county has to run. Oh, it makes me so mad that J. Lawton Benscoter won't advertise. He's so stubborn."

Spur nodded. "Maybe if you go and see him, have a talk. His long fight was with your father, not with you. You might be able to establish a friendlier attitude. He must know that he should be advertising. Might be worth a try."

Gypsy brightened. "Spur McCoy, you're a good man to have around. I'll have to show you my appreciation by cooking a dinner for you. How about tonight at my house at six-thirty."

"Miss Pinnick . . . that is, Gypsy. I'd be delighted to have dinner at your house tonight."

When they arrived at the tent, she opened the frame door held in place only by a hook and eye.

"If anyone wants to steal anything inside, all they have to do is cut a hole in the tent. It's not my tent, so I leave the door open. So far, nothing is missing."

They went in, and Spur spread the paper over a small table. There had to be some clues in these papers. All he had to do was find them.

Chapter Four

The tall man watched from his second floor window on Main Street as Spur McCoy and Gypsy Pinnick went into the tent just across the thoroughfare.

"Who the hell is he and what's he doing here in town?" the thin man asked as he turned from the window. "Especially I want to know what he's doing with Gypsy. He came in town on the stage yesterday and before dark he had talked to the lady owner of the newspaper. What the hell's going on?"

Loophole Larson glared at the man across the room from him. "I've got a lot riding on this deal. If it doesn't work because of some wild-eyed stranger who drops into town after all of our plans are made . . ."

Larson let it hang in the air as he dropped into

the leather executive chair behind his ponderous desk. The irregular shaped top was made from two huge slabs of cherry wood, polished to a mirror sheen and then varnished to a gloss. It was one of his treasures.

Across the room, J. Lawton Benscoter chuckled. "Larson, I thought you had nerves of steel, but I'm beginning to doubt it. We put this together so nothing could go wrong. You came up with the legal moves yourself. You know it's as solid as it ever was." Benscoter was nearly a foot shorter than Larson at five-seven to the lawyer's six-two.

Benscoter walked over to the chair beside the desk and gave a grunt of pain as he sat down. "Damn gout. I'd like to cut that right big toe off and throw it away. It's hot and swollen and hurts like old Billy Hell."

"Sign of high living," Larson said and scowled. "Now, what the hell do we do about this gent who is getting friendly with Miss Pinnick?"

Benscoter eased back in the chair. "Relax, Larson, relax. You'll have a coronary or catch the tremors or fly all to pieces, and we'll have to pack you off to the loony bin in Phoenix." Benscoter eased a ten cent cigar from his suit pocket, snipped off the end, then licked the outside tobacco leaves and sniffed it.

"Damn wonderful thing, a fine cigar. Enough to help a man get up in the morning just thinking about that first smoke." He lit the cigar with a match from a long thin box on the lawyer's desk. When he had blown out two or three big drags of smoke, he settled back.

"First off, Mr. Larson, I don't like this attitude you're taking. You came into this project on my recommendation, and you stand to gain your ten percent of the profits. That does not entitle you to make policy, to run off at the mouth, or demand that something be done. You carefully worked out all of the legal jargon about how to make it foolproof and workable. I'm the man who gets the spade work done, and our other friend is the third cog in the machinery who enables all of this to take place."

He stopped and took another long pull on the brown stogie. J. Lawton Benscoter turned his face upward and blew a perfect smoke ring that floated slowly toward the ten-foot ceiling, at last breaking up near the top of the room where the June heat gathered.

"To ease your mind, Larson, the man's name is Spur McCoy. He listed his work as salesman in the hotel register and showed as his employer a Denver firm I've never heard of. Not quite sure what he does, but the clerk said he makes out like he's a cowboy but has the manners and talks like an educated easterner. So, you see you have little to worry about. My guess is that he's in the printing trades and is here to talk with the lady about her printing plant. Perhaps he wants to help finance her reconstruction for a part of the ownership."

Larson snorted. "He sure as hell won't get far doing that. Two days after the fire, I suggested that we have a community owned paper. I told that pretty lady I'd be glad to set up the company and make shareholders of all those who wanted to finance her new building and equipment. She turned me down flat. Said she didn't want any partners. She wanted to be able to write any story she found. No partners, no control, strictly independent."

Benscoter nodded. "Heard about that. She's getting as pig-headed as her old man was, but she can't be as strait-laced as he was. I'm thinking of putting in an ad in her new small paper to help her along. No reason I have to fight with her—at least not yet. Might forestall any unfavorable comments for a time."

Lawson stood, went to the window again, parted the curtains and watched the tent across the way. The site had been cleaned up but not much else had been done. "I still say my advice to you a week ago is the best. Buy her out now. Offer her two thousand dollars cash and take over any outstanding bills and receivables. You're buying the name of the paper, any existing back files, what equipment has been salvaged and the paper's goodwill. That way you can put in your own editor, and no one will know that you own the paper."

Benscoter blew another smoke ring. "Yes, I thought about it. Interesting idea. Control the press and you control the people. But it would cut out the good fight that I enjoy with the press. If I'm not mistaken, the young lady and I will have a time of peace, then arrows of doubt will slant from her pages and soon we'll be back in a toe to toe battle again. I enjoy a good fight, Larson. Haven't you figured that out yet?"

"So what do we do about this Spur McCoy?"

"I've telegraphed the company in Denver. Should have an answer soon about who they are and what they sell. I didn't mention McCoy, since they might notify him about the inquiry. When we find out what he's up to, we'll know what to do."

"The man is going to be a problem. I sense it," Larson said. "Something about the way he walks, that holster tied low on his leg like he's a gunsharp.

He's no more a salesman than you are. I don't trust him, and we need to watch him."

Benscoter grunted his approval. Larson was acting dangerously near to losing his nerve on this project. This was the first time that Benscoter had needed a lawyer for one of these projects. Oh, he had worked various ploys and schemes in his time, but this would be the biggest and the best paying.

He and the sheriff would share in the profits after Larson had his ten percent. He wasn't sure of market value, but the appraised value was interesting. This scheme would net him more than he could make in another lifetime.

Benscoter heaved out of the chair. He was putting on some weight and knew it. At 51 years of age he should be given a little bit of leeway. Not that his wife appreciated it. He was still having some trouble with her in bed, and it riled him. He liked to do her when he was sure she was safe. He'd had two too many kids already, and they had not been happy experiences.

Benscoter waved at the lawyer. "Loophole, you keep one hand on your crotch now and don't lose your nerve. This is rolling along on schedule. The paper is down so that eliminates one of the problems. Now we simply carry on with the notice and nothing can go wrong. You worry too much."

The town's major mover left the lawyer's office, shuffled across the hard-packed dirt street to the boardwalk, walked four doors up from the burned-out newspaper and went into his office building. It was the only one in Pine Grove built especially for offices. On the ground floor was his real estate firm and land office. Next to it, facing the street, was Doc Johnson's office.

An outside staircase led to the second story

where his offices took up the entire floor. He'd hired a decorator to come up from Phoenix to furnish and finish the inside of his three offices.

The first was an outer reception area where Alice sat at her desk, deftly received visitors, screened those wanting to see him, and kept a list of any appointments or visitors he had for that day. Alice was 49 years-old, plump, wore spectacles and frumpy clothes and called herself an executive assistant. She was so good at her work that Benscoter paid her $40 a month, $15 more than anyone else in town doing the same kind of work earned. She was worth it.

Alice greeted him when he walked in the door. Often he went in a rear entrance down a short hallway, but this time he needed to see Alice.

"Mr. Benscoter, a Paul Wainfield was here to see you, but he had to leave to make another appointment. He'll stop back this afternoon. You have a meeting with the sheriff at noon, lunch he calls it, at the Del Rey Café. Nothing else. The mail isn't sorted yet.

"Oh, yes, the postmaster sent a note by a young lad. He'd like to see you at your convenience at his office. The note's on your desk."

"Thank you, Alice. Anything else?"

"Your first appointment is in your office. You said to send her in whenever she came."

"Yes, Alice, I'd forgotten." Benscoter smiled with warmth at Alice, went through a door marked "Private" and closed it softly. He pushed a bolt into place and turned around.

"Clarissa, sorry I'm late. Business."

Clarissa sat on a sofa that filled half of one wall. It had been specially made, the back crowded with pillows. She patted the spot beside her, and when

Benscoter sat down, she pushed her thigh against his.

"Now, J. Lawton, last time we were talking about what excites a woman, because when you sense that your partner is getting all sexy and hot and ready to go, it will affect your own desire as well." As she spoke, Clarissa unbuttoned the white blouse she wore and her breasts came into view.

"You . . . you mean I need to get her hot, so I'll get excited, too?"

"It works out that way. Now, we talked how most women just love to be kissed—long, hot, sensuous kisses with your tongue in her mouth. Some women think that when she lets your tongue into her mouth that it's like being penetrated down below. It's a signal that it's all right to enter her vagina."

The blouse hung open to her waist.

Clarissa had one hand on his thigh, and she woved it up to his crotch. She frowned slightly. "J. Lawton, didn't unbuttoning my blouse get you excited? Looking at the edge of my bare breasts doesn't help you?"

"A little. I've seen a lot of tits, Clarissa. Maybe I'm just getting old and can't get it up anymore."

"Nonsense. I know a man who is seventy-eight and still humps his wife every Thursday night. Your little problem is in your skull, not your prick." She reached up, undid his fly and worked her hand inside.

"Good, you're starting. Take off my blouse. That will help."

He slid the blouse off her shoulders, and she let it hang there, showing both her breasts.

"J. Lawton Benscoter, you've got to want to fuck before you can fuck. Most men are wild to go as soon as they see a tit. You can still perform, but you've just got to want to fuck more. Think how good it feels when you pump off and climax and the woman squeals and yells with delight. Nothing in the world better."

"Show me again."

She stripped him, then took off her own clothes and tried to teach him the best way to make love to a woman. It took him almost an hour to get a passing grade.

As they dressed she shook her head at him. "J. Lawton, what you need is more practice. I can come in three days a week if you'd like. Or better yet, you should be humping your wife twice a week. In a couple of months you'll be chasing the young girls down the street like a stud bull."

"Damn, I hope so." He took a five dollar bill from his wallet and gave it to her. "Let's try that three times a week here first—Monday, Wednesday and Friday—but make it at four in the afternoon. I work better then than mornings."

Alice nodded when Clarissa left. Alice had never said a word about the treatment sessions or about Clarissa, who worked nights at the Lucky Seven Saloon in the cribs upstairs. Clarissa always used the backstairs so no one would see her come and go.

J. Lawton dressed and combed what was left of his graying hair. He had that noon talk with the sheriff. Nothing unusual. They had been getting together for lunch now and then for eight years.

He made it on time at the Del Rey Café and waved at Sheriff Ben Willard who had claimed a table in the back. Usually they ate by the front window. Sheriff Willard looked pensive today. His pinched face seemed to spell out worry, and his pot belly touched the edge of the table.

Benscoter slid into the chair, signaled for a cup of coffee and looked at the sheriff.

"We're on schedule," he said so only the lawman could hear.

"Damn well hope so. After this is all over, some folks are gonna be looking and poking around, trying to say it was illegal."

"That's why we have Loophole. He says the fact that the paper burned down and printed only a single sheet letter-sized paper on the date we needed is a legitimate reason for not advertising. There wasn't any advertising, and it was more a letter than a newspaper.

"Loophole says we're on solid ground. He says intent is the big thing here. We turned in the ads to the newspaper and scheduled it for publication, listing all the involved parties. It wasn't our fault the advertisements never appeared. Our intent was legal. The letters were mailed registered the same day the ads were to come out. We're legal as anything can be."

"But they never were published."

"Sheriff Willard, drop it. Loophole says we're on solid ground. He had four cases when much the same thing happened down in Phoenix, and the judge ruled that the intent had been there. Circumstances out of the control of the sheriff occurred, but the law had been followed as best it could be. Forget it and be ready to do the rest of your job."

The sheriff sighed. The waitress came and took their order, then hurried away.

"I tell you everything is working out the way we want it to. Just hold tight. In a little over a week it should all be played out, and we'll both have a bundle of cash."

"Damnit, I hope so, J. Lawton. Some of them due bills go back ten years, and it's high time. Oh, damn, I guess we're into this too far to back off now."

J. Lawton's hand came down with sudden force, pinning the sheriff's arm to the table.

"Sheriff, I don't want you ever to say that again or even think it. You're in this up to your neck. Why in hell do you suppose I contributed more than half of your campaign fund the last two elections? We work together—or come a year next November, I'll get a new sheriff elected. Understand?"

The sheriff nodded. J. Lawton smiled again. It wouldn't do for the town folks to see the two most powerful men in the county having an argument.

J. Lawton had worried a little about Sheriff Willard, but he was the vital link in the chain. Without him there would be nothing. He had to be along and had done his bit so far. The end of the campaign was the most important. He had his man, and he wasn't going to let him go.

Right after lunch with the sheriff, J. Lawton walked over to the post office that operated out of the J. Lawton Benscoter General Store. The postmaster also managed the store, since the government paid little more than a modest salary for the right to be the town's mailman.

There was a wall of boxes for the mail behind a partition with a window in it. Mail was sorted alphabetically, and residents called at the window for their mail daily or when they expected something.

Jessie Ferris looked up when Benscoter came in the store. He swallowed hard and waved his boss behind the partition. Ferris was short and wiry, with a full beard he kept trimmed to half an inch.

He wore spectacles and needed dental work.

"About these registered letters. I did what you told me to, but now what am I supposed to do with them? I got the forms signed off and everything, but you didn't tell me what to do with the damn letters."

Benscoter grinned. "No big worry, Jessie. Seems to me it's getting a little chilly in here. About time to start up your heater in the back room. Them letters make damn fine kindling, don't you think? Let's take care of them right now so there won't be any misunderstanding."

"I don't know, Mr. Benscoter."

"Hell, Jessie, you done the crime already. You failed to deliver registered U.S. mail. On top of that you forged forty-seven signatures and X's on delivery chits. You can't get in any deeper, Jessie. Besides, I already paid you that one hundred dollars in advance, right? Then you have four hundred more coming when it's all over. You're bought and paid for, Jessie, so now do your duty. Let's burn up those letters and stir the damn ashes so there isn't the least little shred of evidence that they were never delivered."

Chapter Five

Secret Service Agent Spur McCoy worked over the four back issues of the *Clarion* for an hour. He found no story of any significance that he thought could lead to murder.

The way the fires had been set at both doors of the newspaper building left no doubt in his mind that someone wanted the publisher dead. Yet there had been compassion, or some other reason, because the daughter had been spared. The fire could have been set at any time, yet the killers waited until the pretty young girl had gone out for supper, a regular occurrence on Wednesday nights that half the town must know about.

Spur leaned back in the chair and laced his fingers together behind his head. What in hell had got the killers so stirred up? He watched Gypsy working at a small table nearby and thought she was as pretty as a butterfly sitting on a fresh red rose.

"You're working hard this morning, Gypsy."

"They had a town council meeting I attended and I'm just writing it up for the paper."

"You'll do another small sized edition?"

"Yes, and every week until I get the big press fixed and have enough paper and ink to print the *Clarion* in its usual size."

"Then you don't expect the people who killed your father to cause you or the paper any more trouble?"

"Not unless they think that I'm stepping on their toes. Since I don't have the slightest idea who they might be, I'll probably write something they don't like soon enough. Papa and I thought alike on most of the important issues around the county."

"What are those important issues, Gypsy?"

"Taxation for one. The county commissioners want to raise the tax base so they can build a new courthouse and pay themselves a salary. Most of us don't want that. Things are moving along just fine."

"What else?"

"The local school district. It's a taxing institution and gets voter approval for new funds. Our schoolhouse is a shame. We need a new one built out of brick or stone so it will last a while. Many older people without children won't vote for more school taxes.

"Then the Methodists are trying to get a no firearms law in the city limits. That's so nobody can carry a gun off their own property without a county permit. They say ten men and one woman were shot dead in the city last year because of the flagrant misuse of firearms."

"That one must make everyone unhappy one

way or the other. I'd just as soon keep wearing my side arm if it's all right with you."

"The paper hasn't taken a position on the gun law yet. It may be put up to a vote of the people, and my guess is it would be voted down."

"Gypsy, there must be something else brewing, something bigger than what you told me about. I'm thinking it must be something that would involve large sums of money, a plan or a scheme or a project that would bring a great deal of money to someone here in town. An increase in taxes would mean a lot of money, but it would all go into the county coffers. That can't be it."

Gypsy wrinkled her brow and rubbed her chin. "I just can't think of anything that would fit your description."

"Maybe that's part of my problem. What we're talking about might not be public knowledge, yet somehow your father found out about it and was ready to break the story. I wish we could have gone through his desk and files. He just might have made some notes on a story this big."

A noise at the doorway brought Spur's head around. He relaxed when he saw a tall man in a business suit duck and come in.

"Well, Mr. Larson," Gypsy said, "how do you like the new offices of the *Clarion?*"

Larson was in his early forties, slender, over six feet and with that lean, hungry look Spur had always associated with coyotes on a sparse range.

"Not quite as fancy as your old place. How's the battle going?"

"Hard, working on getting the press into operation. Until then I'll put out the small paper."

"Any room for ads yet? One of my clients is interested."

"No, I can't offer the space or the circulation, so I decided not to run ads until the regular paper comes out. I'm losing money, but it seems the only fair way."

"Highly public spirited of you, Miss Pinnick." Larson turned and looked at Spur.

"Oh, I'm sorry," Gypsy said. "Loophole Larson, this is Spur McCoy."

Spur nodded at the man. "Loophole . . . that mean you're a lawyer?"

Larson laughed. "It does. I gained a reputation for finding holes in the system and in contracts and the moniker just stuck to me. I decided to utilize it."

Spur took a closer look at the lawyer. He must have seen the other small paper and knew there wasn't any advertising. Was he just curious about what was inside the tent, or did he have some other motive? It was easy to be suspicious of everyone in this situation. Spur could not read the man as friend or foe. A lawyer in a town this size would carry considerable weight. He'd see what he could learn about Larson.

"I hear we may have an old-fashioned barn raising one of these days to put up your new building," Larson said.

"Only a dream right now," Gypsy said and grinned. "Unless, Mr. Larson, you want to donate about two hundred dollars worth of lumber and supplies."

He chuckled. "Not right now, lass, but I'm a fair hand with a hammer and saw when the time comes." He looked around again, then nodded. "Well, I better be about my duties. Let me know if there's anything I can do. I understand your father had no insurance. It's expensive but sure can be handy." He looked at Spur. "Good meeting you, Mr. McCoy. I better be off." He smiled at Gypsy and hurried out the framed door.

Spur frowned at Gypsy. "What do you suppose that was all about?"

Gypsy brushed her long hair away from her eyes. "I have no idea. I've always got along with Larson well. He's the city attorney when they need one to interpret the laws and such. Seems friendly enough."

"Has he ever advertised in the paper?"

"No, but he does place an ad for a client now and then." She paused and studied him. "You're still coming to supper tonight?"

"Wouldn't miss it. A home cooked meal. I'd juggle three eggs and stand on my head for that."

Gypsy laughed, and he could see traces of the little girl in her. "Good, I'll hold you to that tonight." She moved from the small table to the type case, pulled out a drawer, and began picking up individual letters and placing them in a holder to set the story in type.

He watched, then moved over for a closer view. "You know where each of those letters is situated in that drawer."

She nodded not missing a letter as she spoke. "It's called learning the case or the drawer. All letters are in the same position no matter what font or kind of type you're setting. That makes it easier. Supposedly the letters are arranged so the ones used most often like i's and e's and a's are closer to the hand. The x and z are way out on the edge."

"Have you thought about any money issue that somebody would get murderous about?"

She shook her head, her long black hair rippling

down her back where it hung to just below her waist. "Not a thing. This isn't a rich town. No railroad coming, no gold mine discovered. Not even silver. I can't imagine what could be worth that much here in Pine Grove."

"What about the timber? I see a lot of pine trees around here."

"Good try, Spur, but the pines are not all that big and not the best for lumber. They make a fine fire, and the young ones are good for fence posts and telegraph poles. Outside of that, not the best money crop."

"Maybe I'm on the wrong trail here. What about some personal vendetta someone had for your father."

"Papa was intense and single-minded, but he really liked people. When he got angry it was because someone was taking advantage of a weaker person. He said the *Clarion* was here for the common man, for the little people who don't have lawyers or money to speak for them. Papa was an optimist. I do think the paper has been a help in the past and will be again, to keep the elected officials honest and to stand up for the common folk."

"I think you're an idealist like your father," Spur said. "I better wander your town, try to get to know more about it. Maybe I'll stumble on something to help us. We probably will never find the men who started the fires, but the man we want is the one who paid them to do so. When he find some big money scheme, we'll find the real killer."

Gypsy blinked rapidly, and when he went to her and put his arm around her, she dropped her head on his chest. He held her tightly.

"I didn't mean to upset you, Gypsy. You're a

strong young lady. I have great hopes for you."

She looked at him, wiped the tears from her eyes, reached up and kissed his cheek.

"Thank you, kind gentleman. I do need a good hug now and then. That should keep me working for the rest of the day." He let her go and she stepped back. "Maybe you could do that again one of these times." Her face was in repose, so vulnerable and open it made his heart pound. The mood passed and she smiled.

"Maybe after dinner, if I do a good job and you're off your guard," she said grinning.

He waved and hurried out the door. This was a girl a man could learn to like so much he wouldn't want to leave her. That kind of a relationship was not in his plans. He walked up the street, wondering what in this small town high in the Arizona mountains held such a secret that it had cost a man his life and his newspaper.

J. Lawton Benscoter stared at the telegram in his hand. "TO: T. L. BENSCOTER, PINE GROVE, ARIZONA. THE FIRM OF SOLOMON AND SONS, OUTFITTERS AND GENERAL HARD-WARE, DENVER, HAS NO OUTSIDE SALES-MEN. IF ANY FRAUD IS COMMITTED THERE BY IMPOSTER, NOTIFY LOCAL AUTHORITIES. HELP US PROTECT OUR GOOD NAME. J. SOL-OMON SENDING."

Benscoter read the wire again, tore it into small pieces and dropped them in the waste basket. So, Spur McCoy was not who he said he was. Now the task was to determine who he was and what he wanted in Pine Grove. Damn bad timing with just a week to go until the project would be complete. His greatest coup in

30 years, and now it all might hang in the balance.

After this paid off, he could sit back and relax, hire some bright young man to run things for him, and move to Phoenix where they had more of the easy life. Yes, in Phoenix he could keep tabs on things up here and yet have some of the luxuries.

It was near the middle of the afternoon, a time when most men would not be in their hotel rooms. Benscoter went to the Pine Grove Hotel, nodded at the clerk and went up the stairs to room 212.

No one was in the hall. He checked the door. Locked. He used his master key, stepped inside and relocked the door. Then he turned the key halfway around so no other key could be inserted to unlock the panel.

He searched the room quickly and deftly. Unless he left some special signals, McCoy wouldn't know anyone had been here. In the bottom of a leather traveling bag he found the spare set of identification that McCoy always carried.

Now Benscoter read the card and accompanying letter that had been signed by William Wood himself. Even Benscoter knew who William Wood was in Washington politics. He scowled as he returned the material to its rightful place, put back everything else as it had been and stepped to the door. Silently he unlocked it and cracked it open. No one in the hall.

Benscoter stepped out and locked the door, then walked down the hall wondering what to do. He had a federal lawman on his hands, a Secret Service man empowered by the federal government to investigate any crimes against the nation, any interstate crime, and any problem where a local law enforcement officer requested aid and assistance. What the hell should he do now?

Benscoter thought about it as he sipped a shot of whiskey at the Blue Goose Saloon which he owned, though few in town realized it. He now owned about half the retail establishments in town, and he wanted them all.

What in hell should he do about Spur McCoy? He could hire any one of half a dozen men in town to blow McCoy's brains out in a dark alley tonight. But would that be the best solution? It would solve the short term problem, but would it open up the way for a half dozen federal lawmen to come trooping in?

Larson was the legal expert; he would talk to him about it. McCoy was sniffing around the newspaper and the girl. Was he here to dig into the fire and the chance that it had not been an accident as the county coroner had determined? Now that would be a problem.

At least the men who struck the matches would never be found. They were well past Phoenix now and on their way to San Francisco. Still something could be turned up that would derail the big project.

The only problem there he could see was Jessie Ferris. He was tied in, incriminated already, but that might not be enough. Benscoter would watch the bearded little man closely. No one was going to foul up this project. Ferris was expendable. He had done his part and could be eliminated any time. In fact, that would be best, making one less witness, one less trouble spot that could blow the whole project right over the moon. He'd think about Jessie. The man was of no use anymore and presented a sizeable liability. Did the liability outweigh the risk? That was the problem Benscoter would have to decide soon.

But first, McCoy. What the hell should he do about this federal lawman breathing down his neck?

Chapter Six

Spur McCoy had walked through the small town of Pine Grove from one end to the other, all three blocks of it, and he had prowled the back streets and alleys. Now he sat in the Home Café sipping a cup of coffee. He had an hour yet before he was to show up for supper at the small white house where Gypsy Pinnick lived.

He had learned little this afternoon. The people he talked to had no idea of any big money plot afoot. Most of them joked about it. Said the town fathers had the gravy train by getting five dollars a meeting for doing almost nothing. Nobody wanted to talk about the anti-gun law except one Methodist who was all for it.

"My cousin came near to death last year when two drunks decided to have an old-fashioned shoot out on Main Street. Both were so potted they couldn't hit the ground and both took five shots at each other. My cousin was a half block away and caught a round in his chest. Could have killed him, but it didn't."

Spur took a pull at the coffee. It was a fair brew, stronger than he liked it but good enough for now. He'd been in town for a little over 24 hours and already the pot was cooking. He had spent a lot of time around the *Clarion* tent hoping that would make somebody nervous, but so far there was no payoff on that ploy.

A land grab? How can you get land for free in a place like this? Most of the surrounding countryside and mountains were federal property. Much of it would revert to the state if and when Arizona gained enough population and met the other requirements to become a state. A land grab didn't seem reasonable, although about 50 sections of land in these mountains should produce enough timber to make the deal worthwhile.

That would require going through congress and the Department of the Interior. There also were several large Indian reservations that were off limits to any kind of land deal.

He finished his coffee, put a nickel on the counter and headed for Gypsy's house. He had no illusions about taking her to bed tonight. She was the kind of lady you took home to mother and put a wedding band on her finger before you lifted her skirts—and rightly so. She was a lady.

For a moment he compared her to Flo Benscoter who was a good time girl who liked sex as much as men did and didn't care where she got it. Flo was a fast tumble in bed; Gypsy was a long term commitment of marriage and family.

He knocked on the door, and it popped open at once. Gypsy stood there, smiling and gorgeous. She must have brushed her waist-length raven-black hair a hundred times. She had trimmed the bangs across her forehead, and her soft brown eyes glowed with a happiness he hadn't seen there before.

"Welcome to the Pinnick place," she said. "Your dinner isn't quite ready but you're welcome to help me finish it in the kitchen." When she reached up and kissed his cheek, for just a moment her breasts brushed his chest.

"Now you're properly welcomed. Do you know how to mash potatoes?"

A few minutes later she watched him with delight. "A little more salt and a spoon full of butter," she directed. "If you were a prospective beau I wouldn't let you within twenty feet of my kitchen. Oh, it's quite simple. I'm not all that good at cooking. Actually Papa did most of the cooking after Mama died. He was good at it. I told him he should open a restaurant."

Spur listened, delighted to hear her running on this way. It told him that she was more than a little nervous having him here for a social occasion rather than work.

She chattered on for another five minutes until he held up his hands.

"Hey, usually you don't talk on and on this way. That tells me you're nervous, and I wish you wouldn't be. This is a business dinner, not social at all. Will that help you relax a little?"

She took a long breath and nodded. "I guess . . . I guess I just sort of got myself all nervous and bothered. Sorry."

Spur chuckled. "It's interesting to see you this

way. You're as pretty as a speckled fawn, and right now about as skitterish. Look, Gypsy, I'm not here to court or woo or seduce you. It's just a friendly little dinner between friends. Nothing to worry about."

He held up the crockery bowl with the potatoes mashed and whipped to a creamy white. "Here is the proof, a topnotch batch of mashed potatoes ready for the table."

Gypsy laughed and brought to the table fried chicken, gravy, carrots, peas and some boiled cabbage.

As they sat down to eat, she reached over and touched his hand. "Thanks for understanding. If it's business, I stay all business, but on the social scene, I get all giddy like a sixteen year-old having her first kiss."

Spur went through the food like a starved man, and she relaxed more. They talked about the problem of the big scam but neither of them had any ideas.

"It can't be mountain land or gold or oil or timber," he said. "I just don't see what else is here that could build up this kind of anger against your father."

"It must be something. I'm sure it wasn't some kind of a personal vendetta. Folks around here face off and scream at each other, and if they're young enough they throw a few punches and the problem is worked out. I just don't understand."

Spur knew she was right. This young lady not only had a nice body and beautiful face, she was smart as well. When the dinner was finished, he insisted on helping her clean up and wash the dishes.

"I'll dry," he said. "I'm best at that."

Twenty minutes later they settled down in the living room.

"Sometimes it seems strange here. Now this is my house. I grew up here and seen a lot of changes. Sometimes I still can't be sure that Papa is gone. I figure he's working late at the paper and he'll come home hungry as a wolverine and I won't have any supper for him."

She looked away, rubbed her eyes for a moment and then turned back to him.

"One thing, I wish I had more self-confidence. Sometimes I'm not sure what I'm doing is right."

Spur grinned and then chuckled. "Gypsy, if you had any more self-confidence you'd be mayor and ready to run for governor. You're doing just fine."

"Well, how nice. Thank you for those fine words. I do know one thing. When I get married it will be for love, and because the man is the kind who will look upon me as a partner and not as something else he owns. My future husband will accept the idea that I am a whole person, that I have the right to run my newspaper after we're married, and that he won't own any of the paper or have anything to do with it—unless he's a professional newspaperman who knows what he's doing."

Spur stood. "Gypsy, even with a list of requirements like that, I'd say you won't last another year before some lucky man waltzes you right down the aisle into matrimony. Now, I thank you for the fine meal. I appreciate it. I better be getting back to my room and figure out what to do tomorrow."

She walked him to the door where she touched his shoulder. He turned toward her. "Spur, would you kiss me please?"

He smiled and bent and kissed her lips, softly

and gently. They parted after a few seconds and she gave a little sigh.

"That was fine, but let's try it again." This time her hands came around his neck, and she pressed hard against his chest. The kiss was fire and ice and lasted longer than he expected. When she at last pulled away from his lips, she clung to him, her face against his shoulder.

She sighed again, then stepped back and laughed ruefully. "I know that was not a smart thing to do. But when I'm around you, I'm not always smart, especially when you're kissing me. I have been kissed before in case you're wondering. I enjoyed it. Perhaps again sometime. Now, like you said, you do have to go."

She opened the screen door and let him outside, then closed it and looked through it. "Oh, yes, Spur McCoy, now that was a kiss to remember. Will I see you tomorrow?"

"I'll stop by your tent, for sure." He turned and walked away with her watching him through the screen.

Spur lifted his brows when he was halfway down the dark block toward Main. Gypsy was a lot more woman than he had thought at first. Somehow he figured she was 19. A lot of suppressed desire flooded out in that last kiss. He wondered if she had ever made love. His first response was no, but as he thought about it, she might have come on too strong to some young man not able to control himself. Could have happened.

It was really none of his business, just curiosity. He pushed it out of his mind. What was left to do tomorrow? He'd covered most of the bases here. He had no leads at all on the murder. He could help organize the barn raising for the new building, but she would still be $1,000 short to start up the *Clarion* again.

Just this side of Main Street, he saw two men in the shadows of the hardware store. They probably would be gone by the time he got there. Then he was near the hardware, and the two men stood 20 feet ahead blocking his path.

"You boys looking for trouble?" he asked stopping ten feet from them.

"Not if you're not," one said. "Give us your wallet and your pocket watch and you're free to go."

"Not a chance." He started to draw, but too late he sensed the loop settle over him and the rope jerk tight, pinning his arms to his side. One of the men jerked the lariat forward with all of his weight, and Spur staggered a step, then stumbled and went down and slid through the dust of the street another three feet before he stopped.

One of the men knelt on top of him, slid the six-gun from leather and pounded his fist into Spur's stomach.

After that neither of the two said a word. The rope held tight as they got him to his feet, looped the rope around him again and tied it off tight. The fists came with practiced ease against his belly, then his face. He took three more shots to his stomach before he saw the opening he wanted. One of the men in front of him backed up half a step for a longer swing.

Spur kicked upward with his right foot as hard as he could. His hard leather toe caught the man along the inside of his left thigh and rocketed upward, crashing into his scrotum, driving it upward against his pelvic bones, crushing both testicles, dumping the man backwards where he lay screaming in terrible pain.

"Oh, shit!" the other tough said and turned and ran down the street. Spur worked at the knots in the rope, and before the man writhing on the ground could stand, Spur had the rope off and found his gun where they had tossed it. He put the loop around the tough's neck and drew it tight.

"Get to your feet or I'll kick you again," Spur snarled. His belly hurt like fire, and he knew he had lost some skin off his nose and under his eye. He'd have a black eye by morning. No matter, this might be his first break on the case.

The attacker shrieked in pain as he stood, then he walked spraddle-legged so he wouldn't move his wounded testicles.

Next to the first saloon, where lamplight spilled onto the boardwalk, Spur pushed the wounded man against the wall and doubled his fist under the man's wild eyes.

"Who hired you?"

"Nobody, broke, needed some cash."

"Not a chance. You followed me to the lady's house, waited for me to come out and challenged me. You're not a range rat. You both knew exactly what you were doing and how to make it hurt the most without killing me. You've got ten seconds, then my fist hits your crotch as hard as I can swing."

"Nobody hired us."

Spur held him with one hand at his throat and fisted his right and swung it back. Just before he started his fist toward the man's crotch, he broke.

"No, no! God, no, not again. All right, I'll tell you. Don't hit me again."

"Who, where?"

"Don't know his name. Asked us if we could use a rope and didn't have any problem with pounding somebody around a little. Paid us twenty dollars."

"Who was he?"

"Don't know him. Bear of a man, over six feet, wide shoulders, red hair, beer belly. Talked with a lisp."

"Where did you meet him?"

"A saloon, don't remember which one."

"You've got twenty seconds to remember the name."

It came at once as the man's eyes turned from side to side as if searching for help. "The Blue Goose Saloon. Down the street a ways."

"Good." Spur pulled the noose tighter around the man's neck until he gurgled from lack of air, then Spur slackened it. "You better go see Doc Johnson about them nuts of yours. They might be mashed up a little. Leastwise you won't want to look at a naked woman for at least three months."

Spur pushed him down the street and went off toward the Blue Goose. A man that big couldn't be hard to find in a town the size of Pine Grove.

The big man wasn't in the Blue Goose. Spur hung around for an hour, drank a cold beer, watched some poker and some faro. He didn't play, but checked every man who came in or went out. The big bear man was not there. Not a redhead in the place. Spur wondered how his own face looked. He could stand the pain in his belly, but his face would show tomorrow.

He went back to the hotel and looked in the mirror. A nasty bruise showed under his right eye and his nose had lost half an inch of skin. He went to the hotel kitchen and talked them out of a six-inch square of river ice and took it upstairs. He broke up some of the ice, wrapped it in a towel and held it against his cheek.

The ice should help reduce the swelling and with any luck would drive some of the blood out of the tissue. He painted his nose with some ointment he had for such small injuries and stared at his face in the mirror again. Tomorrow everyone would know he'd been in a brawl.

In certain quarters, that might prove to be an asset. His first task was to find the redheaded bear. Somebody would know him, maybe the man at the post office. He saw every person in town on a regular basis. Yes, good choice.

Spur stripped down and tried to sleep, but his gut hurt too much. He got up and smoked a thin brown stogie, watching the saloons out his window. It was a quiet night without a single gunfight, and only one fisticuffs erupted all the way to the street out of a saloon.

A little after eleven he checked his watch with a match. Hopefully he'd sleep for a while before morning. A few minutes later a knock sounded on his door. He drew his six-gun from its leather and went to the wall next to the door.

"Who is it?"

"A friend with gifts," Flo said. He let the hammer down gently on the round and unlocked the door.

"Were you sleeping?" Flo asked.

"No. I'll light the lamp. I'm not decent."

"Good, I won't be either for long."

He lit the lamp, put on the chimney and turned down the wick to a steady flame.

Flo looked at him wearing only his short cotton underdrawers.

"You look fine to me. Maybe a little over-dressed." She held out a sack. "Look inside."

He found a bottle of wine, three kinds of cheese and three apples.

"I figured we might get hungry after."

"Look at my face," he told her.

She did. "Tsk, fighting again. Naughty boy. I should spank you." She looked at him for a reaction.

"Not tonight, sexy lady." He told her about the two saddle tramps who had jumped him. "Somebody in your fine little town doesn't like me. Oh, do you know a big bear of a man over six feet who has red hair?"

"Sure, everybody knows Red Kenny. He's one of the guys who beat you up?"

"No, he hired them."

"Oh, gawd!"

"What?"

"Red has worked for my husband from time to time. He's good at a lot of things, kind of a handyman around town. Works for a lot of people."

"Know where he lives?"

"Not the slightest idea. Now, let's get naked and get down to doing some wild, strange and wonderful fucking."

Spur pointed to the bruise marks on his belly.

"I'm having enough trouble just breathing tonight, Flo. Better postpone our party until I'm feeling better."

"You just lay on your back. You don't even have to move."

He reached out and fondled her breasts through the thin dress. "Not a chance, lady. Have you ever been beaten up? No fun, and it takes some recuperation time. Tomorrow night about the same time?"

She kissed him, gently felt his crotch, then picked up her sack of food and went to the door.

"Don't do anything foolish with Red. He out-weighs you."

Spur held up his Colt .45 which he hadn't put back in leather.

"Probably, but he doesn't outweigh this."

"Oh, gawd, you men and your toys." She turned, slipped out the door and closed it after her. He locked it and put a chair under the knob.

It was a long night but he finally fell asleep.

Chapter Seven

When morning came, it took Spur McCoy five minutes to get out of bed. He couldn't remember being so sore or weary. The dozen blows had left a lasting impression. His first try to get out of bed as usual resulted in a searing pain in his gut and dropped him back on the mattress.

After remembering the pounding he took, he rolled over and pushed himself up with his hands, then sat down on the edge of the bed. The room spun for a moment, then righted itself. Spur took a long breath of air and let it out slowly. His face hurt, his belly hurt, even his knees hurt. He was getting too old to be beaten up that way. Next time he'd draw first, no more damn lariat around his torso pinning his hands at his sides.

Spur reached his pants and pulled them on both feet, then knew he had to stand up to

finish putting them on. He stood slowly, kept
his balance and pulled up the brown town
pants. His body shrieked and he groaned, but
he maintained his balance. The shirt was harder to get into. Damn but he was getting soft.
He'd have to pick a fight a week just to stay in
shape.

By the time he finished dressing and walked six
steps to the mirror, he felt a little better. Then he
looked at his face. The bruise under his left eye had
extended upward giving him a beauty of a black
eye. The scrape on his nose had sheened over with
a layer of protective scab.

He'd live, but he'd be hurting for a few days.

Shaving was a chore, but once it was done he
looked forward to breakfast and then a talk with
the county sheriff. Most elected lawmen have a
keen idea of what's going on in their area. He
hoped he hit a good one.

At breakfast in the dining room below, the waitress looked at him and frowned, then took his
order without any questions. He had walked into
the dining room holding himself tightly, sat down
with great care and leaned back before he could
relax. It paid off. The bacon and French toast and
a side of applesauce were good, and he poured on
the hot syrup and layered on butter and ate like he
was getting ready for a marathon.

Just before nine that morning, Spur walked with
less and less difficulty into the sheriff's office and
asked to see the top man. After a quick conference
between two deputies, one went to a door and
knocked.

Spur had no idea what to expect when he walked
into the man's private office. Ben Willard did not
look like the ideal sheriff. He was on the thin side

but with a bulging belly and a pinched face. He did not wear a gun or gunbelt. Willard pushed a paper aside and looked at his visitor.

"Don't believe I know you," Sheriff Willard said. There was no warmth in his voice or attitude, only a steely eyed inquiry.

Spur took out his identification card with the silver shield on the back of it and handed it to the lawman.

Sheriff Willard read the card, looked at the shield and then read the card again.

"Secret Service? Never heard of it. Card says you're a federal lawman with jurisdiction in every state and territory. Noticed you around town for a couple of days. What you interested in here in Pine Grove?"

"The death of Andrew Weston Pinnick. How did your office list the death?"

"Pinnick, the publisher of our weekly newspaper. Coroner found no wrong doing or suspicious acts and listed the death as accidental due to fire."

"As I understand it, there were signs of coal oil being used on the only two doors to the building to start the fire. How could you or the coroner possibly decide that the coal oil and the matches to light the fluid both came to be there at the same time accidentally?"

"Coroner called it an accidental death, and I go along with his verdict. I don't go hunting trouble."

"You don't go hunting murderers either, Sheriff Willard. Pinnick was murdered by persons unknown. It's your job to find who they are and prosecute them. I strongly suggest that you reopen the case and try diligently to find the two men who started those fires, and just as important find the man who hired the killers.

"If you don't do this, Sheriff, I'll file an official complaint with the United States Attorney General as well as with the Territorial Attorney General, who I'm sure will have a team of investigators up here within three days."

The sheriff stood and walked around the room, stared out his window and then came back to his desk. He sat down and shook his head.

"No sir, I don't believe the Territorial Attorney General will come up here. This is strictly a local problem, and he don't mess in local affairs lessen he has to."

"Sheriff, this is a matter of the violation of Pinnick's constitutional rights, both a local and a federal matter. It involves not only the illegal death of Pinnick, but the violation of his rights to exercise the freedom of the press. That's why both attorney generals will be extremely interested in this case, once I present it to them."

"Freedom of the press. Nobody told him he couldn't print what he wanted to."

"It's hard to print anything once you're dead, Sheriff, which you are well-aware of. Now, I'd like to see your file and all applicable papers and orders on Pinnick's death."

"We don't got no files on it. No cause. Coroner done his report and showed it to me and put it in his files. If you want to see files, go see Doc Johnson. He's the coroner."

The sheriff stood. "Now that's the end of it. You do whatever you want. This office has closed the case, and now I'd like you to close the door when you leave. This conversation is at an end."

Spur remained seated. "Sheriff Willard, I'll leave when I'm through with my business here. I've seen several lawmen like you before—highhanded, self important, undertrained for the tough job they have, unbending. Let me remind you of something. Every territorial constitution is patterned for the territory by the federal government.

"In each is a provision for the Territorial Attorney General to remove any local sheriff, town marshal, police chief or other local law enforcement officer whether elected, appointed or hired, in case of malfeasance in office or other just cause when it is in the interests of the people in that community. Sheriff Willard, don't believe that it can't happen here. I'd advise that you reopen the Pinnick case and start tracking down the two men who set those fires and the man who hired them. You have twenty-four hours to get the investigation under way."

Spur stood, turned sharply and, without any word or gesture of farewell, left the room and walked back to the street. He felt damn good again. That sheriff would be no help in his work here. In fact he could be a hinderance.

The man was not only uncooperative but was downright hostile. Was he only angry because a federal lawman was in his jurisdiction, or was it something deeper?

By that time, the saloons were open. Spur walked into the Blue Goose and looked around. A dozen men were there. Half looked to be out of work cowboys, miners or drifters. Two dark-suited business men huddled in a conference over coffee at a back table. One game of draw poker had just started.

Spur bought a beer and watched the poker game. He refused an offer to join in. His mention of lack of funds stilled their interest in his participation.

Red Kenny was not around, but Spur figured he'd give it two hours. He was on his second beer when the redhead came in the back door.

Spur watched him as he talked to the barman, then went to a back table and sat down. Spur got up and stood across the poker table from Kenny.

"Red, you and I got some talking to do. Let's go out back."

"Who the hell are you?" the big man at the table asked. He dropped his hand below the table and Spur drew his .45 so fast the redhead scowled.

"What the hell? I can talk. No hogs leg needed. Let's talk right here first. What about?"

"You know damn well what about. My name is Spur McCoy, and you hired two saddle tramps last night to beat me up and slice me open. I don't like that."

"Afraid you have the wrong man. If I wanted you smashed up a little, I'd do that job myself."

"Why didn't you? Who hired you to hire the tramps? You're not smart enough to work up some big scheme, you're just a cog in the wheel somewhere. Who hired you?"

"Nobody. If you still want to settle this, we can move out to the alley like you said. Then no bystanders get hurt."

Spur wondered what his ploy was. He'd denied hiring the two thugs, so what more could he prove? Spur nodded, keeping the six-gun leveled on the man. "Yeah, let's go outside where I can cut you down to size a little easier, without breaking up the furniture."

Red stood with no sudden movements and kept his hand well away from the six-gun on his hip as they walked to the back door. Once there, Red went out first, then slammed the door backwards against Spur and darted into the alley.

Spur kicked the door open but stayed against the wall. Three shots jolted into the heavy wooden door as it swung out and one came through the opening. All missed Spur. He ducked, kicked the door open again and fired around the side. Spur caught one man moving from a box to the side of a building and hit him in the thigh. He went down screeching.

By that time the apron from the bar was at the back door with the sawed-off shotgun he kept to tame down fights.

"What the hell's going on back here?" he demanded, holding the shotgun ready.

"Somebody in the alley started shooting at me when I started out the door," Spur said. "Damn unfriendly town you got here. Think I'll use the front door before they run around there." Spur reloaded the empty chambers in his Colt, holstered it and walked through the saloon to the front door. Nobody tried to stop him, and no guns barked as he went out the swinging doors to the street.

He leaned against the store front next door for a minute to gather his thoughts. He didn't get far with Red Kenny, but he knew there would be another meeting with that bear of a man. In the meantime, he'd check out all possibilities. Maybe he'd had more instructions from the general in Washington D.C.

Spur pushed away from the store front and walked across the street to the Pine Grove Hotel.

A quick look in his box showed a message. The room clerk handed it to him, and Spur saw it was a plain envelope, not a telegram. Inside he found a message on lined paper.

"Spur McCoy. Understand you're a federal lawman. I know why you're here. I know what they are up to. I'll give you all the details on the scheme if you promise me total protection and that no charges will be filed against me and no public revelation made of my small part in this swindle. Come to the old stage stop about six miles out of town on the road north toward Flag at two P.M. today. I'll be waiting." The note had no signature, only the initials, J.F.

Spur checked his pocket watch and saw it was slightly after ten o'clock. Plenty of time. He always liked to get to a meeting like this well ahead of schedule to check out the lay of the land and to watch the other party arrive.

He had a thick roast beef sandwich at the Home Café, then rented a horse from the livery, borrowed a repeating rifle and a box of rounds and headed out the north road. It wound along a ridge line for several miles, and he saw the old swing station a mile before he came to it. The time was a little before one o'clock so he'd have a wait.

He stopped a quarter of a mile from the burned-out remains of the swing station. There was most of a barn left, part of the cabin, a well house and what might have been a chicken coop. Fire had gutted most of it except the barn. Might be a good spot to hole up and wait for anyone coming up the road. Loose boards on the upper part of the barn would give him a fine view down the road toward town.

As he turned the bay mare and moved toward the barn, he saw a glint of metal to the left behind a small rise and a pair of pine trees. Automatically he grabbed the rifle out of the boot and dove off the bay.

Just as he dove he felt a bullet whip through the air where his head had been a fraction of a second before. The sound of the shot came almost on top of the bullet and with it came another pair of shots. He hit the dirt on his hands, did a shoulder roll and flattened out in a small drainage ditch at the side of the wagon road.

Spur heard his horse screaming and saw her go down, shot at least twice. Then the sound of more shots came from the half-burned barn. He was out of sight of the gunman in the pine trees, but the one in the barn could see half of him. A bullet slammed into the dirt near his left leg, hit a rock and ricocheted off with a nasty whine.

Spur pulled his leg to the left out of the line of fire. He lifted up and sent one round into the barn's second floor about where he figured the gunsharp would be, but there was no reaction.

The gun from the trees blasted again twice, and this time one round came close enough to make Spur gasp. He screamed as if in sudden pain and then let the screams grow weaker and weaker until they faded out. He drew his six-gun, held it by his side and waited.

The old decoy game might work. He heard boots crunching on the road before he saw anyone. He waited, his eyes wide open in a motionless stare at the spot where the man should appear. It was all Spur could do to keep his eyeballs still as a gun-man came in view, still holding the rifle aimed at Spur.

A voice came from far off, and the man turned his head for a fraction of a second and shouted something. Spur lifted the six-gun and fired.

The rifleman's finger triggered a round automatically. The round jolted through Spur's left forearm halfway down. Spur bit his lip to hold in the pain. He had seen the rifleman slam backwards from the force of the heavy .45 round.

Now Spur edged up from the ditch he lay in and looked at the roadway. A man lay there without moving. Spur had had little chance to aim, but now he saw that the round had evidently entered on an upward course under the rifleman's chin and took half of his skull off.

The rifle by the pines spoke again, and Spur slid back into the ditch to protect himself. He rose up and returned two rounds into the trees, then dropped down. This time there was no return fire.

Now it was waiting time. One man dead, his own horse dead, one more rifleman in the trees. Would he fight, or wasn't that in his plan? Maybe he figured he could cut down Spur from long distance in the deadly crossfire and go collect his blood money.

While waiting, Spur tended to his left arm. The bullets had penetrated an inch and a half of his arm but missed the bone. He used his handkerchief as a pad and his neckerchief to bind it up. He covered the wounds on both sides of his forearm and figured the tight bandage should stop the bleeding.

With his teeth, he tore the end of the kerchief so he could tie the two ends around his wrist and hold the bandage on tight.

After what Spur figured was 15 minutes, he lifted up again and fired into the pine trees. There was no response. It could mean the ambusher was gone. Knowing that kind of person, Spur figured there was little chance he would still be waiting for a chance to finish his job.

Spur looked at his rented bay, lying on the ground not moving. She must be dead. He eyed the barn. The two could have left their mounts there or in the trees behind the swing station. He got up, carried the rifle and six-gun and ran flat out toward the barn.

The first few steps were the worst, but he heard no shots, and soon he finished the 200 yards to the barn. Behind the burned-out relic he found where two horses had been tied. One mount remained. He checked the barn, then what was left of the cabin. Nobody was there, dead or alive.

He wondered now if the note had been an honest one. It could all have been a simple ploy to get him out where they could kill him. On the other hand it might have been an honestly conceived notion of this J.F. to get out of some kind of conspiracy and illegal operation.

If so, the boss of the operation must have caught him writing it or delivering it and used the note as a way to eliminate McCoy. If so, then J.F. was little better than a walking corpse—if he was still alive.

The initials might not have stood for anyone in particular, just a way to bring more credibility to the note. Either way, he'd find out soon enough.

Spur mounted the remaining horse, rode out to where his bay lay dead and pulled off the saddle and bridle. He perched them on the back of his mount and rode for town. He didn't use the easy track of the wagon road. Instead he angled off the road down a canyon and stayed a half mile off the road to be sure that the unsuccessful bushwhacker didn't get another shot at him. The six mile ride gave him lots of time to think about the case.

Chapter Eight

Just after four o'clock that afternoon, Spur turned
the horse in at the livery. He said his horse had hit
a gopher hole and went down, so he had to shoot
it. He tried to convince the owner that the horse he
brought back was as good as the one he left with.

"Besides you get a fifteen dollar saddle and bridle thrown in," Spur said. He didn't explain why
he brought back another horse, and the livery man
wasn't all that interested. He soon was convinced
of the wisdom of the deal and charged Spur a dollar
for the use of the rifle and the cartridges.

Next stop was the county coroner and medic,
Doc Johnson, who had fairly new offices in the
Benscoter building. The sawbones was in his sixties, spry and sharp-tongued. He stared at the open
wound and nodded.

"Rifle wound, not a handgun. Seen a lot of them

in my time. Supposed to report such to the sheriff, but he don't even want me to anymore. He don't seem to be paying a whole lot of attention lately to his job."

The medic cleaned out both wounds and applied some antiseptic solution that hurt like fire. Then he put on some salve and small pads over the wounds and wrapped it tight enough to keep everything in place.

"Don't use that arm for at least a week. The slug missed the bone, but not by much. Got some major muscles in there with big holes in them."

Spur nodded. "I can do that, Doc. I have a question for you. Your report says that Andrew Pinnick's death was accidental due to fire. Did you do any investigation or hold a hearing before making that determination?"

"You're sounding like some damn lawyer, son. Fact is I went on what the sheriff and the deputies told me. Time they got there the whole damn building was on fire. Bucket brigade couldn't even hold down the smoke, let alone put out the blaze. Better get that pumper truck or this whole wooden town will burn down one of these days. Hell, no, I didn't do no investigation. They don't pay me enough to hold a real coroner's inquest, if that's what you're thinking about."

"Did anyone tell you that those first on the scene smelled coal oil at both the front and the back doors, and later on cans were found that could have held two gallons of coal oil each?"

"You don't say?" The doctor shook his head. "Nobody told me that, so I figured it was accidental." He walked to his bench, arranged some instruments and came back.

"Mean to tell me that somebody deliberately

torched that building and made damn sure that the only two doors out got set on fire first and both at the same time?"

"That's what witnesses I've talked to tell me, Doc."

"Be damned. I'm changing that death certificate to death by design by person or persons unknown. Means the case should be open."

"Just what I told the sheriff, and he didn't like it one bit. I'd guess he'll leave it open but won't do much."

The medic looked concerned for a moment. "Hell, I just went by what they told me. You're that federal lawman, I'd reckon. Heard you were in town." He took a step toward the door.

"Well, if there's nothing else . . ."

"No, that's all unless you tended another man for a gunshot wound this afternoon."

"You're my first, and I hope my only."

Spur eased out of the chair and went back to the street. His aches from this morning were still there, just muted a little. The doctor hadn't said a word about his face. Maybe he thought Spur always looked that way.

The newspaper tent was just ahead. He swung open the door and looked inside. Gypsy sat at her small desk working on a proof. She looked up when he came in and smiled.

"About time you got here. I have good news." She hurried to him and grabbed both his hands. "Really, really good news. Come out here."

In back of the tent they walked through a few stray beams to the spot where the press stood. The floor had burned through under it, and now the big press sat directly on the rocky ground. It was nearly level, and a young man in oil and greasy overalls worked on one of the levers.

"That's Mike from Phoenix. He's a whiz with presses. Says he can have mine up and running before dark. Isn't that wonderful!"

Spur enjoyed her enthusiasm. Her face lit up like an octogenarian's birthday cake, and her eyes sparkled.

"Good news, Gypsy. One more step in getting back to normal. Now you need that building and your printing supplies."

Her light mood vanished and she scowled. "Yes, both those things, and my bank account is starting to give out. It's my dowry money I've been spending. I could always sell the house. It's free and clear and should bring maybe twelve hundred dollars—furnished, of course."

"Don't sell the house. We'll figure out something. How about a small building first that you can expand later on? One just big enough for the press and some supplies, maybe twenty by forty feet set in the middle of the space here."

"Lumber, nails, roofing. I can't pay for a building that size."

"How about a basket social? All proceeds go to the new building for the *Clarion*. Make a basket and help the town get back the newspaper that it deserves."

Gypsy squinted slightly, thinking about it. She rubbed her chin, then looked up at him. "It just might work. I could print off some flyers and post them around town, then talk all the women I can see into making a basket. We'll have it Sunday afternoon in the park."

"Sounds good. Minimum bid two dollars. No limit on how high the bidding can go. Gypsy, your basket alone should fetch twenty dollars. Do you realize how many two by fours you can buy for a twenty dollar gold piece?"

"Yes, let's try it. I'll get the flyers set in type and proofed tonight, then print them off by lantern light. I could use some help if you're going to be around."

"Try to be."

She looked at him then stepped forward and touched his shoulder.

"That's a bandage around your arm. How did you hurt it?"

"A small disagreement with a man shooting a rifle. Nothing fatal."

"Oh, and your poor eye. I bet you didn't put any steak on that, did you?"

"Guilty, your honor."

"Your nose! I didn't even notice I was so excited about the press. Mike is charging me just for one day's work and the fare on the stage. Not even any new parts, he said. When the roof fell in it sagged away from the press before it dropped. Otherwise it could have ruined the whole machine." They walked back to her office area.

"Now, let me look at your nose. You sure you've seen a doctor about this?"

"Yes, I have. Don't mother me. I'm fine. You get to thinking about your box social. Talk it up with the women and get them to promise to come. If the married women all come their husbands will have to, and it'll work out fine."

"Oh, I hope so. I'm going to write the flyer right now and lay it out with some great big huge type. Wish we still had the circus wooden letters. Oh, well, we have some two inch." She waved and hurried off to work on the flyer.

Spur felt the pain boil up from his arm. The nerve endings had come out of their shock and now complained bitterly about being cut in half by that damn rifle slug.

He thought of going to the doctor for some pain killer, but usually the medics gave out laudanum. He'd come too close to getting addicted to that heroin derivative once. He wouldn't touch it now.

Instead he'd have a big supper at the fanciest eatery in town, then invent some games to take his mind off the pain and get to bed early. Sleep would be the best thing for him tonight.

By the time he walked to the Eagle's Nest Restaurant down near the end of Main, they were serving dinner. He had a fine meal of steak and pheasant, with all the trimmings and side dishes. It was delicious. The price was $1.75 and he nearly choked at the tab. How was he going to explain that meal on his expense account? He shrugged. They didn't believe half the things he claimed anyway.

He strolled the long way back to the hotel and arrived there slightly after eight o'clock. There were no notices in his key box, and he went directly to his room.

Spur went through his usual routine for opening the door, and this time when he pushed it in hard, he saw that two lamps were burning and Flo Benscoter sat on the bed smoking a long thin cigar.

He went in, closed the door and stared at her.

"I didn't know that you smoked cigars."

"I didn't either, until tonight. I got tired of waiting for you so I prowled around in your suitcase until I found your stogies. Flo, light the damned thing, I told myself. So I did. First few times I coughed and choked half to death, but by the time I got the second one smoked halfway down,

I got the knack of it. Not a bad tasting cheroot, old man."

"You're impossible."

"I know, McCoy. That's why you love to love me. I brought back the cheese and the wine."

"Good timing. I got shot today."

She jumped off the bed. "Poor darling. Who shot you? Where?"

"I don't know who, because he got away. The round went through my arm, so take it easy on my left one."

She pushed up his shirt-sleeve, kissed the white dressing and pulled him to the bed.

"You look like a man who needs some of my special brand of tender loving care. Just let Flo take care of everything. I know you're still hurting, but I won't make you hurt more. Not unless you bust a blood vessel when you come so hard. You just have your supper?"

He nodded.

"Good I slipped out for some sustenance as well." She unbuttoned his shirt and helped him ease the sleeve off his left arm, then pulled it away.

"Say now, I like manly chests, and yours is just fabulous. Enough hair and red nipples and muscles you haven't even used yet."

She knelt in front of him where he stood next to the bed. "Now, folks, we come to the good parts. Yeah, inside his pants. Want to see?" She opened his gunbelt buckle, took it off and hung it on the bedpost. She undid his belt and then his fly and in two more minutes had him stark naked and spread out on the bed like a sacrificial male virgin.

"Aye, that's more like it, laddie," Flo said.

"You're not Irish."

"And you're not English but you wear an English tweed."

She pulled off her clothes and eased down beside him.

"See how gentle I am so I don't hurt the poor warrior." She knelt beside him and lowered one breast to his face. "Hungry for a little dessert?" He chewed contentedly for a minute. Then she moved back and put her face close to his.

"Let's do something wicked and dangerous tonight, something wild and misguided, something absolutely wanton."

Spur put his hands under his head and let his gaze wash over her face and what of her naked body he could see without moving.

"What suggestions do you have?"

"I do have a young friend I share many things with. If you like I can go bring her in. She's seventeen, bright and nicely formed."

Spur shook his head. "I think one fine lady will be all I can handle tonight, even with the wine and cheese. Perhaps some other time."

"We could do it around the world. You ever done around the world before?"

Spur frowned. "Not that I know of. Explain."

"We pick out six countries, and then we make love in a fashion that's typical of that nation. We start with me on top for the first country, America. Then we go on to England and the proper missionary position. From there we bounce to France and we do it eating up one another."

Spur grinned. "I hope we get to Russia."

"That's next. You hit all three spots in one go round, and it's like a Russian bear. Then comes China, and we wind up in Mexico to the tunes of a mariachi band."

"We have to go in order?" Spur asked. His hands found her breasts and began caressing them, feeling the heat of them build and build.

"Hell, we can do them in any order you want to," she said, her breath coming in panting gulps now, her hands working on his erection, teasing him, stroking him.

"Stay on top," Spur said, and Flo gave a little cry of joy and moved down to position herself over his thrusting hips. She found the right place, held his erection straight up and eased down on him, his prick slashing upward into her slot until their pelvic bones ground together.

Flo let out a long low moan as they slid together. She kissed him and kept her mouth covering his as she lifted upward with her hips and dropped down on him. Her hips pounded against his, her mouth gasping for air as the whirlwind of her passion steamrolled over her, grinding her, shaking her body.

"Oh, my gawd!" Flo shouted. She gave one more powerful thrust of her slender hips and collapsed on top of him like a billowing tablecloth settling down on a rocky picnic spot.

She lay there panting. He figured she was nearly unconscious after her series of climaxes. He stirred, but she remained the same. He lifted one of her hands and let it go and it fell lifeless to the bed.

"My God, one fuck and she dies right on top of me," he said.

She giggled.

"Guess I'll have to get this ton of sexy flesh and bones and holes off me."

She rolled to the left of the bed. A moment later she sat up, worry clouding her face.

"My gawd, I didn't let you have your turn."

"Relax, I did mine while you were far out in space somewhere past our sun. How was your flight?"

"So good, you'll never know, because I can't describe it in mere words. I'd need an artist's pallet and a full stage of actors and musicians and dancers to show you how fine it was."

"What's left? Sounds like you experienced it all."

Flo shook her head. "No, no, no. Not all. I just can't wait for China's turn."

Spur had his hands clasped behind his head again. It gave him a strange sense of mastery. He didn't understand why. "China. You're waiting for China? We can't possibly get there until we hit France where we eat to our soul's content. Hey, naked lady, I sure as hell ain't gonna miss France."

Chapter Nine

Spur McCoy lay in his bed taking stock as the light at last turned dawn into day.

The lady had left sometime before.

His arm still hurt like fire and had awakened him.

His belly and chest felt better but still hurt with certain movements.

He was getting old, over 30 now.

Damn, what a night! He didn't care if he saw another naked lady for two or three days, at least.

They had tried to kill him twice now. He was stepping on some mighty big toes.

He wished he knew who the toes belonged to.

He had the name of Red Kenny to try to get some answers.

The initials on the note—J.F.—might be the real

thing or a fake. It was a possible second lead.

It was almost six A.M. and he should be getting up.

Spur McCoy summed it all up in a rush.

"Get your body out of bed, shaved, dressed and fed. Then see where Red Kenny lives and track the bastard down." He nodded. It sounded good saying it out loud.

It was nearly an hour later that he left the Home Café. Terri, the owner, had a big sign up about the basket social for the *Clarion*. Good. Now who would know where to find Red Kenny? The postmaster. He or she would know most everyone in town.

When he walked into the Benscoter General Store, he saw a new man behind the counter.

"Yes sir, what can we do for you today?"

"Is the postmaster around?"

"Mr. Ferris was called out of town. Just not sure when he's coming back. Mr. Benscoter made me the acting manager for the time being. That means I have to do the mail, too. Not a big job, but I like it."

The man speaking was not a day over 21 and had an open, honest face and what sounded like an ounce or two of common sense.

"Maybe you can answer my question. I'm looking for Red Kenny, big guy with red hair. You know where he works or where he lives?"

"Stayed at Ma Carlson's boarding house last I knew. Big Red is a man hard to miss. You might try Ma. She's the blue-trimmed white house a block up from the Pine Grove Bank on the corner of Main and Third."

"Obliged," Spur said and hiked out the door and down toward Third Street.

Ma Carlson shook her head. "Sorry, Red ain't

here. Was here up to yesterday, but he said he had a new job in Phoenix and had to get right down there. Gone lock, stock and britches."

"Well, reckon I won't talk to him any, that being the case. Thanks for your time."

He walked back to Main and leaned against the corner of a building and pondered his situation for a minute. Not a damn sight better than it had been when he woke up. Spur pushed away from the building, strolled up the street and into the *Clarion* tent. When Gypsy saw him she rushed up, threw her arms around him for a tight hug, then kissed his lips hard and fast and stepped back.

"Thank you, thank you, thank you! That idea about the basket social benefit is catching fire. Half the merchants have up signs and have stacks of flyers and are really getting behind the idea. I have you to thank for the whole thing."

"Well, another kiss and hug would be nice. That was so fast it didn't count."

Gypsy grinned. "I think you like this kissing stuff."

"I confess."

She reached up and without touching him kissed his lips with a light, gentle touch like a soft summer breeze. It stirred him more than anything had in a long time.

"Now the hug," he said with a hoarseness creeping into his voice. She put her arms around him, pushed her breasts firmly against his chest and lay her head on his shoulder. He guessed her eyes had closed. She held the hug longer than he thought she would, then she sighed and let go and stepped back. Her eyes glistened.

"So, that's part payment. I'm so excited about the box social I can hardly get any work done. Oh, you didn't make it back last night to help on the flyers. I hope you have a good excuse."

"I'll bring a note from my mother," he said, and they both grinned.

"Mike left on the morning stage. The press is all ready to go as soon as I get regular paper stock and a five gallon can of ink."

"Where can you get that?"

"Mike said he'd ask the paper in Phoenix if they'll lend me some paper and ink. I usually order it out of a supply house in San Francisco. Takes about a week to get here even on the train and stage."

"So another small paper this week?"

"Yes. Any progress on the fire?"

"Not much. I had a lead, but he suddenly left town for a job in Phoenix."

"That sounds familiar. Papa used to say that sometimes when he was chasing down a story."

"Right now I'm chasing in circles." Spur walked back and forth in the confines of the tent and finally what had been digging away at the back of his mind but never quite surfacing came out.

"Gypsy, did you father ever do any work at home? Did he have a small desk there or a table where he left things?"

"Yes, a small desk in the living room, a secretary I think it's called. He said it was for home things, not business."

"Sometimes the two get mixed up a little. Can we take a look at it?"

"Right now or after dinner tonight? No, damn, this is press day if I ever get this story finished. How about right now?"

"Better than fine."

When they reached the house, she showed him the desk in the living room. It had a swing down lid that served as a writing table. Above were two glass doors in front of four shelves for knick knacks and below three drawers for storage.

"Papa told me he kept some records and important papers here."

"I'm hoping he left some of his notes or information about the big story he was working on."

"You take all the time you want. I haven't had a chance to go through it yet. I better get back to the paper."

"You're leaving a stranger alone in your house?"

She smiled and walked up to him slowly, letting her breasts sway and bounce as she came. "Hey, cowboy, you're not a stranger. I've kissed you twice, and you're a Secret Service man. How can I lose?"

"Maybe by getting kissed again."

"Deal!" she said and pressed against him and lifted her face for his kiss. Her eyes closed and she sighed and clung to him after the hot kiss ended.

"Oh, damn, McCoy, you turn my knees into jelly and make me feel so wonderful I don't want to leave your arms." She leaned back and looked at him. "Yes, I know a girl shouldn't tell a man he affects her that way. I'm new at this loving. Give me a little time to learn what to do and what not to do." She shook her head and stepped back. "Oh, damn," she said softly, then turned and ran out of the house.

He watched her go with a smile. Some little woman. She had aroused him in that short exchange. True, she should be more careful talking that way when she was in a man's arms.

He shook his head, sat down and began the job of going through the dead man's desk. He found some things that surprised him, but so far nothing that would give a clue about the big money swindle he was afraid was about to take place in town.

He had finished going through the drawers and had two more small pigeonholes to search when he came across a note scrawled on a piece of newsprint.

"Check county clerk for legal owners on commercial property." Below those words were these notes: "31 commercial properties. Owner of 17—Benscoter. Owner of 14 houses—Benscoter."

Spur stared at the notes. Why did Pinnick check out who owned what in town? He seemed only to be interested in which buildings and business firms Benscoter owned. Was that part of the Swindle or had something to do with it?

Spur didn't know but he saved the notes on the properties. Was it a waste of time? He wasn't sure and couldn't be until he had a meeting with Benscoter and evaluated the man himself.

"Oh, damn," he said softly the same way Gypsy had said earlier. He needed some kind of a break in this case. He was damned if he was going to let it beat him.

J. Lawton Benscoter glared at Loophole Larson who was sprawled in the chair on the other side of the cherry wood desk.

"What the hell do you mean Jessie wasn't on the morning stage to Phoenix? He's a walking dynamite bomb just looking for an excuse to go off. You saw what he said in that damned note. He was ready to sell us out for immunity. The little bastard would have dumped us right into prison to save his own neck. He's got to be out of town on the afternoon stage or else."

"J. Lawson, don't threaten me. I've been worked over by experts and they didn't find a chink in my armor. Look at it this way. I didn't just stop a prison sentence for you. I delivered into your hands a new partner—me."

Loophole stood, put his hands on the desk and glared down at the businessman. "Benscoter, I'm giving notice right now. I'm not risking prison for any damn ten percent. I know the sheriff is in, and that makes three of us. I want a third of the take. We split it three ways."

"Not a chance. The sheriff and I are the ones at risk. We could go up for a long time. You're just on the fringes of the conspiracy. Jury wouldn't hurt you much. This is foolishness. You advised us on the methods, we did the deed. Not acceptable at all. Forget it."

"Benscoter, you're forgetting something. I didn't send Jessie to Phoenix because I own him. He's mine. I can dust him off and take him to the district attorney any time I want to. I can telegraph the State Attorney General, tell him the situation and have you and Sheriff Willard behind bars in a day and a half."

"You threatening me?" Benscoter said, disbelief bursting out all over his face.

"Damn right. Either I get a third of the profits, or you and Willard go to prison. Take your choice."

Sweat seeped down Benscoter's balding head, running into his eyes. His face distorted, and he bellowed with rage.

"Damnit, Loophole, we had a deal, an agreement."

"On your terms. I did my work, now I want my fair share. I can get immunity from the attorney general by turning in you two. Jessie and I will both testify and you won't stand a chance. Take your choice."

Benscoter tried to calm himself. Storming into a bigger rage wouldn't help any. Loophole was tricky, sneaky. He knew that. This was the first time that it had been used against him. He tried to compose himself.

"Loophole, damnit, I hate this, but I can see your point. As a conspirator you stand to get the same sentence I would. You take the risk, you should get the benefits. All right. I agree. You get your share, one-third, after we pay off Jessie." Benscoter held out his sweaty hand. "Agreed?"

Loophole laughed, grabbed the hand and shook it. "Damn right, partner. How much do you think this should involve over the long run?"

"I'd say at least a hundred and fifty thousand dollars, more or less. That would mean fifty thousand for you."

Loophole laughed again. "Damn but that sounds good. At last I'm going to make some real money."

"Now, this brings up the problem of Jessie. Will it be enough to send him to Phoenix? What do you think, Loophole?"

"I been considering that. He tried to double-cross us by going to that Secret Service agent. He had the note written and was going to the hotel to deliver it when you caught him. Maybe we don't need him anymore."

"True, his part in the scheme is over. Friday morning it should all be completed and we'll be rich," Benscoter said.

"Then why not make sure he doesn't tell anybody—ever?"

Benscoter stared at Loophole. "You take care of that little task. You have him."

"Me? Hell, no. I don't do that kind of thing. Not a chance. I could hire somebody, but I wouldn't know where to look."

"You found the two riflemen to go after Spur McCoy on short notice."

"Lucky chance, J. Lawton. I'd rather leave this sort of thing up to you so it gets done right."

"Hell, Loophole, you're a full partner now. You should be doing your share of the work and take more risks." Benscoter stood, walked to the door and came back. He shook his head. "Hell, Loophole, I guess I can find somebody. I'll get it done. You bring Jessie here, up the back stairs. We can put him in that back room without any windows until it gets dark."

"Yeah, sounds good, J. Lawton. I'll go get him right now. Won't take fifteen minutes. Meet me at the head of the stairs."

"Disguise him somehow. A big hat or something. We don't want anybody happen to see him brought up those back stairs."

Loophole nodded. "I'll be back in fifteen minutes."

When the lawyer left, J. Lawton Benscoter scowled and wrote two names down on a pad—Jessie and Loophole. He drew a thick black line through Jessie's name and hesitated over the next one. He lay down the pencil.

Now he had to come up with a reliable man to do the job on Jessie. It would be better if no one ever found the body. One of the sinks or one of those little lakes to the north in the mountains. Yes, that sounded good. Some chain and some heavy rocks should do it for 20 years. By then he didn't care who found the skeleton.

J. Lawton took a deep breath. Yes, things were

moving along a little faster than he thought they might. Not exactly what he expected, but with a lawyer as smart as Loophole, he should have figured there would be complications.

He decided on the man he wanted. Plenty of time to notify him. He'd be at the Blue Goose, holding down the bar. Good man, but he drank a little. Hell, everyone drank a little.

Benscoter reached in the bottom drawer of his desk, took out a .45 derringer and slid it in his jacket pocket. It hardly showed. He liked to be armed now and then, especially when dealing with unpredictable men. He hadn't the slightest idea that Jessie would turn yellow on him. Damn. Now Loophole was kicking up his heels. Time would tell.

He heard a buggy coming round as he stood on the top of the back stairs up to his offices. Those back stairs sure had come in handy dozens of times.

When the rig pulled in Loophole got out, went to the other side and helped a man down. Benscoter couldn't tell who the man was. He appeared to be in pain. A large hat on his head shaded his face so Benscoter didn't recognize Jessie even though he knew it had to be him.

Loophole half-carried the smaller Jessie up the steps. Benscoter unlocked a room halfway along the corridor and all three went in. Benscoter lit a lamp on a small dresser. There was a single bed with mattress and blankets. A chamber pot showed under the bed. The room was ten feet square and had no windows and the one door.

Benscoter pulled the hat off Jessie Ferris's head. The man's hands were tried behind him. Benscoter backhanded him without warning, and

Jessie's head snapped to the left.

"Bastard!" Benscoter roared. "You tried to sell me out. If Loophole hadn't found you in time, we'd all be in jail by now. You damned fucking ingrate!" Benscoter's right fist slashed into Jessie's jaw, jolting him sideways. He stumbled and fell on the bed.

"Don't worry about screaming," Benscoter said, his breath coming fast, his face red from the fury. "You'll have a gag on soon enough."

Benscoter turned to Loophole. "Now that we have him here, are there any other traitors running around I don't know about?"

Loophole grinned and shook his head. "Hell, not a one. Just the three of us left. Sheriff ain't going nowhere, and neither am I. We just wait until Friday afternoon and start collecting."

Loophole paused. "Oh, you find the right man for the job?"

"I did," Benscoter said. "One I can trust and have trusted before, not one to see a chance to blackmail me and get away with a lot of my hard-earned cash."

Loophole frowned. "Hey, J. Lawton, you aren't insinuating that I was disloyal to you? Oh, God!"

J. Lawton Benscoter stood four feet from the lawyer who could see the derringer in the merchant's hand with the muzzle pointed directly at him.

"You really didn't think I'd let you blackmail me like this, did you, Loophole? You know me better than that. You got too big for your own good. Just because you can hoodwink and cheat and con these common folks around here is no reason to think you can do the same thing to me. I offered you a reasonable wage for your efforts.

You would have made fifteen thousand dollars. No, you wanted more."

"J. Lawton, I can't believe you're doing this. I'm your friend."

"I have no friends."

"I'm your lawyer. We've worked together for ten years."

"You've sponged off me for ten years."

Loophole began to sweat. Moisture popped out on his forehead and made little rivers down to his eyes and nose.

"What can I do, J. Lawton, to set this right? I'll go back to the ten percent. Fine. I can do that. I'll work for you for a year with no fee at all. Any legal work you need. Just don't leave me here."

"You don't have a chance in hell, Loophole. You betrayed me just as much as Jessie there did."

Loophole must have thought he saw a chance. He looked to the side, then when he must have thought Benscoter's eyes also turned that way, the tall lawyer charged the shorter, heavier man. The derringer fired. The round struck the lawyer in his belly. Loophole stumbled forward into Benscoter, his weight driving the smaller man back a foot. The muzzle of the small gun jammed into Loophole's chest.

Benscoter regained his balance and pulled the trigger again. The .45 caliber round smashed through a rib and rammed into the lawyer's heart, killing him in a second and a half.

J. Lawton Benscoter pushed the corpse away from him and let it fall to the floor. He turned the gun on the small man lying on the bed, his face white, his eyes wild with fear.

A moment later Jessie Ferris vomited on the floor, retching again and again.

J. Lawton Benscoter decided not to put a gag on the small man. It was nearing five o'clock. Everyone would have gone home soon. He had to get to the Blue Goose and tell his man he had a small job for him. Benscoter scowled and looked at the dead body on the floor. No, not one job—two jobs for him to do.

Chapter Ten

Spur McCoy walked the dusty streets of Pine Grove wondering what he should do next. He had to see J. Lawton Benscoter sooner or later to set his mind at ease. He should stop by at the courthouse and inquire of the county clerk about who owned certain properties in town.

He also had a commitment to help Gypsy run off the paper tonight on the proof press. He didn't even want to think how many times he would have to push that heavy roller back and forth to create the small newspapers. Only four pages tonight she said, so that was four times the number of issues—200? Already his arms hurt.

He settled for the courthouse and found the county clerk's office.

The clerk's office was filled with large volumes of records that held a detailed account on every piece of property in the county that had been bought, sold, a lien filed against or any legal action taken against. It listed chapter and verse on all of them.

The county clerk was a heavy-set man with a forward jutting chin and small black eyes not wide enough apart. His brows grew together in the middle, and his black hair licked at his forehead as if trying to take over new territory.

"You want to know what?"

"Wondered how many pieces of property are owned in the county by J. Lawton Benscoter."

"You a reporter or something?"

"No, just interested."

"Oh, yeah, now I got it. You're that government lawman who's been nosing around. Don't have to look up the legals on Benscoter. Fact is the paper's publisher—ex-publisher I figure I should say—came in two weeks ago asking the same question. He put in about two days going over the volumes. Came up with seventeen business firms and fourteen houses."

"That seems like a lot," Spur said.

"I don't judge, just keep the books all legal and square and in order like I'm supposed to. Used to be a county clerk back in Illinois. Not much different here, just fewer people and fewer pieces of property. Most of it is still federal land. Lots will go to the state if and when we ever get enough people to qualify."

"How many does it take?"

"Sixty thousand souls in the state, and got to have all regular elected officials. Hell, we got the counties and officers. All we need is more people."

"Any idea how Benscoter got all these properties?"

"Ain't my job to know. I just record the transactions." The clerk looked up, squinting one eye. "Official or unofficial?"

"Oh, unofficial, by all means."

"Some folks say he cheated a few out of their houses. He runs the bank, too, you know. Then he foreclosed on a couple of business firms that didn't quite make a go of it. All legal and proper, just in a shitty way on some of them. Couple of months overdue on payments and—Wham, he forecloses."

The clerk closed one of the big books that held the records.

"Anything else I can do for you?"

"Can't think of a thing."

"See you spending time with that sweet little Gypsy. You planning on needing a marriage license, I issue them here."

"Not in my plans, but thanks."

Spur grinned as he left the courthouse and stopped by the sheriff's office. A deputy said the sheriff was gone for the day and would be in about ten the next morning.

It was five o'clock. Spur headed for the Benscoter building, went up to the second story and pushed open the unlocked door of the office of Benson Properties.

Alice had just finished clearing her desk for the day. She looked up and smiled. "Yes, sir, what can I do for you?"

"I'd like to see Mr. Benscoter. Is he in?"

"I believe he's still here. Just a moment. Who should I say is calling?"

"Spur McCoy."

She nodded and went through the door marked private after a quick knock. Spur could not hear any conversation through the door. He looked around the reception area and saw two chairs, a soft couch, a vase with some nearly wilted flowers and two framed prints on the walls. The place had touches of quality.

Alice came out the door and nodded. "Mr. Benscoter will see you, Mr. McCoy, but he has only five minutes. There's a meeting he has to get to. this way, please."

He went into the office. It had a carpet on the floor, curtains at the large windows, a sofa at one side with several pillows and a large desk and leather chair. Benscoter stood behind the desk but didn't offer to shake hands.

"Yes, Spur McCoy. I've heard you were in town. You're some kind of a federal lawman?"

"Yes, Mr. Benscoter, I'm with the Secret Service. We're empowered with jurisdiction in every state and territory as well as the unimproved lands across the West."

"What can I do for you?"

Plenty, Spur thought, if you only would. "I'm interested in the death of Andrew Pinnick. I've encouraged the sheriff to reopen the case since it is reported that coal oil was used to start fires at both the front and back doors of the newspaper office at the same time, trapping Pinnick inside. That's murder. Denying Pinnick his ability to exercise his freedom of the press rights is violating his civil rights, also a felony and a federal crime. I'm wondering what you've heard about the case."

Not a flicker of an eyelash, no intake of breath, no nervous hand movements. Either Benscoter had nothing to hide or was a master at controlling himself.

"Pinnick, yes, he's been here a while. He and I never saw eye to eye on everything, but he did put out a good paper. He was concerned about the city, about our people. A lot of things we did agree on, like when the railroad built as far as Phoenix and stopped. They had grade surveys all the way to Flag, but claimed it was too expensive to build and their land grants from the government for putting down the rails weren't big enough for this tough mountainous country. We both fought them on that a few years ago, and we lost."

Spur waved one hand to get Benscoter's attention. "I'd say you both were on a tough nut on that issue. Any reason you can think of why somebody would kill Pinnick?"

"Been doing some thinking on that. He was a prominent man in town. I'm a bit of a prominent man as well. Wondering if somebody has his sights on me. Not that I worry about it. Just a thought."

Spur had made up his mind and stood up. "Well, I better be moving on. Have a few more people to talk to. Good to meet you." Spur didn't offer to shake hands and neither did Benscoter.

Outside, Spur walked down the steps to Main and wandered down the boardwalk. He came to a place where there was a vacant lot for someone to build on. Since there was no store there, there was no boardwalk in front of the lot. Each store owner put up his own boardwalk out front. On hills the boardwalks sometimes mismatched and were not level.

Here, Spur stepped down to the dirt, went across it and up to the boardwalk on the other side in front of the bank. Benscoter owned that, too.

His impression of the town's richest man was not favorable. The man was a talker, a salesman of the first order, and with that gift of gab, he could sell a lot of things that shouldn't be sold.

Spur simply didn't trust the man. He had a feeling in his gut that he was looking at an enemy, but he had no proof what-so-ever. He wasn't afraid of Benscoter, but he knew he was a man to watch.

Spur turned and walked back to the Pine Grove Hotel, slipped into the dining room and had the specialty of the day, elk steak with a special sauce. The elk was cooked exactly right, not over-done. It was the best elk steak he had eaten in years. Somebody had bled the big animal soon after killing it to keep the blood from seeping into the meat.

He had some of the newfangled ice cream sprinkled with fresh strawberries. By the time he got to his room he was ready for a quick nap before he decided what to do for the evening.

Just as he put his key in his door, Flo came out of a room down the hall and waved at him. He closed his eyes. Not tonight, he implored. He wasn't in that good of shape.

Flo timed it perfectly. She walked toward him, and the minute he stepped into his room, she slid in after him and closed the door.

"I've missed you," she said.

"How could you? It's only been about ten hours."

"Hours and minutes mean little to me. I live for the moment."

"Good. Tell me about your husband. I just met him and had a short, unsweet talk. He's rich, I know, but what does he do all day to take up his time?"

"Plans how he can get richer."

"Does he ever talk about his plans?"

"We don't talk a lot. Now and then he tries out an idea on me to see how I react."

"What kind of ideas?"

"Moneymaking schemes. Once he had a mortgage on the hardware store. He wanted the store, since it was making money. He started a whispering campaign that the owner had been a rebel captain during the war in charge of a prison camp where a lot of Yanks died. The man's business fell off. Then he spread rumors about the man's wife, said she slept around. The man was furious. His business suffered. J. Lawton came up with one little plan after another to harass the man, and he got so worried and confused that he forgot to make a mortgage payment. J. Lawton pounced, and the next day he foreclosed on the note. The man couldn't pay up, so J. Lawton took the business and has been running it ever since."

"Your husband sounds like a real winner."

"He is, if you like money. I do. I like money and what it can buy, and I like a man hot and sweating, pumping away on top of me. Why are you looking at me that way?"

"Because I'm too tired and too sore and my arm hurts too much where I was shot. Which means no sex tonight."

"Oh, fuck!"

"Figured you'd be understanding about my condition."

"So what do you want to do tonight?"

"We could search your husband's office."

"Yeah?"

"You could help get me inside and we could see what kind of dirty tricks he's working up. Does he spend much time in his office at night?"

"Not usually. He puts in time at the Blue Goose, his saloon. He plays cards in the back room and plays with a fucking whore's tits when he isn't at the card table."

"Do you want to?"

"Want to make love right now? Fuck, yes."

"No, do you want to help me search his office?"

"Oh." She shrugged. "I guess so. Might be exciting. I've never done any burglary before. We going to steal money from his safe?"

"No, just look through the place. I think something big is about to happen in Pine Grove. I think your husband is behind it or has a hand in it. Something must be written down."

Flo stood and opened her blouse, letting her breasts swing out, and then walked up to Spur. "Kiss my girls a little first, just to make them feel better. They figured on a wild fucking time tonight."

He bent and kissed them, then nibbled at the brown nipples until she squealed.

"Oh, yeah, my girls like that. Now, you want to break in or use my key to the back door?"

They stood in deep shadows 50 feet from the back stairs of the Benscoter building. When first they came up the alley they had seen a buggy leaving.

"Did that rig leave from your husband's building?" Spur asked.

"I didn't see it any better than you did. Nobody's around now if they did come from there. No lights on front or back. Let's go up there and play."

They walked the rest of the way through the alley and went up the back steps as if they belonged there. Flo dug a key out of her reticule, and Spur opened the back door. When they stepped inside Spur touched her shoulder to keep her still as he listened.

He heard nothing. "Where's his office? Toward the front?" She nodded and led the way down a short hall to a door. She pushed it open. Inside the room had only one window that faced the side of a two story building three feet away.

"Nobody from the street could see a light in here," Flo said. "What are you hunting for?"

"I don't know. When I find it, I'll let you hear."

Spur struck a match, found a lamp and lit it, then turned it down low. He put it on the big desk and pulled out drawers looking for files, papers, notes, anything. He found a bottle of Scotch whiskey, a derringer that had recently been fired, and a lot of papers, cards and envelopes.

On top of the desk sat a small square cardboard box three inches deep. In it were papers and two pencils. Some of the papers were fastened together with a straight pin pushed through two places.

One was a contract to buy a piece of property west of town. Another was an agreement to furnish water from a runoff stream to a farmer's small acreage. Spur sat in the big chair behind the desk and shook his head. He had no idea what he was hunting.

"I'll be damned. Look at this," Flo said. She brought it over closer to the light. It was a small poster like one Spur had seen in San Francisco's Chinatown. It showed 116 different sexual positions featuring well-endowed oriental men and women.

"J. Lawton, you old dog. We'll just have to try some of these. Damn, wish I could keep this. He'd miss it. Maybe I can take it now and bring it back later. Yes!"

Spur made one more look, this time through some files in a long box. He found documents about houses and buildings and businesses, but that was about it. He was just ready to turn out the lamp and give up when he saw an envelope sticking out from under a blotter on the big desk. He pulled it out and looked at it.

In the upper left-hand corner was the return address. It was county stationery. The hand-written name on the envelope was not that of Benscoter. Stamped on the envelope was an official post office mark that read "Registered". In an empty box was a handwritten number in ink.

What was a registered letter to Amos K. Rondell doing in Benscoter's office, mostly hidden under a blotter? He noticed that the end of the envelope had been cut off.

Gently, Spur shook out the letter inside, and he and Flo both read it.

It was handwritten on county letterhead. It said: "Mr. Amos K. Rondell, this is your third notice that your property is in default on county taxes. If your arrears bill is not paid in full by Friday, June 23, the county will take appropriate legal action."

There was a the legal description of the property, and the statement that he owed $146 in back taxes. Then the letter was signed by the county treasurer.

"This mean anything to you?" Flo said.

Spur frowned. Something seemed to register far back in his mind, but it slipped away. He wrote down the name and address and the amount of the tax and the registered number, then put the letter in the envelope and the envelope back under the blotter.

"Let's get out of here. I just struck out again. One of these damn days I'm going to have to hit a homerun or I'll get thrown off the team."

"You're still at bat on my team," Flo said trying to rub his crotch. He leaned away from her.

"Maybe tomorrow. I told you I'm plumb fucked out for today."

"Damn, Spur, you ain't no fun no more."

"Woman, when a body hurts, it just isn't fun."

They slipped out the back door of the office, made sure the door was locked and went down the rear steps.

At the bottom, they went down the alley where Flo pulled Spur to a stop and kissed him.

"Spur, violating J. Lawton's office just made me all sexy as hell. How about a quick one, standing up, right here? Nobody ever comes through this alley. Hey, you ever fucked in public this way before? A real kick, a wild thrill. Makes me shiver just thinking about it. Come on, spoil-sport, just a quick one right here, right now."

She backed against the wall of a building in the shadows. Flo lifted her long skirt and bunched it around her waist. She caught his hand and pulled him over to her.

Flo put his hand to her crotch. Spur laughed softly. "You ain't wearing a damn thing under your dress."

"So, take advantage of the chance, right now. Might not happen like this ever again."

Spur McCoy was suddenly so sexually excited he could hardly keep from shivering. He ripped open the buttons on his fly and pulled out his penis. He had a full erection. Flo giggled, then leaned against the wall, laced her fingers together behind his neck, jumped up and fastened her legs around his back.

"You've done it this way before," Spur said.

"Once or twice, but never outside in public. Come on, Spur, right now, fuck me hard."

It was an offering that Spur could not turn down.

Chapter Eleven

Spur McCoy and Flo left the alley laughing softly and feeling like teenage kids who did something naughty in public.

"That was a first for me," Spur said. He studied the woman beside him who so recently had been one driving, grinding mass of sexual excitement.

"I'm not in the habit of copulating in public places either. What a hoot!"

"Oh, damn!" Spur said.

"What, what?"

"I forgot I had an appointment tonight. Sorry I have to just fuck and run, but it's important."

"Hell, I got the best part of you. Run along. Maybe we'll get together again, like tomorrow."

"Maybe. I have to go." He turned and hurried up Main Street. He saw Flo sticking to the shadows as she walked in the opposite direction. He realized he had no idea where she lived, where the Benscoter house was.

He forgot about that when he saw the lights on in the *Clarion* tent ahead. He looked inside, but saw no one. Around the side of the tent he saw three lamps where the proof press had been positioned in the center of the burned-out newspaper office.

There he saw Gypsy rolling the heavy proof press cylinder. He walked back, calling out from the darkness to let her know he was coming.

"Hello, there. I'm late." He walked into the light. She had a smudge of ink on her nose, another on her right cheek. She blew a stand of her long hair out of her eyes and frowned at him.

"You are extremely late, but then so am I. I haven't even finished the first page yet. You're welcome to help, if you want to."

"Why I came."

He watched her put the sheet of paper over the inked type, roll the cylinder across it, peel off the printed page and put it on a box to one side.

"That's all there is to it. If you can do the rolling, I'll put on the sheets and take them off and ink the roller. It'll go faster that way."

Again he compared this sweet young girl to Flo. Their ages weren't all that much different, but the different quality was something to see. Gypsy wore a smock over her dress, but it didn't conceal her good breasts and tight little waist.

"Think you can manage this?"

"I think so. Just make sure I don't flatten your hand against the type."

"Not a chance. I'm faster than that."

They began to print the pages which soon came down to a rhythm, and in five minutes they had finished the first page.

"I'm only doing two hundred copies," Gypsy said. "We won't have time for much more than that. Anyway I'm running out of the small paper. I mooched paper from everyone I knew. Tomorrow I'm going down to Phoenix to try to get some larger paper and a can of ink."

He put the second page on the proof press, and they started the job again. Halfway through she looked up.

"You hear the latest news? Loophole Larson, our town's best lawyer, got himself killed tonight. Evidently it was a brawl in back of a saloon. The barkeep at the Blue Goose said he heard some wild yelling and shots, and by the time he got into the alley, Loophole had two holes in him, one through his heart."

"Is Larson important to help us find the arsonists?"

"He could be. Larson was Benscoter's lawyer. He'd worked with Benscoter on several questionable deals. Papa said he knew something wasn't right with them, but they were legal and there was nothing he could do. Maybe a falling out of thieves?"

"Maybe. But why a back alley brawl? Doesn't quite sound in character for this Larson."

"Not at all in character. But if you've got a body on your hands it makes a good cover-up." Gypsy missed placing the page straight on the type, and he stopped the roll. "Another interesting fact is that Benscoter owns the Blue Goose and can tell his barkeep what to say and what to tell the sheriff."

Spur talked as he rolled the cylinder, printing page two on the back of page one.

"This is starting to pile up evidence against

Benscoter. It must mean we have the wrong man. He's the richest man in town. Someone who does handyman work for him and who hired two shooters to put lead in my body suddenly leaves town. A dead man turns up in back of a saloon he owns, and the barkeep swears he had been inside moments before and went out back to settle an argument or some such.

"Just too much of it. He's either in the wrong place at the wrong time or guilty as hell. Hey, what would you think if I told you I prowled Benscoter's office tonight and found a registered letter addressed to someone else half-hidden on Benscoter's desk?"

"You broke into his office?"

"Not exactly. I used a key. The whole thing wasn't lawful, but nobody is watching me. What about a registered letter?"

"Might have been delivered and the person it was sent to showed it to Benscoter for some reason."

"True, might be. Wouldn't hurt to ask the man it was sent to if he ever got it. Just a hunch I have."

"You always play your hunches?"

"Usually."

"Well, I have a hunch side two is done. Now on to page three."

They finished printing about ten o'clock, then collated the two pages and folded them in half so they would stay together.

"You going to help me deliver them?" Gypsy asked, her eyes sparkling.

"Now? In the middle of the night?"

"Best time, then the subscribers have the paper bright and early in the morning."

"Who gets the papers?"

"Every store and every house as far out as we want to walk."

"No subscribers?"

"Some, but we need the circulation to charge for the advertising. You don't know much about running a newspaper, do you?"

They finished delivering the last of the papers about one A.M. They had covered every door in the town. He walked her back to her porch and collapsed on the front steps.

Gypsy sat down beside him.

"Nice night?"

"Tired night. I'd be more at home delivering those papers on horseback."

"The cowboy who never walks when he can ride his horse. You're not really a cowboy."

"Did a trail drive once, about a hundred miles. Enough to make me know I didn't want to do it again."

"What now?"

"Oh, something you might know. I got a note from somebody with the signature of J.F. You know anybody in town with those initials?"

"Mmmm, let me think. F. That could be Feldon, Franklin or Fife. No, wrong first names. Ferris, hey, Jessie Ferris, the postmaster. That's his initials."

"The postmaster. Jessie Ferris went to visit his mother. Isn't in strange how everyone I want to talk to is out of town.

"Or dead. Loophole Larson, for instance."

He stood. "My next visit is going to be to the man who was supposed to have received the registered letter. I've got his name here somewhere." He found the scrap of paper.

"Amos K. Rondell. That name mean anything to you?"

"No, not at the moment. There is a family of Rondells here. I went to school with one of the girls, I think. Yes, they own a little ranch not far out of town. A homestead. Mr. Rondell wasn't much of a farmer but he did prove up on it."

"I'm going to go see Mr. Rondell first thing in the morning. Which direction out of town?"

"South."

When he stood and helped her up, she pushed up close to him.

"Time we get to bed," he said. "In separate beds," he added quickly.

She nodded, leaned in and put her arms around him. He bent and kissed her upturned face. A polite kiss. She made a growling sound in her throat, and he kissed her again like a lover. She sighed when they broke apart.

She looked at him a moment, then put her head on his shoulder.

"That was more like it. Sometimes I dream about you, Spur McCoy. Sometimes. But not tonight, I'm too tired."

She reached up, brushed her lips across his, stepped into her house and closed the door.

The next morning, Spur rented a horse, got directions to Amos K. Rondell's small ranch and rode out. The fresh green of the pines invigorated him. He loved the open country. Two grouse kicked out of some brush and took off with a furious flapping of wings. He trained an imaginary shotgun at them and fired. He would have nailed the second one.

The ranch house was little more than a one room cabin with a lean-to on the back. No barn, no corral. He found a one row walking plow and a fenced pasture for three cows and a pair of young steers. Meat and milk. A big garden was next to a small stream that wound its way down the slope.

A big dog barked a greeting as Spur stepped down from his mount. The screen door slammed and a man in overalls and a faded wide-brimmed hat came out of the side door. He carried a rifle over one arm, aimed at the ground.

"Morning," Spur said. "Mr. Rondell?"

"The same. Who you be?"

"Name's Spur McCoy. I'm a federal lawman. I need to ask you a few questions if you've got a moment."

"Got all day. Mind sitting outside here?"

Spur said he didn't, and they sat on a log across a sawhorse.

"Hear your homestead is all proved up," Spur said.

"About the size of it."

Rondell was a man with arms and legs that didn't seem attached right. He was loose-limbed and lean with a full beard in need of trimming. His hair had been long, Spur guessed, but now had been chopped off around the back to collar length.

"What about taxes, Mr. Rondell, your county taxes? Have you been paying them every year?"

"Taxes? Don't understand much about that. Figure I done my bit by proving up the land and it's mine. Don't need to pay nobody for owning it."

"There are county land taxes, Mr. Rondell. That's how the county raises enough money to hire a sheriff and county recorder and the essentials of county government."

"Don't vote for none of them, so don't reckon I got to pay taxes to them."

Spur nodded. Just what he had been afraid of. "Mr. Rondell, what I'm going to ask you is extremely important. Think about your answer before you tell me. Have you received in the mail in the last two or three weeks a letter from the county that was registered? That means you have to sign your name for the letter on a slip of paper at the post office. Did you sign for and pick up a letter like that lately?"

"Nosiree. Even if one of them registered ones come, I don't collect it. Don't take any mail with the county's name on it. Nope, don't believe in no county."

"You're sure you didn't sign your name on a receipt for a registered letter from the county?"

"Damn sure, son. Told you once. Don't like to chew my cud twice."

"Then nobody has told you that you owe the county a hundred and forty-six dollars in back taxes."

"No sir. Don't pay taxes. Ain't right."

Spur nodded. "Seems like a man should own what he owns, but that isn't always the case. Do you know that if you don't pay the taxes, the county sheriff can sell your homestead, land, house, the whole thing? Sell it to the highest bidder over a hundred and forty-six dollars?"

"Nope, don't know that. Anybody tries to move in or move me off got about three rifles and two shotguns aimed right down their gut to stop them."

"I'm sorry about this, Mr. Rondell, but it's the way our laws are written. I just wanted to find out if you received the letter or not. There's some skullduggery going on in town, and I'm trying to put a stop to it."

"Good, but I'm still not paying any damn taxes.

My land, I proved it up. The United States government said I own it. Got me the paper in the house there."

Spur stood and nodded. "I'm due back in town. Somebody will be out to talk to you about the taxes again. Don't shoot them. Talk with them. Make some payments and do it all in time. Otherwise you could lose your 'stead here."

Spur waved and stepped into his saddle. So the registered letter was never delivered. Were they mailed? As he rode back he knew that one was mailed—Rondell's. It had a stamp on it and a hand canceled postmark. Were other letters sent? The county treasurer was the man to ask.

Spur couldn't wait to get back to the courthouse to ask the treasurer about it.

A little over an hour later, county treasurer Paul Sedgwick nodded. "Absolutely, Mr. McCoy. I addressed about half of those letters myself. I personally selected the forty-seven county citizens who were at least two years in arrears on their tax payments and sent them letters showing the amount. The letter also warned them that appropriate legal action would be taken if they did not respond within fifteen days. I send out letters like this every year. Strange this year, though. Not a single one of those forty-seven has responded. Seems damn strange now that I think of it."

"Did you mail a letter to Amos K. Rondell?"

Treasurer Sedgwick chuckled. "You know our man Amos? Yes, he got a letter. Every two or three years I go out and reason with him. He at last gives in and sends us a beef or some hogs or some grain that we can turn into cash and apply against his taxes. He just doesn't understand about how taxation works."

"All right, I'm getting myself oriented here, Mr. Sedgwick. Now what happens if these forty-seven don't respond by the deadline?"

"Simple. I can turn them over to the county sheriff and instruct him to conduct a sheriff's sale of the properties in question at no less an amount than the taxes owed. Usually this is done with an auction, with the owner of the property free to make a bid. Often a man buys back his own property for the cost of the taxes."

"But anyone can bid?"

"Oh, absolutely. Sometimes I'll hold a property off the sale if the owner in good faith says he's trying to pay or makes a partial payment. We have a certain amount of leeway here."

"You notify the owners by registered mail. Isn't there more to it than that?"

"You bet. Three weeks before the sheriff's sale, the properties have to be listed in an advertisement in the official county newspaper, notifying all property owners that they are behind in their taxes and that a sale will be held if they don't respond."

"Did you place the ad?"

"Oh, yes, right on schedule. In fact I'd say we had it in and the proof approved three days before the paper's deadline."

"Mr. Sedgwick, do you have a copy of the printed advertisement? Isn't that a part of the permanent records you must keep?"

"Yes, indeed. I'm sure it's in the file. Let me take a look." The treasurer went to a wooden filing cabinet and leafed through some folders. He frowned and checked again. When he came back he had a folder with the date on top and opened it.

"Here's the folder with the selected taxpayers

who are in arrears. Also I have a copy of the letter that went out and the date. But nowhere do I find a copy of the advertisement."

"What was the date the ad was supposed to run in the paper?'

"Let's see, it should be here. Yes, it was to run on May 25th."

"I'm not sure, Mr. Sedgwick, but wasn't that just two days after the fire at the *Clarion*? I don't think your ad ever ran. The ad and the copy and the whole paper burned up on May 23rd and killed Mr. Pinnick."

Sedgwick looked at a calendar and scowled. "Damn, you're right."

"Then, Mr. Sedgwick, any sheriff's sale wouldn't be legal, would it? The proper procedure for advertising the indebtedness was not carried out."

Paul Sedgwick's eyes went wide. "But I already certified the properties, all forty-seven of them. They are to be put up for auction this afternoon at four P.M. on the front steps of the courthouse."

"You've got to stop it, Sedgwick. Amos Rondell swears he never received any registered letter from you. I saw the envelope with a postmark on it and your letter inside it on the desk of J. Lawton Benscoter last night. The only way it could have been there is for the postmaster to have stopped delivery on those registered letters. I think he did that and then destroyed the letters. In effect, none of the forty-seven property owners on that list were notified of this sheriff's sale in either of the two ways the law specifies that they must be notified."

"But I can't stop the auction. Once I've certified them to the sheriff, it's out of my hands. Only

the sheriff can call it off once things have gone
this far."

Spur grabbed the treasurer by the arm. "Come
on, Sedgwick. You and I are going to go have a serious talk with Sheriff Ben Willard. It eleven o'clock
already. We don't have much time."

Chapter Twelve

The county treasurer and Spur McCoy rushed down the corridor to the other side of the courthouse where the sheriff's offices were. A lethargic deputy looked up at them when they raced into the room.

"Got to see the sheriff," Sedgwick snapped.

"Sheriff?"

"Yes, Sheriff Willard. Is he here?"

"Oh, the sheriff. Nope, he's not in right now."

"Where did he go?" Spur asked.

"Don't rightly know. Said he'd be back about four o'clock this afternoon. Might try the Blue Goose."

Spur talked quietly with Sedgwick. "He's holed up somewhere until the sale. He's planned it this way. No chance to stop the sale if we can't find him."

"Let's check the Blue Goose," Sedgwick said.

They were halfway there when Spur saw a horse being led down Main Street. The man and horse had a string of six or eight boys chasing after him and pointing. Something had been slung over the back of the horse.

They stopped to watch and soon realized that the horse carried a body, head down, over the saddle.

"Not another body," Spur said. He and the treasurer went out to check. Sedgwick lifted the man's head and grunted.

"Yep, know him. Jessie Ferris, our late postmaster. He must be the one who stopped my registered letters. He must have signed for them as well, forging all of those signatures. If he was in on the conspiracy, somebody made sure he won't talk about it."

"Benscoter. It has to be Benscoter. How does he profit from all of this?"

Sedgwick explained it. "Simple. They have the auction, but nobody knows about it. One man shows up and makes a bid for one dollar over the amount of the tax on each property. The bidder picks up property, buildings, ranches, houses at a tenth or a fiftieth of their value. A lot of folks will protest if this happens. Then all the facts would come out. The lawyers would argue that there was an honest attempt to comply with the law, but the newspaper burned down. Somehow the letters that were mailed in good faith never got delivered. Then the lawyers would argue the case for months, maybe years in the courts. So we have to stop the sheriff somehow before it gets that far."

"Can you give me a list of those property owners, all forty-seven of them, who face the sheriff's sale?

"Why?"

"We need to have them at that auction if it takes place. Then at least they can buy their property back. Exposing the secrecy of the plan just might be enough to topple it. But we have to contact those property owners."

Sedgwick turned around. "Let's go back to the courthouse. Take about ten minutes to get the list together with their addresses. Then I'll go hunting the sheriff."

"You think the sheriff is in on the scheme?"

"He has to be or it wouldn't work."

"All right. You get me that list. I need to send a telegram. Meet you there."

Spur ran to the telegraph office a block down from the courthouse. He sent the wire to the Arizona Territorial Attorney General, in Phoenix.

"Sir. Complete law and order breakdown in Pine Grove. Sheriff Ben Willard engaged in gigantic fraud to hold auction of property for taxes without notifying property owners. Request you send deputy attorney general to take over Sheriff's duties until a new one can be appointed." He signed it Spur McCoy, United States Secret Service Agent, number 0041.

The clerk read it and scowled. "Is this true?"

"Damn right. You know anybody who's delinquent in his property taxes, you better have them get right over to the county courthouse."

Spur paid for the wire and ran back to the courthouse. Sedgwick had the list ready with businesses in one group and homes and ranches in another.

Spur ran to the newspaper and briefed Gypsy. "We've got to notify these people as quickly as we can. You take half the businesses and I'll take the other half, then we'll see if we can find the houses."

"So that's the conspiracy. They burned down the paper so we couldn't publish that list of threatened properties. It was a long list. I prepared the ad, but forgot all about it with the paper burning— and all."

"Right. Now we've got to rush. You ready?"

"Yes, absolutely. We've got to stop this scheme before it ruins those forty-seven families."

They hurried toward the first stores on their list. There were six for each to contact.

Spur talked to the saddle maker and leather shop owner.

"Hell, nobody contacted me. Ain't they supposed to send a registered letter? Did last year."

Spur told the man to be at the courthouse by two o'clock and hurried on to the next one. It was almost an hour later before Spur and Gypsy met back at the newspaper tent.

"Now what about the houses?" Gypsy asked. They divided them so they each had half the town.

"Have the people be at the courthouse at two o'clock," Spur instructed.

It was nearly one o'clock before they both returned to the newspaper.

Spur grinned and kissed her cheek. "Hey, thought you said you were going to Phoenix today to get newsprint."

"I was, but I overslept and missed the stage."

"Good. This is going to be the biggest story of the year. You know somebody found Jessie Ferris shot to death."

"I heard. He must have been the weak link. He must have been the one who wrote that J.F. note asking you to meet him to tell you about the conspiracy."

"So now we have the conspirators for murder as well—Jessie and probably Loophole Larson."

"Then Loophole would have been in on it to steer them around any legal problems," Gypsy said.

"Looks like it. He might have told them by burning down the newspaper they could prove that they tried to have the advertisements run. Then they could claim mailing the letters, since the treasurer did that and would testify accordingly. They just might convince the court the legal requirements had been met. The postmaster was a vital element in the conspiracy."

"Let's get over to the courthouse."

As they walked that way they saw little groups of people and noticed that several of the men had rifles and shotguns. He didn't want this to turn into a mob.

By the time they got to the courthouse, there were 20 people on the steps waiting. The treasurer, Sedgwick, was there talking to the people quietly.

Sedgwick saw Spur and told him he couldn't find the sheriff. "He's hiding out somewhere, waiting to come at the last minute to hold the auction."

"I doubt if the people here will let him do that," Spur said. "We don't want a mob, but I'm not sure we can stop it if it starts to get out of hand. A lot of these people are furious at the underhanded scheme the sheriff tried to pull. They don't know anything about Benscoter, but since he had that registered letter, he has to be one of the main partners."

"Think he'll come and do the bidding?" Gypsy asked.

"Not a chance," Spur said. "He'll send one of his clerks or a dummy of some kind to do his bidding."

The crowd increased in size.

"Where's the sheriff?" somebody bellowed.

"Let's string up the bastard!" another voice screamed.

Spur went to the top of the steps and fired his six-gun twice in the air. That quieted the crowd.

"Listen to me, you people," Spur thundered. By then there were about 100 people milling around the front of the court house. "My name is Spur McCoy. I've met a lot of you. I'm a United States lawman. I work with the Secret Service directly under the president. I came here to get this situation straightened out."

"Then let's do it by hanging the crooked damn sheriff," somebody in the crowd shouted.

"That's exactly what we won't be doing," Spur bellowed. "Two wrongs won't set things right. What we have to do is to stop the sheriff's sale— and do it legally. Then everyone wins. Now settle down, put your guns away, and let's get this done properly. First I have a couple of questions. Was anyone here notified about being delinquent in your taxes in the last two or three weeks by registered letter, the kind you have to sign for to get from the post office? Anybody?"

Not a person raised a hand or called out.

"All right, that's important, because by law, the treasurer must notify you before a sheriff's sale can be held. The treasurer will swear that he mailed the letters at the post office. We believe that the postmaster, Jessie Ferris, who was just found today shot dead, received those letters and then collected them and burned them so they couldn't be delivered."

There were some shouts in the crowd. One man bellowed out clearly. "Good riddance then to the bastard."

"We think the conspirators shot Jessie to keep him quiet. He tried to come forward and tell me about the swindle, but they caught him and killed him. Secrecy about the sheriff's sale was the most important thing. Without it the whole scheme falls apart."

"So where's the sheriff? I want to arrest him and pitch him in his own jail," a man called out from near Spur.

"We're wondering the same thing. One more point. The law also states that before any sale to recover taxes can be made, the delinquent property owners must all be listed in a notice published in the official county newspaper. That's why the conspirators in this case burned down the *Clarion* three weeks ago so the notices couldn't appear."

The telegraph operator came pushing through the crowd and handed Spur an envelope. He opened it and read it then held it up.

"Help is coming. Listen to this. I wired the Attorney General, the top cop in the state. Listen to this: TO SPUR MCCOY, PINE GROVE, ARIZONA. UNDERSTAND YOUR PROBLEM. SENDING MAN TO RUN SHERIFF'S OFFICE ON MORNING STAGE. ARRIVE TOMORROW AFTERNOON. AVOID ANY MOB ACTION. THE LAW WILL PROTECT THE PEOPLE OF PINE GROVE. HARTLEY WESTOVER, ARIZONA TERRITORIAL ATTORNEY GENERAL."

"So let's find the sheriff so he don't get out of town," somebody yelled.

"Spread out, everyone, and search for the no-good. Don't let him get away."

"Remember, no violence," Spur shouted. "If you find him, bring him back here or to the jail."

The crowd broke up. Some moved down the street looking in the saloons. Some went to the sheriff's house. The livery stable man said he wouldn't rent the sheriff a horse or a rig.

"What about Benscoter?" Gypsy asked. "I've a notion that he's the main conspirator behind all this. Let's not let him get away."

"I doubt if he'll be running," Spur said. "He's got too much invested in this town. Let's go pay him a friendly social call."

They went up the steps and knocked on the door to Benscoter's office, then went inside. His secretary looked up from her desk and smiled.

"Miss Pinnick, how nice to see you," she said.

"Is Mr. Benscoter here?" Spur asked.

"Fact is he stepped out about half an hour ago. Told me he had some things to do and would be gone the rest of the afternoon. He didn't mention any specifics. May I help you?"

"No, we need to see him. Any chance that he went home?"

"I doubt it. He's seldom there except at night. Do you wish to leave a message?"

"No, I don't think so," Gypsy said.

Spur stepped forward quickly and opened the door marked private where he had met with Benscoter before.

"See here!" the secretary said.

Spur pulled the door fully open and looked inside. No one was there.

"Just checking," Spur said. Then he and Gypsy went outside.

"Where does he live?" Spur asked.

Gypsy pointed the way. The street was alive with people chattering about the big scandal. Several men still carried shotguns and rifles. Spur heard that two teams of men had left for the north and south roads out of town to prevent the sheriff from escaping that way.

He'd be found sooner or later. Spur wasn't sure what would happen to the sheriff if the crowd turned ugly again. Down two blocks and over one, they found the Benscoter home. It was the biggest house on the block, three stories of wood and glass, well-painted with lush landscaping around it.

Gypsy lifted a heavy brass knocker on the front door and let it fall. They waited a reasonable time, and Spur dropped the knocker three more times. At last someone opened the door.

"Oh, Mrs. Hartung," Gypsy said, "is Mr. Benscoter at home."

"No, ma'am, just me doing my Friday cleaning. Nobody here. Haven't seen him since morning. She went out about noon someplace."

"Thanks, Mrs. Hartung."

They walked slowly back to Main Street.

"So where is he?" Gypsy asked.

"I'd say hiding somewhere he feels safe. He must have heard and seen what's going on. He knows the secret is out. Not a chance in hell they can have the sheriff's sale now. The whole thing has blown up in his face."

"From that one registered letter you saw?"

"That was part of it. There were too many loose ends he couldn't tie up. He tried hard, had two men killed and still couldn't cover it all."

"It's almost two-thirty," Gypsy said. "Still an hour and a half to the time set for the sheriff's sale. I won't feel that this is all over until that time is past."

"Or we catch the sheriff and throw him in his own jail."

"We can do that?"

"Just watch us. Let's go down to the sheriff's office. I'm taking over as the highest ranking, legally constituted, law officer in the area not under suspicion. I can do that. Had to once or twice. Usually there isn't trouble. How many deputies work with the sheriff?"

"Three, and none of them strong-willed men."

"Good."

They walked in the door of the sheriff's office and found three townsmen there with drawn revolvers.

"Oh, it's you, McCoy," the tallest of the men said. "We're just kind of keeping the peace here and waiting for the sheriff to show up."

"I'll take over here. You three get outside and look for the sheriff."

They nodded, holstered their weapons and went out the door.

"Who's the top deputy here?" Spur demanded. One man came forward. He didn't have a weapon on his hip. Spur looked at the rifle rack and saw that it had been emptied.

"Deputy Higgins, Marshal."

"I'm not a marshal, Higgins. I'm with the Secret Service. You three men know anything about what the sheriff seems to be up to?"

"No sir. Don't know, and nobody will tell us."

Spur filled them in quickly. "What the sheriff has agreed to do is illegal and can get him into a territorial prison for ten to twenty years. He's guilty of conspiracy to defraud if nothing else. If he had anything to do with the two dead men, he's in worse trouble yet. My name is Spur McCoy.

I'm taking over this office until a man gets here tomorrow from the Territorial Attorney General's office. You three understand?"

"Yes sir," all three said.

"Fine. If Sheriff Willard shows up here anytime day or night, he's to be detained, arrested, handcuffed and then put in a cell. Then notify me at once. I'll either be on the street or at my hotel room. We have two men we're hunting, and nobody has the slightest idea how to find them."

"I know how to find at least one of them," someone said from behind Spur. He turned around and saw Flo Benscoter standing in the door of the sheriff's office, smoking a long thin cigar and smiling.

Chapter Thirteen

Spur McCoy looked at Flo Benscoter and chuckled. "You know where to find your husband?"

"I've been married to him for five years. I know most of his small quirks and habits."

"So, Mrs. Benscoter, where is he?" Gypsy asked.

"He went rushing past me on the street a block from his office about half an hour before the big meeting at the courthouse. He figured you'd found him out. He had his hat on with the earflaps. Whenever he puts that on I know he's going up to the cabin. He likes to ski and fish up there. Bought some of those weird long slats and goes sliding down the mountain."

"Can you take us to the cabin, Mrs. Benscoter?" Spur asked.

"I could, if I wanted to." She looked at Spur, her face drawn now, no humor left in it. "Is it true what

I think he planned on doing, the sheriff's sale?"

"We think he was the brains behind it, Mrs. Benscoter," Spur said. "The sheriff isn't smart enough to plan something like this, and Loophole Larson doesn't have the nerve to do it by himself. The postmaster was just a pawn. that leaves J. Lawton as the best candidate."

"What happens to him if I take you up there?"

"Depends on him. If he tries to run again or shoot it out, he'll get hurt. If he surrenders, he'll go to prison for a long, long time."

"Maybe. Your case is a little weak. Two of the conspirators are dead. The only witness you have is the sheriff, if he decides to testify. If he won't talk, you have no case. Or if he gets hung by that mob out there, you also won't have a witness. Chances are looking better and better that J. Lawton could go scot-free in the end. So I'll take you up to the cabin. That way you might not be here when they find Sheriff Willard, and there might be a necktie party before we get back."

Twenty minutes later, Flo had changed into riding pants, boots and a rough jacket, and she and Spur were about to step into saddles.

"I still want to go along," Gypsy said.

"You have a job here, an important one. If you spot the sheriff, you tell him exactly what I told you. Make sure that nobody shoots him or hangs him. He's had a small part in this swindle so far. Tell him we'll guarantee him total immunity from prosecution if he'll testify for the prosecution."

Gypsy nodded and took the .38 revolver out of her reticule. She checked the loads, put it back and waved as the two riders moved west down

Main Street. They didn't take the north or the south road, but headed into the rugged mountains directly west of town. Sharp spires and purple peaks in the distance outlined some of the highest mountains in Arizona.

"Is there really a cabin up here, or is this just a ploy to get me out of town?"

"Oh, there's a cabin all right, and my best bet is that J. Lawton is there, probably with that *puta* he's been fucking, that little slut Clarissa from the whorehouse. Sure, I know all about her. She isn't half the woman I am, and she gets paid for it."

"Then why are you leading me up there?"

"J. Lawton has done some mean things in his time, but cheating these people out of their property and most of their life's savings is too much. Besides, I want to see him squirm when I catch him with that bitch."

"Love conquers all," Spur said.

"True love, not fucking love," Flo said. "Besides, maybe we could tie him up and make him watch me seduce you and then fuck your brains right through your skull. I'd enjoy that. It would make him go crazy wild."

"You could live with him doing twenty years in the territorial prison in Yuma?"

"Easy. He's still the richest man in town, and the court would give me control of everything he owns. I've got lawyers, too."

"That would make him even unhappier, wouldn't it?"

"Knowing that I was spending his money while he was in prison would drive him insane and he'd never last six months in jail." She snorted. "Do I look stupid to you?"

It took them nearly an hour to get to the cabin, about four miles up some rough trail that degenerated into a single line track up a narrow canyon.

"He skis down there in winter. Sometimes I thought he'd break his neck. He used to bring me up here before we got married. Now he brings his sluts."

They came around a small bend in the trail and could see the log cabin 100 yards ahead. She stopped and held up her hand. Smoke came from the chimney, and two horses stood at the tie rail at the side.

"Damned if I wasn't right. He knew the situation had gotten out of hand. If the sale went through, he'd be in clover. If it didn't, nobody would think to look for him up here."

Flo slid off her horse and ground tied it. "We walk from here through the woods so he can't see us coming, not that he'd be looking. He's still probably humping that little whore of his. Damn, I hate that slut."

They came up to the side of the cabin that didn't have any windows. Spur ordered Flo to stay back, and he edged around the corner, ducked under a window and made it to the door. He grabbed the knob and turned it. Not locked. He eased the panel open half an inch. No squeak. He peered through and saw a stove, a table and three chairs.

Another inch crack and he spotted the bed. Two naked forms lay there, pumping up and down, low moans and squeals coming from the pair.

Spur pushed open the door and stepped inside, his boots hitting the wooden floor. J. Lawton, on top, looked at Spur and bellowed in anger.

"What the hell are you doing up here?" He scrambled off the girl and toward a shotgun that leaned against the wall near the head of the bed. Spur put a round into the weapon's wooden stock, blasting it off the wall and skidding it six feet away down the side wall.

"Bastard!"

The girl sat up on the bed, not trying to cover herself.

Flo ran in through the front door, a six-gun in her hand.

"Well, well, look at the lovers. Isn't this just too damn sweet for words? True love, at last you've found it, Jethro, up here in the woods with your fucking little slut."

"Flo, you brought him?" Disbelief pulsed through the words as J. Lawton looked at his wife with anger and shock.

"Get your pants on, lover. You're going down to town to stand trial for conspiracy, for bribing a postal employee, for extortion, for trying to swindle the good folks out of their property, and, oh yes, for the murder of Jessie and Loophole."

"You out of your mind, Flo?"

"Won't take much to dig up the scum you hired to ride Jessie out of town and kill him. Probably at the Blue Goose right now. As for Loophole, that was stupid. That barkeep will see the light and admit he never did see Loophole in the bar or behind it until somebody found his shot-up body. Hell, Jethro Lawton Benscoter, you're gonna hang so high it won't be worth missing. People will come from miles around just to see your feet twitch and your tongue stick out and your eyes bulge as your neck snaps."

J. Lawton stood there, clenching and unclenching his hands. At last he let them drop to his sides.

"The lady is right, Benscoter. You better get your britches on and dress for a ride. You'll be in jail tonight."

Flo walked closer, still holding the Colt. "Jethro Lawton, you'll be in jail tonight or in hell. You call it. Which one do you want?"

"Put down the gun, Flo," Spur said. He was too far away to do much about her weapon, and he certainly didn't want to shoot her.

"Call it, Jethro Lawton. You want me to kill you or just shoot you up a little? You remember I was with a Wild West show as a pistol shot before you married me."

His eyes went wide, one hand coming up to cover his heart. He reached out with his other hand.

"Flo, you wouldn't do this. You can't do this."

"The hell I won't. Jail or hell, you bastard?"

"Jail," he said, so softly that Spur barely heard him. Spur lunged toward her, but Flo fired the .38 revolver twice. Both rounds found their mark. One smashed into Benscoter's right knee and one into his left knee. He screamed in agony and hatred and fury as he crumpled to the floor, naked and now bleeding from his smashed knees.

"Oh, God!" Spur said.

Flo flipped the weapon over in the air, caught it by the barrel and handed it to Spur.

"Come on, whore, get your clothes on. The party and the pay days for you are over. Jethro Lawton, I guess the least I can do is help you get dressed. I'll let the federal lawman here bind up your knees so you don't bleed to death. There must be some old sheets around here he can use for bandages."

Two hours later they rode into a wildly celebrating Pine Grove. There were lanterns strung across the street. A wide swatch across it had been swept down to the hardpan. An impromptu orchestra beat out a dance tempo, and two dozen dancers kicked up their heels across the dirt floor.

Spur and the three others rode down to the jail. Flo found Doc Johnson and had him go to the jail, then she went to her house to relax in a hot bubble bath.

At the jail, Spur found one deputy holding down the place with Gypsy beating him at a game of poker with matches for chips.

She bounced up, long black hair flying, her dark eyes checking on Spur who came carrying Benscoter over his back. She guided Spur into a cell and only then saw the bloody bandages on both of Benscoter's knees.

Without saying a word, Spur let Benscoter down on the bunk and stepped out of the cell, then closed it and locked the door.

"Doc will be over soon," he said and walked back into the main office.

"So tell me!" Gypsy said, grabbing at his sleeve.

Spur took a cup of coffee from the pot on the small stove and drank it half down, then he recounted the uneventful capture.

"She actually shot him in both knees?"

"From about ten feet and so fast I'd swear it was one long sound in that cabin. Maybe she did used to be a Wild West show gun shooter."

"Would she have killed him if he told her he wanted to go straight to hell?"

"I thought so at the time, but on the way back she confided that she wouldn't have done that. I'd have had to arrest her for murder, and then she wouldn't get to enjoy all of Benscoter's money. She said she figured he might be able to beat the conspiracy charges and the fraud charges, if the sheriff got killed as he was captured or if he refused to testify against Benscoter But she said she figured he would be convicted of the murders of Loophole and Jessie. He had the motive and the opportunity with Loophole, and she's sure he hired someone to shoot down Jessie."

"So the chances are high that Benscoter will hang and she will inherit his fortune, which must be considerable even without what he was trying to steal," Gypsy said.

"Right. Now all we have to do is find the sheriff and we can wrap this up. Why the big celebration? I figured somebody must have captured the lawman and had him in jail."

"Nope, not yet. They decided that since the sheriff didn't show up for the sale at four o'clock, he'd lost and they wanted a celebration. They got it started about five, and there's more whiskey and barrels of beer and cornjack out there than I've seen in years. Two bunches of musicians are going to play all night just as long as anyone wants to dance."

Doc Johnson came through the door, and Spur took him to the cell.

"Afraid we have a nasty pair of wounds, Doc. Benscoter got himself nailed in both knees by a sharpshooter—not me. See if you can fix him up well enough so he can walk to his own trap door on the scaffold complete with a hangman's noose."

Doc Johnson took off the makeshift bandages and shook his head. "Somebody did a hell of a job on these knees. Not one chance in ten that he'll be able to walk in six months, let alone in a month when the gallows will be ready."

Spur talked with the deputy in charge, warning him that if Benscoter got out of jail the deputy would hang in his place.

Spur and Gypsy walked up Main to the celebration and took a quick two-step whirl around the street. They visited the punch bowl and found it was cider generously laced with whiskey. After a sip, Gypsy put her cup down.

They sat in chairs brought out from many of the stores and watched the dancers.

"What's the chances of finding the sheriff?" Gypsy asked.

"Not too good. Come night he can slip out of town fifteen dozen places and be halfway to Phoenix by morning. With a good horse and a clear night, he'd make good time."

"Oh, the lawman coming from Phoenix sent a wire to the mayor. He said he was bringing two additional men with him to insure they could maintain law and order in Pine Grove. All three will be here tomorrow afternoon on the regular stage run."

"More the better. Want to dance?" he asked.

"Not really. You want to come to my place for a nice quiet piece of cherry pie?"

"With whipped cream?"

"Out of whipped cream, but you can have two pieces of pie."

"Done."

A short time later in Gypsy's house, Spur stretched out in an overstuffed chair, put his feet on an ottoman and took a second bite of the best cherry pie he'd had in months. Cherry pie was one of his failings. He'd die for a fine cherry pie.

"You like it?" Gypsy asked.

"Good enough to eat," Spur said, using a line he'd learned years ago, but it still got a laugh now and then. Gypsy laughed. She had a piece herself, and when she finished it, she carried her dish and fork back to the kitchen and returned with a second slice of pie for Spur.

"I was just joking about another pie," Spur said.

"You were not. Cherry pie is your favorite."

"How did you know?"

She smiled. "You told me in a weak moment."

He ate the second piece. They talked about the hunt for the sheriff, which would continue in the morning outside of town. Somebody must have seen him. It didn't matter a lot if they caught him or not. No real damage was done on the sheriff's sale that didn't happen, and they had plenty of evidence to convict Benscoter of murder. Spur would get going on that first thing in the morning.

"Let's sit in the porch swing," Gypsy said.

"You like that swing."

"I had my first real kiss out there when I was sixteen."

"Lead the way."

He let her sit down first and pushed her a while.

"I can see the moon through the trees," she said. "Come and take a look."

He sat beside her and kept the swing moving with his feet on the porch floor. It was dark out, but they were splotched with the moonlight coming through the trees.

"Why do people think the moon is romantic?" Gypsy asked, turning toward him.

"Not sure, but a guess would be that a lot of romantic things like first kisses take place at night in the dark under a moon somewhere.

Moonlight means darkness, and a lot of people do things in the dark they wouldn't try in the daylight."

"Good explanation. I'll remember that." She moved closer to him. "Remember how I told you how I felt when you kissed me so long the other day?"

"I remember."

"Did it make you feel all kind of warm and cozy and wanting things, too?"

"Lady, you're getting on dangerous ground here."

"I know, but it's dark, and people try things." She moved over and kissed him. Her mouth came open and her tongue teased his lips until they opened. She sighed and melted against him, her breasts pressing hard on his chest.

He came away from her lips.

"Don't stop," she said and kissed him again. Her hand strayed down to his leg and lay there on his thigh, not moving, just making contact.

He eased his lips from hers. She caught his hand and put it over one of her breasts.

"Gypsy."

"Hush, it's dark. Who's to know. Please, pet me. Make me feel like you want me. It's important to me right now."

She kissed him again before he could reply. Her mouth was open and her tongue darted into his mouth.

He eased away. "Gypsy, this is not what I should be doing."

"Spur, don't talk. I'll tell you if I have to. I'm not a virgin, Spur McCoy, and I bet you aren't either. You're not stealing something from me. I've made love before, and I swore I'd be sure I wanted to the next time. Right now is the next time. Spur McCoy, I want to show you my gratitude and my thanks for finding out what happened at the newspaper and to my father. Let me do that for you."

Chapter Fourteen

Spur's hand seemed to have a mind of its own. Gently it caressed her soft breast, and she nodded.

"Oh, yes! That feels so fine. Kiss me again and keep doing that. Oh, yes!"

He kissed her, leaving room for his hand to work. He could feel her nipple harden under her dress. He found a button and undid it, then a second one, and his hand crept inside her dress.

He touched something silky, a chemise. It was loose. He pulled it up, and then his hand crept upward and touched the edge of a breast.

Gypsy trembled. Her tongue darted deeper into his mouth, then she sighed again and her lips left his. "Darling Spur, you don't know how long I've wanted you to touch me, to pet me that way. Yes, yes. Don't ever stop. Oh, great lord, that is so fine."

His tweaked at her nipple, and she pushed her hips against him. He caught her hand and moved it over so it covered the growing bulge under his pants. Her eyes widened in the dappled moonlight, and then she smiled and snuggled against his hand under her dress.

He stroked and caressed both breasts and kissed her again.

"Gypsy, it might be better if we went inside."

"Oh, yes!"

She stood at once, caught his hand, hurried him through the screen door and led him to her bedroom.

He let go of her hand and lit the lamp there. She ran out and brought back two more lit lamps and put one on the dresser and one on a nightstand beside the bed. She grinned.

"I want to see everything," she said. Gypsy checked to make sure the blind was drawn tightly over the bedroom window, then she came back to him and hugged him so her entire body pressed hard against his. Her lips found his and she kissed him with that light feathery touch, then let go of him and lay on the bed.

He stretched out beside her. They were both still fully clothed, only the two buttons open on her dress. He took her hand and put it on the erection bulging his pants.

"Open the buttons," he said.

She nodded and undid his belt buckle, then the buttons on his fly. Her hand slid inside his pants over his underwear, and she gasped when she felt his erection.

He kissed her again, held her tight and whispered, "Do you want both of us to take off our clothes?"

"Just you first," she said, grinning.

He pulled off his boots, then slid out of his pants and removed his vest and then his town shirt. He wore no undershirt.

She sat up and touched his chest, running her hand over the hairy surfaces, brushing his nipples, smiling and running her hand down the hairy patch that led inside his underwear at his waist.

He touched her dress. She nodded and sat up and pulled it off over her head. She left the chemise in place, hiding her breasts. She wore some of the newer bloomers, loose, halfway to the knee. A strip of bare flesh showed between her bloomers and the bottom of her chemise. He ran his hand under the silky cloth and caught one breast.

She gasped, then nodded, and his other hand captured a breast. She touched the bulge in his short underwear.

"Oh, my!" she whispered. "I've never felt this way before, like I wanted to stay here the rest of my life. Like nothing is important but what we're doing right now. Like I'll love you forever and ever no matter what happens."

His hands left her breast, and gently he lifted the chemise up to her chin. She nodded, and he lofted it over her head and trailed it down her back until it came free of her waist-length black hair.

Her breasts showed with pink areolas, brighter now with sexual arousal, her nipples a deeper red and erect, pulsing when he touched them.

Spur bent and kissed the swell of one breast, and she gasped. He kissed it again and again as he fondled the other with his hand. He licked her breast and then nibbled at her nipple with his teeth.

Gypsy gasped and her eyes went wide, then she grabbed him and fell on top of him on the bed.

Her breath came in small gasps and her hips pounded against his, then her whole body shook and vibrated as a spasm shot through her, exciting every nerve ending. She moaned low and soft, then louder until it rose to a keening wail as she jolted against him another dozen times as the spasms rolled through her again and again and again.

Spur held her tightly, one hand still on a breast. She gave one last moan and lay still, her breath coming in a long series of gulps and gasps. At last she lay quietly on top of him. She opened one eye and stared down at him, then pushed back so she could focus on his face.

"Nothing like that has ever happened to me before. What a wonder you are! You kissed my titties and I went wild." She bent and brushed her lips across his cheek. "Miracle man, you truly are a miracle worker."

She sat up and urged him up, then pulled down on his short underwear. He lifted his hips off the bed and she tugged the cloth down until it slipped over his penis which swung upward, stiff and ready.

"Oh my!" Her eyes went wide, and she looked at him. "He's so . . . so huge!" Gypsy's hand moved toward it, then stopped.

"I like to be touched, too," he said. She smiled then and brushed the shaft with her hand, then held him and gripped him tightly for a moment.

"Oh, so big."

He kissed her lips lightly. "Don't worry. We'll fit together. You'll have lots of room."

She looked up at him, her face edged with worry, then a slow smile broke through. "Of course. Women have babies and they come right out through—" She stopped and giggled. "Through the same place."

She pulled the underwear off his feet, then lay down again and pulled him on top of her.

"Just lay there a minute. This is all happening so fast. A girl dreams of this for years, and then when it happens, she needs to slow down a little and think about it and wonder and feel how good it all is." She smiled up at him.

"It's just as good as I dreamed. I told you I wasn't a virgin. That first time was when I was seventeen and the boy was sixteen and we didn't know what we were doing. He tried, but I'm not sure he ever actually got inside of me. He made a mess of sticky stuff all over my legs and then he yelled and grinned and got up and ran away."

"I won't run away. Promise."

She looked at him, and the delight turned her face into one of total beauty. She kissed him hard on the lips. "Make me naked like you are," she said.

She helped him take down her bloomers. Her hips had a little more womanly flair than he had guessed, and her swatch of black pubic hair made a rectangle up from her crotch more than a V. She looked down at her naked body and lifted her brows.

"Now you know. This is all of me, naked and ready for whatever you want."

He kissed her, warming her breasts as he did, then one hand moved down to her crotch and she trembled. He worked up both inner thighs, then eased one leg away from the other. She looked at him, then pulled his face to her and kissed him. As the kiss lasted he brushed his fingers across her heartland.

He felt the moist outer lips, and she jolted when he touched them. Her mouth left his.

"Oh, lordy, do that again!"

He brushed them, then again, and each time she responded. Gently he found her hard node and stroked it back and forth.

She looked at him curiously. "Oh, my!" He stroked her clit again and again, and she yelped in total delight. Her hips began moving against him and then she wailed and kicked into a furious climax that shook her body. It was over quickly, and she frowned and looked at him.

"That's a little trigger down there that sets you off in a hurry," he said.

"There's so much to find out, to learn about." She sat up. "Let me look at you. I've never really looked down there before."

She explored him, fingered his heavy scrotum and stared in wonder again at his long tool.

"It just gets hard this way when you get excited?"

"Yes. Otherwise it would be tough walking around."

"Not fair. Women's breasts are big all the time."

"But they get bigger when they fill with milk for a baby. Haven't you noticed with mothers?"

"I guess. I've never thought about it."

She lay down and pulled him over her. "You really think it'll fit?"

"I think so."

He massaged her outer lips and stroked one finger deep inside her slot. She yelped when he did it, but he brought out her juices and wet her more.

He spread her legs, knelt between them and lifted her knees. Her eyes sparkled as she watched him.

"Soon?"

He nodded, bent and placed himself against her lips and eased forward. For a moment there was resistance, then he edged in a little and the expression on her face blossomed into rapture.

He edged in more and more, and her juices welcomed him. In an instant he sank in until their pelvic bones nudged together and he could penetrate no farther.

"Oh, I'm gonna melt!" Gypsy whispered. "That's just the most wonderful thing—ever!"

Slowly he began to ease out and stroke back in. Her face beamed then her hips picked up the motion and worked upward to meet his downward strokes.

"Oh, yes," she whispered. "How can people say this can be wrong when it feels so wonderful?"

With each stroke he brushed across her clit, and after a dozen ministrations she burst into another climax, shaking and jolting and wailing like the end of the world had come. He kept stroking as she tapered off.

Sweat beaded her forehead. She still panted like a small steam engine, and her smile was magnificent. She closed her eyes and rested a moment, then her hips worked again and she looked up at him.

"Isn't it your turn? Don't you do something, too?"

Spur grinned. "Yes, but it takes me a little longer."

"Can I help?"

"You are." He drove in harder and faster then. He felt her knees around his sides as she lifted them higher. He slipped in deeper and increased his speed. The pressure built slowly, then higher and higher. He knew the juices were coming, the gates opening, the dam about to burst.

Spur grunted and panted and whispered again. "Oh, yes, yes, yes." Then the whole world exploded, and he came again and again in great spurts.

As his body stopped shaking, he realized Gypsy had climaxed again as well. She eased down from her ecstasy, and her eyes opened. She smiled. He'd never seen a more wonderful, happy, contented smile in his life.

They both eased down from their peaks holding each other tightly, then trying to relax and bring their breathing back to normal.

After a time, she touched his face and he opened his eyes and looked at her.

"Spur McCoy, this is so marvelous, so beautiful, just so, so wonderful, why do adults ever do anything else but make love?"

"That's a question I never can find an answer to. Maybe it's because people have to eat, and that takes work and forces the man and woman apart to get the work done to obtain the food. The problem is the more they make love, the more babies they have and the more food they need, so it takes more work."

She giggled. "I guess that makes as much sense as anything." She pulled his face down and kissed him, long and soft and possessively.

"Now, Spur McCoy, you're here and it's dark out and I don't want you to risk going back to the old hotel, so you have to stay here with me all night."

"You sure? What will the neighbors think?"

"I don't care. Anyway, you can leave just as it gets light before any of them get up." She kissed him. "You know that I love you, Spur McCoy? I know it's a just-getting-fucked kind of love, but I love you."

"You said the bad word."

"It seemed right. I've said it before, when I was alone, practicing so I'd be able to say it when I needed it."

"Shameless."

"You made me that way. I've often wondered how I'd feel after my first real lovemaking. It's nothing like I figured. I don't feel all that different. More like I have learned something, experienced something that I'll understand and use the rest of my life. But it didn't make a different person or anything like that."

"You thought it might?"

"A girl never knows. I've been dreaming about this since I was thirteen. That's a third of my life."

"Oh." He lay there with her head on his chest, his hands laced behind his head. He usually put his hands back there when he was waiting for a woman or after he'd made love. He wondered why.

"Can I ask a question?" he said.

"Yes, anything."

"Do you have any more of that wonderful cherry pie?"

"Only if you'll stay all night and make love to me again and again until we're exhausted."

He frowned. "How about a fresh pot of coffee to keep up our strength?"

"You got it," Gypsy said. She crawled over him, her long black hair trailing behind her as she scampered, naked, for the kitchen. Spur McCoy ran lightly after her, feeling like a kid of 18 again. He gloried in the feeling. Too soon morning would come and with it the harsher realities of finding the sheriff.

"Hey, where are you, McCoy?" Gypsy called.

Spur hurried into the kitchen.

Chapter Fifteen

Spur McCoy opened up the Home Café the next morning at six A.M. He had coffee, a high stack of flapjacks, three eggs and six slices of bacon. Then he went to the courthouse and checked with the deputy sheriff on duty, the youngest of the three who had drawn night duty.

Benscoter still lay in his cell, bellowing and complaining. He shut up as soon as he saw Spur.

"Benscoter, you going to take this prosecution all alone, or do you know where ex-sheriff Willard might be hiding?"

"Bastard ran out on me."

"You ran out on him first, didn't you? You high-tailed it up to your cabin."

"Yeah, so sue me. Throw me in jail. You can't hurt me any more than you have, damn you!"

"Now that you've got that out of your craw, do you know where Willard is so we can put him in a cell beside you?"

"Hell, yes. He's got a place two miles north on the road to Flag, but it's a damn fortress. He's got all sorts of weapons up there and traps and pits and a dozen ways to keep a whole posse off his land."

"Two miles north. Which side of the road?"

"To the right, up a skinny little canyon that ends at a sheer cliff nobody can climb up or down lessen you want to dangle on a rope for two hundred feet."

"He alone?"

"Think he took Ruth with him. She's one of the girls at the saloon he likes. Nice looking little whore."

"Might just pay him a visit. How are the knees?"

"Hurt like hell."

"Good, you deserve it."

"I want to see my lawyer."

"You don't have one. You shot him, remember?"

"The other lawyer. I'll pay him good."

"Guess that's your right. I'll tell the deputy."

An hour later, Spur left on a horse from the livery. He had the repeating rifle again, with a box of shells, a rope, five sticks of dynamite all capped and with 15-second burning fuses.

He rode out for what he judged was two miles and found only a flat gentle valley as he worked along the ridges and slopes toward Flagstaff. He kept moving. A half mile beyond, he discovered a valley to the right that quickly rose and turned into a narrow canyon that ended in a sheer rock wall maybe a half mile away.

He slid off his mount and checked his gear. He put the rifle around his back on its sling, adjusted his .45 Colt in leather and checked the extra box of rounds for the .45. He had the rifle rounds loose in his jacket pocket and eight in the weapon ready to fire. He tied the lariat rope to his belt at his side. Time to go.

Spur worked along an easy trail for 300 yards, then felt it was time to leave the track. He angled 20 yards into the woods so he could still see the trail and parallel it, watching for tree falls, pits, tied back saplings or young trees, anything that could be a lethal trap for the unwary. He found nothing like that along this stretch.

He took his time. He had all day. He had all week. No reason to rush except he didn't bring any food with him. There would be food in the cabin.

After he had worked another 200 yards forward, he moved cautiously back to the trail. From there he could see a cabin, maybe a quarter of a mile ahead. No smoke came from the chimney. This could be an exercise in futility.

He stayed closer to the trail this time and moved forward. It was early. Maybe the sheriff was still asleep. Spur was no more than ten yards from the trail now, and directly ahead he saw a small pine tree bent back. He stopped and examined the ground in front of it.

Spur picked up the trigger at once—a piece of twine stretched from a small stake in the ground to another stake where it wasn't tied, only positioned around. The first time an animal or a man kicked that twine, it would release the tied back tree and some lethal device would be slammed forward with great force and impale or crush the victim. He didn't look to see what the weapon was.

Spur found a half dozen rocks and threw them one at a time at the trigger twine. The fifth one hit the string and drove it forward.

The result was quick. The pine tree rammed forward with a swishing of the air and a six-inch thick log three feet long slammed forward with it chest high. The log would have crushed anyone's ribs into their chest.

Spur went around the trap, faded another ten yards into the brush and woods and worked forward. Had these traps been here all the time, or had Willard recently set them up?

It took Spur ten minutes more to work his way to within 50 yards of the small log cabin. Now a stream of smoke came from the chimney and Spur nodded. Someone was inside. All he had to do was find out who it was. If it was Willard he'd arrest him and take him back to jail in Pine Grove—if he was lucky. It depended on how desperate the sheriff was.

Spur lay in the brush looking past a small pine tree at the cabin for ten more minutes. It was a recon, judging the target, figuring how to take it, what risks were involved, how best to attack the problem, trying to find any weakness.

Plug up the chimney and make the stove smoke was always good, but he had no available material to use on the chimney. Pine boughs might work, but if the fire was hot they would simply burn away and the smoke would escape normally. Besides, there was no good access to the roof.

He wondered what areas would be set with traps. He moved so he could see the rear of the cabin. There was a second door with two horses tied there. Willard wouldn't risk any traps around the horses. First Spur would take the horses and hide them. There was no window in the back, so he should be able to get away with the horses.

He moved cautiously to the edge of the timber, but saw no places where the leaves or needles of the forest floor had been disturbed. He found a dead branch four feet long and jammed it into the ground in front of him as he walked. He was within 20 feet of the rear door when the stick suddenly sank into the ground right in front of his foot. He drew the stick out and looked. A thin lattice work of branches held up some netting that had been covered carefully with leaves and twigs and pine needles to make it look natural. He probed to the side and found it went about four feet wide.

Cautiously he worked his way around the pit, then headed again for the horses. He spoke quietly to them as he came up to them. At once he saw the bells attached to the mounts' bridles. Ordinary head movement did not ring the bells, but a sustained walk or gallop would make them ring.

Spur cut the leather leads that held the bells on the mounts and checked them again. Nothing else. He caught the reins of both animals and with his probe, followed the hoofprints the animals used to walk into the area.

Five minutes later he had the horses hidden 50 yards from the cabin. He went back and stared at the place again. Two sticks of dynamite wedged tightly at the bottom of the door should blow the panel inward. He could be just around the corner of the cabin and rush around and cover the stunned sheriff inside.

Before he placed the dynamite he went over his route with his probe. He found no pits dug, but there was a small pine tree bent back and tied. It took him five minutes to find the trigger. The weapon was a two inch thick pole, two feet long, that had 30 or 40 sharpened sticks protruding from it at many angles. The sticks were strong enough to kill a man if it struck him anywhere in the belly, chest or head.

Cautiously, Spur cut the leather thongs that held the deadly spiked log. He cut three of the thongs and then held the log by one end and lowered it to the ground. Now tripping the twine would do nothing but release the tree to swing forward.

His route was clear. Spur set the two sticks of dynamite and pushed the end of one of them into a crack under the door. He wedged the second beside it, then lit one of the 15-second fuses with a match and hurried around the corner of the cabin.

One fuse would set off the dynamite cap pushed into the one stick of powder which would set off the other one instantaneously.

The fuse burned for 20 seconds, then a cracking roar ripped through the peaceful quiet of the morning. With the explosion, Spur raced around the corner of the cabin, his .45 out. Smoke still hovered over the whole door opening.

Spur heard a six-gun fire and sensed the round blast through the smoky doorway. He ducked low, pushed through the smoke and tried to see something. The small cabin had filled with the vapors from the explosion.

It blew out both front windows as well, and a breeze soon thinned out the smoke so he could see.

Sheriff Ben Willard lay on the floor near a bunk on the far side of the cabin. He had the six-gun in his hand but it sagged toward the floor. His leg stuck out at an odd angle. Broken, Spur decided.

A woman got up from the bunk. She held her head and stared around as if not sure where she was.

Spur advanced on the sheriff slowly. He worked around a broken table, past a tumbled chair and a splintered half of the door.

The sheriff didn't move. He was fully dressed. Breakfast was cooking on the small wood burning stove to the far side. The sheriff's pants leg was red with blood. The six-gun fell from his hand and the force of the fall dropped the hammer on a live round. The firing made a thunderous sound in the small enclosed cabin as the bullet thudded into the wall.

Spur jumped over to the man and covered him with his .45. Sheriff Willard didn't move. He looked down at his right leg through glinting eyes.

"My damn leg. Part of the door, I think."

Slowly and with care, Spur eased up the lawman's right pants leg. Then he saw higher up where a giant splinter from the door had ripped through the heavy part of the lower leg.

Blood gushed from the wound. Spur hurried to the small kitchen and found two dishtowels. He tore them into strips, came back and bound them around the wound—leg, splinter and all.

"Better get you to a doctor soon as we can," Spur said.

Ben Willard's color was better though he'd lost a lot of blood. He rubbed one hand over his face. "You know about the sheriff's sale due for yesterday?"

"It all came out. We've got Benscoter in jail. You'll get a cell beside his. You're just as guilty as he is."

"How much time will I get?"

"I'd say two years. Depends on the judge. Also depends if you testify for the prosecution."

"I'll testify if I don't get charged with the crime."

"I can't do that. Talk to the District Attorney when we get back. Maybe you can work out something."

Spur picked up the gun from the floor. "You have any more weapons in the cabin?"

"No, just that one."

"I'm going to go get the horses. If you try to keep me out when I get back, I'll ride for town and let you rot up here. By morning that leg will drive you insane."

"Won't try nothing. Get the horses. Oh, watch them pits. Got a few of them. Follow the hoof prints, best way."

Nearly two hours later, Spur arrived at Doc Johnson's office with his prisoner. The whore had not been hurt, only dazed, and she gratefully went back to her saloon.

Doc Johnson took a look and said, "Have him patched up in an hour. Send a deputy over to take him to the jail. He won't be walking. Better bring a wheelbarrow."

When Spur walked into the sheriff's office he found more than a dozen people there. Gypsy had her notebook and pencil and came over and grabbed his hand. She led him to a tall, silver-haired man.

"Spur McCoy, I'd like you to meet Jerico Domero. He's the assistant Attorney General for the territory and has come to take over the county law work until we can elect a new sheriff."

The two shook hands. Spur liked this tall, bronzed man with the white hair. He didn't look over 35.

"Hear you've been doing your share of rounding up the bad guys," Domero said.

"Figured I'd help out a little until you got here. Ex-Sheriff Ben Willard is over at Doc Johnson's office getting a log cut out of his leg. You might want to send a deputy over there to bring him back. Oh, Doc said to bring a wheelbarrow."

Domero nodded, moved away and talked to one of his men.

"Things been happening fast and furious here," Gypsy said. "The stage left Phoenix at three A.M. so it could get here early. Domero has been whipping things into shape fast. He's already charged Benscoter with two counts of murder as well as the sheriff's sale fraud. He said it will be grand larceny and conspiracy."

"Sounds like he has things well in hand."

"Let's leave here. I want to talk to you."

They went out into the soft noontime sunshine and walked in the mountain air.

"You were really terribly wicked last night, Spur McCoy, to lead me on that way until I just let you do anything you wanted to do with me."

Spur chuckled.

"I guess I seduced you, didn't I? I just wanted to make love so much that I couldn't control myself. So I want to thank you."

She squeezed his hand.

"Your thanks are noted and appreciated."

"More thanks will come later in a more personal, intimate fashion. Now, it looks to me like Domero has things well in hand. He'll want to talk to you again, I'm sure, to get more details about what you've done here, but that can wait until tomorrow. Right now I want to take you to dinner, lunch, whatever you call it. My treat, I get to pay. Let's go to the Home Café. Terri is a special friend of mine."

He told her about the capture of Sheriff Willard.

"Domero might let Willard off easy if he can testify or give any eyewitness evidence about Benscoter talking about killing either Jessie or Loophole. We'll see. Now about us."

"Us?" Spur asked.

"Of course. You don't think you can toy with a lady's affections that way, violate her most precious treasure, and simply kiss her on the cheek and walk away."

Spur looked at her sharply, and she giggled. "I figured that would get your attention. What I really want to know is how your wounded arm is. Bet you haven't had it checked since the doc patched you up. Really, McCoy, you need a full-time nurse. I suggest that you wire your superiors in Washington and tell them that this case is wrapped up, but you'll need to stay here two or three days to give testimony and talk with the new law officers. Also you have an arm wound that needs some healing time."

"When I do this, who would I get to be my private nurse to watch over me night and day?"

Gypsy flipped a handful of black hair over her shoulder and smiled at him. It was a smile and a face he would find hard to forget.

"Oh, we might be able to find someone who could do those difficult tasks. Might even find someone who would do them all with no charge to the government, not even for the board and room."

"I can't imagine who."

"Oh, another development. I had a talk with Florence Benscoter. She's in charge now of all of her husband's businesses. She says her husband's feud with Papa was silly. As soon as I get the regular paper going again, she'll want to talk to me about advertising. Which means I'll be in much better financial condition."

"Any more news running around?"

"Well, one little thing. The box social is set for day after tomorrow, and you better be there. I'll tell you what my basket looks like. All the funds will go toward my new building for the *Clarion*. Mrs. Benscoter says she knows that her husband had a hand in how my father died, and she's guaranteed that if we don't raise at least three hundred dollars, she'll make up the balance. She also said the bank would be more than happy to give me a no interest loan to rebuild the *Clarion* office and even get a new press and the printing and paper supplies I'll need. So, looks like some good might come out of all of this after all."

When they had finished their lunch, she stood and headed for the back door that led to the alley, motioning him to follow. In the alley she looked around and saw no one.

"I just had to kiss you right away or I knew that I would explode. Do you mind?"

She put her arms around him and kissed him hard. When she eased away, Spur McCoy smiled.

"Don't mind the kissing at all. Fact is, I kind of like it. About that board and room and nurse care. Does that include any cherry pie?"

Gypsy Pinnick laughed and nodded. "Cherry pie every day is a specialty of the house. That and a wonderfully soft feather bed every morning and evening."

"It works for me," Spur McCoy said and grinned.

TWICE THE FIGHTIN' AND TWICE THE FILLIES IN ONE GIANT SPECIAL EDITION!

GIANT
SPECIAL EDITION

SPUR

COLORADO
CHIPPY
Dirk Fletcher

It seems everyone in Colorado wants Spur McCoy. Uncle Sam wants Spur to shoot some bank robbers to hell. The desperadoes want McCoy cold in the earth. And a hot-blooded little angel wants to take him to heaven. But Spur isn't complaining. It is his job to uphold the Secret Service's record. It is his duty to aim straight for the renegades' heads. And it is his pleasure to bed down every fiery vixen in the Wild West.

_3911-7 $5.99 US/$7.99 CAN

Dorchester Publishing Co., Inc.
65 Commerce Road
Stamford, CT 06902

Please add $1.75 for shipping and handling for the first book and $.50 for each book thereafter. NY, NYC, PA and CT residents, please add appropriate sales tax. No cash, stamps, or C.O.D.s. All orders shipped within 6 weeks via postal service book rate. Canadian orders require $2.00 extra postage and must be paid in U.S. dollars through a U.S. banking facility.

Name_____

Address_____

City _____ State_____Zip_____

I have enclosed $_____in payment for the checked book(s).

Payment <u>must</u> accompany all orders.☐ Please send a free catalog.